# MOUTH of the DRAGON

**The Perseid Press**
P.O. Box 584
Centerville, MA 02632

**Mouth of the Dragon**
Copyright © 2017 by Thomas Barczak.

First Perseid Press trade paperback edition, 2017
First Perseid Press hardcover edition, 2017
First Perseid Press electronic edition, 2017

Cover Design, Roy Mauritsen
Original Drawing by Thomas Barczak
Interior Design, Christopher Morris and Janet Morris
Book Cover Image copyright © 2017, Perseid Press

Trade edition: ISBN-13: 978-0-9977583-9-9; ISBN-10: 0-9977583-9-2
ePub edition ISBN-13: 978-0-9977583-8-2; ISBN-10: 0-9977583-8-4
Kindle edition ISBN-13: 978-0-9977583-6-8; ISBN-10: 0-9977583-6-8

Printed in the United States of America

10 9 8 7 6 5 4 3 2 1

*For Shannon, Olivia, Jaxon, Nicholas, Kayne,
Maxwell, and Julian.*

# TABLE OF CONTENTS

*Acknowledgments*

*Thank you to God, for the privilege and ability to write.*
*Thank you to my family, for allowing me to. I know it is not without sacrifice.*
*Thank you to Janet and Chris Morris at Perseid Press for your continuous support, for forging the literary path ahead, and then taking the time to share what you've learned.*
*Thank you to Cas Peace for her editorial prowess.*
*Thank you to Sarah Snyder Gray Hulcy for her constant Musing.*
*Thank you to the shark-diving Roy Mauritsen for his amazing cover design.*
*Thank you to Norman Galaxy of Writers and to OWFI. You taught me I never have to write alone.*
*Thank you to my writer friends, with a particular thank you to Seth Lindberg, Walter Rhein and Nick Lyon, who keep me coming back.*
*Thank you to all my friends who light my spiritual path.*
*Thank you to New Beginnings.*
*Thank you to my boss.*
*Thank you to my readers for believing in me.*
*Thank you to the story for continually unfolding before me.*

# MOUTH of the DRAGON

# THOMAS BARCZAK

## Prophecy of the Evarun
## Mouth of the Dragon

*A hundred years have passed*
*Since we were awoken.*

*A hundred years have passed*
*Since the Wyrm was driven away.*

*A hundred years have passed*
*Since we remembered why we were saved.*

*Close your eyes behind the veil.*
*Of the truth, you cannot tell.*

*Go to sleep, go to sleep.*
*In the warmth of dragon's fire.*

## Chapter One: Blood

Chaelus, once Roan Lord of the House of Malius, now vessel of the Giver reborn, crumpled beneath the legion boot slammed against his spine.

He didn't cry out.

He had come to save his brother, and win a kingdom back.

The blood red glare of the setting sun filled the hall of the tower from the oculus high above. The light pulsed with the harsh clamor of a drumbeat sounding from beyond its walls; a marshaling call for war.

Above him, his younger brother, Baelus, scarcely more than a boy, drew his crimson robes about himself, sinking into the expanse of what had once been his, and before that, their father's throne. Baelus traced his long fingers along the deep carvings upon its arms, woodland branches stretched wayward across pallid stone. Even the stone bled in the mournful light.

Their father's sword, Sundengal, now Chaelus' sword, waited just out of reach in its scabbard where the legion-naires had thrown it across the rushes beneath Baelus' feet; the sword their father had used to take the life of the Giver before Chaelus, the sword Chaelus had defeated the Dragon with—the Dragon that had possessed him and his father both, the same Dragon that now possessed his brother.

"You look older, Baelus," he said, straining. "You're no longer the child I once knew."

Baelus stared back at him.

It was a cold but not an empty stare that came from beneath their father's simple crown, a band of cold steel woven like dragons. The shadow of the Dragon, the Dragon of legend, the Dragon reborn, swirled around Baelus like a cloud. Black tendrils of it drifted across his eyes like oil. It rippled just beneath the surface of his haunted skin.

Chaelus knew the Dragon well because it had once possessed him. It had once possessed their father, Malius. Malius, first among the twelve Servian lords, who, if not for his martyrdom, would have been counted as one of the Fallen Ones like them, as well. He already knew the Dragon because he had been defeated by it, and in so doing had defeated it, once before. Yet still the Dragon remained.

He alone, Chaelus, vessel of the Giver reborn, could see it. Not Baelus, nor anyone else around him. They wouldn't see it. None of them could see the Dragon. Not yet. But soon, every one of them would.

Such was the way of the Dragon.

Such was the way of prophecy.

Baelus smiled, a feint, a lie.

"Welcome home, brother."

Two more legionnaires seized Chaelus, one at each of his arms. Over their chainmail hauberks, the crest of Malius marked the iron clasps of their crimson cloaks; twined branches over the sigil of the Servian order, a single point and then a line, followed by the sinuous curve of the Dragon.

They were foreigners, all of them. By their look, by the cast of their skin and the wide set of their eyes, by the long knotted braids of their beards, they were most likely from the south, probably from one of the provinces of Goarnn; probably gladiators, or mercenaries come through the western port city of Tulon.

He didn't know them. He didn't know their faces. But he knew the shadow that held them. It was the same shadow as his own. It was the shadow of the Dragon that swirled about them and through them, like a wisp, the same shadow that held his brother now, just as it held everyone here, everything here, just as it had once held him, just as it would soon hold all of the rest of the Pale as well.

The men of his own legion, from when he had ruled here, were no more. Baelus had apparently learned enough from his older brother to know that you only kept close those loyal to your own, whatever the cost. Baelus had certainly murdered them all. Just as Chaelus once did to the men who had served his father before him.

The heat of the open hearth behind him, around which the twelve Servian lords had once sat in council here, long ago, washed over him like a tide. Its smoke brought a sharp sting to his eyes.

Yet even the smell of burning pine did nothing to abate the rot of loss and shame that clung about the place. The warmth of a fire did nothing to heal the chill of his brother's—of the Dragon's—stare which now held him in its grip. Its light did nothing to heal the darkness that consumed his brother's soul right now before him, the selfsame darkness that had once consumed Chaelus', and their father's before them both.

It was why the Mother, the matriarch of the Servian Order, the order of knights that now served him, had warned him—no, had *told* him not to come here. His House, his throne, the throne of their father, the throne of the House of

Malius, she had said, was already lost. She had told him there was nothing left here but poison, like that from an old, festering wound.

Yet he had come back anyway. He had come because he had to. He had to try, even if there was no hope, try to save his brother and win his father's kingdom back. He had to try, even if there was no hope left for those things he had already given up for the sake of prophecy, even if he could never have these things for himself.

Baelus leaned forward.

"I see that even death cannot take you, my brother. You can't imagine what horror I felt when I found your tomb was empty but a few months ago."

No more than the horror Chaelus had felt, raised from the dead by the hand of a child Servian knight, only to discover that an even greater darkness than death had consumed him. No. No more than horror he had felt when he eventually learned that to save the very things and the people he loved, he had to abandon them all, give them up, for the sake, for the will, of a prophecy he had never believed in.

Yet it wasn't sincerity that passed now across his brother's lips, only guile.

"It wasn't death that claimed me," Chaelus replied. "It was the Dragon's whisper. It is the same whisper that succors you now, that holds you in its shadow, my brother."

"A whisper?" Baelus smirked. "That's all?"

"A whisper, and you know it all too well. It is the same whisper that once ministered to our father, and then again to myself until the time of my passing. The same whisper that came to you before what should have been the long hours of your mourning for me. It is the whisper in the dark that you know so well, and though you haven't heard the wizard's whisper in months, it is in the darkness that still whispers to you, long after he's gone."

"Who? Magus? That old wizard left when your corpse did. I wonder now if it wasn't you perhaps that finished him off."

"My brother, Magus was only a veil of the Dragon, and he was no man. And though the veil has been lifted, its deceit remains. I have come to warn you, brother. The veil of the Dragon has descended upon you now. Very soon, the Dragon's Sleep will come to claim you, just as it claimed me."

Baelus grimaced. "I have heard all the tales of what you in all your newfound piety have done. I see the mark of the Dragon that is etched upon your brow. But I don't believe in any of it. Nothing. Just as I know that you come to me now only to supplant me. You speak of deceit, brother, but I know all too well the spies you have already sent against me."

Baelus flourished his hand and the sleeve of his robe. It billowed out like that of a troubadour who has already rehearsed a movement too many times.

Another legionnaire emerged from the burgeoning shadows behind the throne. He was a foreigner too, a mercenary just like the men who held Chaelus. His face a scowl, he tossed a dark spotted sack on the rush-covered stones before Chaelus. It landed with a thickened thud and fell open. The red-bearded head of Cullin, Roan Lord of the House of Soloth, his friend once lost then regained, rolled free from it. Cullin's eyes stared back at Chaelus, rent open in death's final pallor.

Cullin's dead eyes stared with the same warning the Mother had given him before he left her. That he should not have come. That there was nothing left here for him to save. They stared back at him with the loss of the only thing he had gotten back since the Dragon had come; the trust of his friend. Cullin's stare screamed back at him like a talisman, like a warding, like a warning, to leave while he still could.

Revulsion filled his gorge.

He turned away.

The legionnaires forced his stare back at the severed head of his friend.

Their boots drove into his back again.

Baelus smiled.

"Go ahead, if you will. Try to raise him."

Shadow poured out of Baelus like oil. The tentacles of the Dragon spread from him like wings, invisible to everyone here, including Baelus, who could do nothing to know of, or to stop, the evil that already consumed him.

Chaelus kept his face still, a feint of his own, holding back his anger for Cullin's death, but even more, for the threat of the loss of the brother he had come here to save.

And he would save him, no matter what.

The warm tremor of the Giver, like a gentle surge of water just before a storm, flowed into his hands. Its power held there, awash in the sacred moment that lingered just before its release, almost like a lover, still unseen by those gathered, unseen by those who would want to know, unseen by his brother, and most of all, unseen by the shadow of the Dragon that had already claimed them all.

He held it there and waited for the disembodied voice of Talus, the Giver from a hundred years before who had last driven the wyrm away, whose spirit now possessed Chaelus but only spoke when he willed, to whisper his truth in his ear. To tell him he could do this. To tell him he could save the damned.

It did not come to him.

Instead, he only heard the memory of his Teacher, Al-Aaron, the boy Servian knight who had saved him, in a long ago whisper heard over burning gossamer; a reply from when Chaelus once asked him why his Teacher had not come to save him sooner.

"You weren't ready," was Al-Aaron's reply.

It was from death Al-Aaron had raised him, not life.

Baelus stared back at him. The sad sting of contempt brimmed around Baelus' eyes.

Baelus wouldn't change. He couldn't change, at least not yet, certainly not on this day.

Chaelus closed his eyes. His lips parted with a sigh. Still, he had to try, before it was too late. He could not refuse to save his brother.

He had to try.

His own crown, the mark of the Dragon, the mark of prophecy, burned in white sigils upon the flesh of his brow. He opened his hands to the rush of azure flame. It surged and flew out from them like rain.

The Dragon's shadow, and all that it threatened to consume, fell like rushes beneath it. The expanding glow of the Giver's flame burned through everything, a resplendent circle of holy fire rising above the cries of men falling in rapture around him, and the searing cries of the hopelessly damned.

The spirit of the Giver ebbed beneath the whispered moans of the faithful that remained.

Chaelus opened his eyes.

Baelus shook, frozen over the rage of the Dragon within him. His hands whitened against the pale stone they gripped. His breath shot out in bursts. He was paralyzed. But so was the Dragon that dwelt within him, paralyzed but far from defeated, far from anything like that at all. The Dragon roared through Baelus' lips. Its shriek thundered and set the pale stones of the tall tower atremble.

Answering cries of men to the Dragon's call descended and rose from both above and beneath them.

Chaelus reached down and retrieved Sundengal from the feet of his brother and stood.

"Then it seemsI must bear our father's sword a little longer, my brother," he whispered.

Sidestepping the writhing faithful and the dead, he ascended the rightmost of the twinned stairs leading to the outer doors.

He felt as much as heard the screams of those behind him, those who had succumbed to grace just a moment before, as they were put to death by the swords of their newly arrived brothers before the malaise of their new faith could spread.

Before him, the outer doors swung open. Four legionnaires burst in, confused and afraid of the sounds they had heard, their swords held at the ready.

He would spare them the fate of their brothers.

The chime of Sundengal, its blade now free, rang out against the tower's white stone. He had come to save his brother, not to kill; whether they be Roan man or mercenary rogue did not matter. His only choice was to persuade them of something else, to let them run. The legionnaires above had not witnessed the fate of the others. They had only heard the cacophony of the dying below. They hopefully wouldn't understand that it was a different fate altogether, a more benign fate, waiting for them—that they might live.

He let loose a cry of war.

The legionnaires broke ranks. Two fled down the other stair. Another stumbled after them. The fourth tumbled off the stair in his haste. His scream silenced as his neck snapped upon the stones and rushes below.

Beyond the door, the courtyard was silent.

Even the drums of war had fallen mute.

Legionnaires waited and watched from the top of the surround. Their spears lowered as he stepped out into the court.

The rest of the legion gathered there staggered back from him, their heads bowed, shaking, falling to their knees around him.

No one opposed him before the outer gate. The saved before him would have built him a bridge of their own bodies if he had but asked them.

He had already done enough.

The rush of booted heels and clang of swords rang up the stairs behind him.

So many more would die on this day for the unwitting piety he had forced upon them.

He turned. The blue light of the Giver still burned like a halo from his hands.

The legionnaires not in thrall to him formed a shield wall as they poured through the open tower door. Two score vomited out from the tower depths. Yet they came no further. Their swords drawn, the light of the Giver reflected in the fear in their eyes, fear of him, and of their punishment for failing to stop him.

Behind them rose the seamless white stone of the tower that no mason born of man could have ever built; one of the twelve towers of the Evarun, left behind by them for the redemption of man. Machinations and hoardings built for war by his father, then Chaelus, and now his brother, dressed it like scars. Its pure stone smoldered like blood in the dying light of the setting sun.

He turned full circle, so that all eyes in the open courtyard and those in the shadows around it, all of them, would see him and bear witness.

"Bring Idyliss to me," he called out.

The legionnaires did nothing, neither the saved, nor the condemned. Perhaps prophecy would not let them.

Against the still, the shadows of the stables stirred. The familiar bray of Idyliss pierced the tense air.

A drab, cloaked servant shambled alongside the silver mare as he led her to him, saddled and ready. Beneath the shadow of his cowl, a slave collar gripped the man's neck. Burns covered the right side of his face, a face that was at once both distant and familiar.

Grovis, the man who had once been his tribune before Chaelus died and Baelus took his throne, smiled. Baelus apparently hadn't killed everyone. Those closest to his brother he had kept to torture; as an example, as a trophy, as a warning.

Above his smile, Grovis stared past Chaelus, his eyes ringed red by the foreshadowing of tears. The Dragon's shadow was strange to be only a ghost within him.

The man would die this day.

Chaelus took Idyliss' reins from Grovis.

"Come with me."

"No." Grovis shook his head.

"Why?"

Grovis' smile stiffened.

"Because I can't."

"Then know at least you are blessed," he whispered, choked.

"I am indeed," Grovis answered.

The converted mercenaries of Baelus' legion kept their places as the last cries of the dying fell away.

The unconverted held their rank before the tower doors.

Leading Idyliss, he pushed open the heavy oak doors of the outer gate.

The blackened stumps of the forest that had once surrounded the House of Malius, Servian lord, betrayer of the Giver and only redeemed of the Fallen, stood up like gravestones above winter's first snow, like a warning, bathed beneath the somber glare of the setting sun.

Like a promise.

Like prophecy.

He mounted Idyliss.

Before the sun would fully set, so many more men would die this day, for what he had done, and for what he had failed to do.

## Chapter Two: Hope

Al-Mariam raised her face to the chill of evening's first call. The sable trim of her hood flickered soft against her. The blush of her skin grew numb.

It felt good.

Like the cold strength just beneath the leather of Aela's graceful hilt. Like the cold bright steel beneath the gossamer binding of her blade, white like the newly fallen snow. Like the grace of Rua that had brought her through her own forge, to be here.

The path of footsteps she had left behind as she climbed out of the shallow ravine away from the other Servian knights, to be alone, was the only mar upon the bright expanse around her. It stretched out away from her, pristine like a halo.

Like a promise.

Like a hope.

"Shabek," Obidae's voice came.

She nearly jumped from her skin. The Khaalish chieftain's single word drifted on the winter breeze. The unwashed musk of his presence settled over her. He stood beside her in his furs and his leathers, leaning on the shaft of his spear, where no one had been just a silent breath ago.

Here, along the silent edge of Sanseveria, and the Garden of Rua.

The southern edge of the forest behind them marked the boundary of their sacred home, of their safety, of their exile. Its deep azure cloak of conifer and ash watched over them from the chalk-white cliffs above.

"It means the great waiting," Obidae offered. "It is the place where the Giver, where the Shoa, resides. It is the hope that is contained in the space within the moment that is left in between."

She steeled herself against her newly-unsettled nerves. She breathed in until she felt the calm chill of the air once more fill her bones, until she felt its peace, like a moment in between.

Obidae nodded, satisfied. He stroked the long dark braid of his hair, stopping at each of the small bright colored stones woven within it. He paused, saying a small silent word, a prayer, at each one of them. He took a deep breath, not unlike her own.

"So tell me, what do you wait for?" he asked.

She felt Obidae's stare wash over her before he turned it toward the waiting emphasis of the white plain below.

"I'm waiting," she replied, "we are all waiting, for Chaelus' return."

"You mean the Giver. But you cannot say that of him yet."

"He's late," she said. "And it's nearly nightfall again."

Three days he had been gone, gone to a place he should never have left for. The Mother had forbidden him to go. But then, that had never stopped Al-Mariam, had it? At least, not in her heart, but Chaelus didn't even serve the Mother the same way she did. The Mother served him. The Mother

served the Giver, served Chaelus, and so too, Al-Mariam reminded herself, did she.

All of them did, didn't they? That was why they were
here.

Twelve Servian knights, one for each of the twelve disciples who had been prophesied to follow the Giver, just as
Talus had raised each of the twelve Servian lords a hundred
years before.

Twelve.

Like the twelve Servian lords before they had fallen.

The number was not the Mother's intended choice, but a
concession made in part to Al-Aaron, the Younger; the child
knight who, because of his near-mortal wound, could not be
one of the twelve to go with Chaelus. Yet it was not for him
alone that the Mother had done this, but rather it was her ac-
knowledgement of the reality of the malaise that had befallen
what now remained of the Servian order.

Twelve.

Twelve who had fallen. Twelve apostates.

It was the same number that the traitor Maedelous had
chosen to take with him. It was the same number of Servian
knights that had chosen to follow him in his abandonment of
their vows, their faith, and their order.

The wounds that Maedelous' betrayal had left ran deep,
and what little remained of the Servian knights' hope had
bled away with them. This was in spite of the fact that only
a fortnight before, the one for whom they had waited a hundred years, the Giver, had been returned to them in the vessel
of a Roan lord named Chaelus.

Yet their faith still wanted a symbol, a number.

So, twelve they would be.

Twelve who would serve. Twelve who would save.

The Mother's decision had been one of faith. It had to be, because the Servian knights who followed her had lost theirs.

For most of the Servian knights who remained, the notion that their faith, their belief, was best served by something they couldn't see had vanished like fall beneath winter. Precious little faith remained for them even for the things they could see. Now, more than ever, they needed to be carried by something.

Al-Aaron knew this. The child knight knew it better than anyone. He always had. In part, it was what had previously driven him to defy the Mother when he raised Chaelus from the cenotaph, raised him from the very dead and brought him, brought the Giver, the first seed of their hope, back to them.

Now it seemed, the Mother, in spite of her own desires, in spite of her own belief, or perhaps because of it, at last knew this as well.

She knew it was the right choice for the Mother to make, to keep the remnants of the Servian order together. This was in spite of the fact that every part of her still screamed against it. The artifice of it all burned within her breast like a lingering, smoldering coal, because if they could only have faith in the things they could see, what kind of faith was it to begin with?

If this was indeed the moment in-between as Obidae had just said, Al-Mariam would be a fool to not be afraid of the fire being kindled within it.

Twelve.

Twelve who would save. Twelve who would fall.

The Mother had chosen each of them, each for her own reasons, and one of them was Al-Mariam.

Twelve Servian knights the Mother had chosen to be guardians of the Giver reborn.

Yet their mortal husks served no purpose for that. Their own vows, her own vows, forbade it. By their vows, they were forbidden to shed the blood of men. But then, Chaelus didn't need them to, did he? Prophecy itself protected him. It needed him. She had seen the power of it, the Giver's power, manifested within him. She had felt it in his very touch upon her skin.

Yet still, twelve the Mother had chosen for him.

The twelve were not to be his companions, either. The mysticism that had already grown around him, around Chaelus, the Giver, forbade that. How could one befriend or love something, or someone, so holy as he? Or could they? Could she?

No. The one redemptive truth was that she and the other Servian knights sent with him were much more than guardians or companions. They were at last what they were always intended to be. They were his servants, and if need be, his sacrifice. That was the purpose for which they had been chosen.

And she would gladly be that.

If not for prophecy, then for him.

The small shadow of a horse and rider broke out of the thin blue veil on the horizon, a mark like a firebrand upon a pristine field of white, like an urgent stroke of prophecy.

Chaelus, the vessel of the Giver reborn, had returned to them.

Chaelus.

Her lips, her cheeks, the very flesh beneath her brow kindled at the sight of him, in the very place where Chaelus had touched her only a fortnight before, when he had held her face and showed her his divinity, the true nature of what he was; when he had touched the very soul of her.

When he had touched her heart.

She had tried to then, but she could no longer deny her devotion toward him. What plagued her heart, though, was the question of its nature. She had been touched by him, by the eternal spirit of the Giver that possessed him, but she had also been touched by something else, something more. She had been touched by the mortal husk that carried it, by the man who so effortlessly and nobly suffered both the burden and the grace of its bearing.

It was his humanness that kept her near to him, that made her love him.

It was he, Chaelus, not the vessel of the Giver reborn but the resurrected barbarian lord of the House of Malius, who had laid such a claim upon her heart.

She stopped her hand as it drew unconsciously near her brow, just above the place where Chaelus' flesh bore the pale mark of the Dragon's crown.

The shuffling cascade of ice and stone down the slope behind her announced Al-Toman's arrival.

Al-Toman's thick merchant cloak swirled about him.

Disguised as a noblewoman's merchant train returning from Tulon, some of them as merchants, some of them as slaves, the twelve kept their Gossamer Blades hidden beyond the warded safety of the Garden, the place of their exile. Obidae, along with Al-Mariam's orphaned mystical brother, Michalas, spiritual twin to Chaelus and somehow part of the prophecy as well, would also play the part of slaves. Chaelus, their prophesied protector, would be their temporal one as well, should ever the eyes of bandits or Hunters, the assassins sent by the Theocracy to exterminate their order, find them.

And, of course, Obidae would be there to help them with this, too.

Al-Toman eyed Obidae and nodded to him.

Obidae, the mastiff barbarian, nodded back.

Al-Toman, unlike most of the Servian Knights, felt no discomfort toward the barbarian chieftain. In fact, a sort of silent friendship had developed between the two in the fortnight that had passed since Obidae and his band of Khaalish warriors joined them.

Al-Toman, like most of the Servian knights, came from a foreign land. In Al-Toman's case, from the Dunnish lands to the east, where the mysticism of the Khaalishite was not so foreign and where both blood and trade had flowed between both peoples ever since the Awakening, a hundred years before.

Together, the two would also help to serve as ambassadors when they arrived in the Khaalishite, so that the Giver, so that Chaelus, could carry the message of his return to them as well. Hopefully, they could do so before the Dragon, which had already darkened the Theocratic States along their border, carried its own.

That was why the Mother had sent them, anyway, if it was true that the souls of the Theocracy were already lost.

"The others are beginning to wonder if..." Al-Toman began. He followed the direction of her stare. His voice softened. "He's here."

Al-Mariam heard Al-Toman's voice change at the sight of Chaelus, in unfeigned reverence at the sight of their, his own, savior.

She heard the call and running footsteps of the other Servian knights climbing the ridge to meet him, to see him.

"He's late," she said.

Al-Toman's mouth waited, open but silent.

Blood and spittle gathered around the corner of his lips. His head hung with a slight bend over where the arrow shaft protruded from his throat and through the back of his neck. The rest of his body sagged, then gave way beneath him.

Her own voice, along with everything else, fell suddenly silent.

More arrows grew out of the snow around her, sprouting like a savage garden. Their fletching was the color of blood. She felt a sharp tug at her cloak and a heavy weight.

She searched in vain for Obidae, for his protection, but only found the muted pleas of fallen knights in the snow around her.

Across the frozen plain, the small shadow of Chaelus seemed to move farther away from her.

The silence cracked at last like a frozen pond around her, exploding in a pain that consumed her, crushing her, bringing her down, dulled only by the mortal sound of her own scream.

## Chapter Three: Ire

Chaelus watched them fall, one by one, like cordwood; five Servian knights brought down to the bristling snow.

Crimson feathers stuck out against the pallor. Even from a half a league away he could see them, like the blood they let. The red fletching of the Khaalish. But Chaelus didn't need the whisper of the Giver to drift through him to know it was a ruse. It wasn't the Khaalish. It was something far worse.

It was the Hunters.

Idyliss bowed her head without his command and flew across the snow-covered plain.

They were still too far away for him to save them.

He held out his hand to reach them with all of the power of the Giver that he held; his palm outstretched, to reach, to ward, to summon, to defend, to rain holy fire upon the men, the evil men, the Hunters who had struck them down.

Nothing came from him. The only thing left was the seeming weight of a hundred stone.

Beyond the scarcest whisper, the spirit of the Giver said nothing else to him. The whisper, it said no.

His shoulders shook with impotent rage. His hand trembled with the desperation of a drunken fool. He knew that was just what he had been; a fool. He had been a fool to leave them here. The Mother had been right, just as she always was.

He should never have gone.

The dark shadow of Baelus' eyes, the eyes of the Dragon, stared back at him like a veil over the distant slaughter before him. The bleeding cries of the Servian knights rushed up to him like some foul incense offered up beneath them.

He slumped over Idyliss' mane. The wind of their flight whistled past them.

The Mother had been right.

He never should have gone.

In a rush, the plain of snow disappeared beneath them.

A shallow vale, unseen against the winter haze, opened up beneath Idyliss' hooves. Together they went, beast and man, tumbling down. Billows of ice and snow exploded around him as they fell.

The ground trembled beneath them.

Idyliss struggled to right herself.

He took to his feet.

Beyond the curtain of settling snow, four archers against the rising slope before him stared back at him in shock.

One of them, the quicker of them, hefted his bow.

Chaelus drew Sundengal as the man nocked an arrow against him. The distance fell away beneath his strides.

Bow and chainmail splintered through the screaming flesh of the Hunter beneath them.

The other three dropped their bows and pulled out whatever they could reach. Sword, axe, and mace.

Yet they were unprepared for someone with drawn steel coming against them, only the helpless cry of the faithful slaughtered. They were only prepared to watch the Servian knights die helplessly before them. They were woefully unprepared to meet him.

One by one, the other three Hunters, just like the Servian knights whose lives they had taken, fell like cordwood. Their cries fell silent as their blood rushed onto the snow amongst the red fletching of their feigned Khaalish arrows, fallen and scattered from their quivers where they died.

*

Michalas, unwitting stepchild of the angels, could only stare at the place where his sister, Mariam, had just fallen with an arrow through her heart.

He took another step closer to her through the trampled, bloodied snow.

Men rushed past him.

The cries and laments of the dying surrounded him, but not his sister's.

She was silent.

The fletching of arrows matted with blood around her. There were too many of them; too many arrows, too much blood, too many dead.

He held where he was, frozen. Not from the cold, but from the sore weight that clung to him like a tomb; a weight and a numbness he was beginning to know all too well ever since the angels had left him.

Because he didn't know. He didn't know anything now, only that he couldn't help her. He couldn't help her because the angels had gone. Because no matter how hard he tried not to see it, all he knew was their absence, the void left behind by the angels who had always been with him until his sister had rescued him, when he had first found Chaelus, the vessel of the Giver reborn.

They were all he had ever known. The angels had cared for him ever since he could remember, even before Ras Dumas had taken him, and ever since he was born. They were like breath to him. But now, even their marking upon his brow was silent, a mirror of the Giver's own, like a hollow ward.

All he could do was tremble at the sight of her, his sister, not knowing if she was alive or dead. Not knowing if she breathed. And it terrified him. Because he didn't know.

Because the angels had gone, and it didn't seem like they were ever coming back, and the only thing he had left was her.

*

Blood on fallen snow.

Chaelus slumped to his knees beside Mariam's still form.

The frozen shadow of her brother, Michalas, the child who would save them, reached out silently toward her.

The gentle locks of Michalas' hair fell over the runes of the Dragon, etched upon his brow like Chaelus' own, the mark of the Dragon that bound him and the boy together under the ubiquitous guiding lamp of prophecy.

There was no guidance from prophecy here, where only the silence of the dead surrounded them.

But Mariam still breathed. Her chest rose slowly. She wasn't dead; at least, not yet.

A broken shaft protruded from her side, just beneath her breast and thankfully, just beneath her heart.

His hand wavered over it. The impotent silence of the Giver surrounded it. Like the silence of the dead.

The vessel of the Giver reborn cried out for help.

Knights ran to him, tunics torn, bringing forth wine to clean and dull the pain of her wound, or her passing.

He cradled her head in his arms. With one of his hands he held the broken shaft.

Michalas held her hand, tears streaming from his eyes. Strange; he had never seen the boy cry before.

Her dim eyes stared into him with all the faith a soul could muster.

He, Chaelus, once Roan Lord of the House of Malius, now vessel of the Giver reborn, stared back into hers with all the courage and faith he could feign, and every ounce of his fear, as her scream let loose upon the frozen Pale.

*

Al-Mariam walked amongst the dead laid out upon the pallid snow.

Obidae staggered toward her from the edge of the camp in a blood-let haze. The blood of more dead dressed his skin and the matt of his furs like a second cloak, even as it mingled with his own. A bright new wound colored the scars on his arm as he held up a medallion swinging from a chain within his fist. The medallion had the writ of Tulon marked upon it.

Hunters.

Mercenaries hired to hunt down the last of the Servian order.

She had heard their screams even as she woke, even louder than those of the knights they killed, even louder than her own, she imagined. Three more assassins, other than the four she learned Chaelus had killed. She had been told that Obidae had kept them alive just long enough to question them. They hadn't said much, but they had said enough.

The four dead Servian knights, who should have been five, lay in repose against the still blanket of snow, their arms folded over the pristine gossamer-bound promise of their blades, their sightless eyes pressed closed by her. The young knight Al-Tomas looked strangely the eldest among them now.

Strange what death can do.

Her own wound beneath her breast burned.

She glanced toward Chaelus, where he stood apart from them all. He stared back at her with mournful eyes, the same blood-let cloak that covered Obidae covering him as well.

The blood-red fletching of the arrows piercing the dead knights fluttered in the breeze; arrows made by the Hunters to cast blame on the Khaalish, to end what fragile alliance of faith they and the Servian knights shared.

Hunters under the writ of the city of Tulon, by order by the Theocracy, which in name and claim ruled over them all.

A flurry of prayerful whispers opened near to her.

The shadow of Chaelus draped over her. The surviving Servian knights around her went to bended knee.

She stumbled, unthinking, toward him. She fell into him, grateful all the more as he took her within his arms. The scent of him washed over her, burning through her like a healing salve, like nothing else she had ever felt.

Chaelus stared into her. His eyes seared red at their edges, hardened at a depth she could never really know, by things she knew only he alone could ever see, and where angels spoke to him alone in whispers.

Not even angels could heal the hurt in his eyes.

Chaelus had failed at the one thing he wanted most. She knew this without him even saying it. He had failed to save someone he loved from the same darkness that once claimed him. He had failed to save his brother. And he had returned from that failure to this, a massacre, and she could tell by his eyes it was one he told himself he should have been here to prevent.

"I'm so sorry," she whispered.

"No," Chaelus' voice choked. "I am."

Chaelus traced the back of his finger along her cheek. He kissed her brow.

Her heart quickened. The salve deepened.

"I should not have let this happen to you," Chaelus said.

She let go of him. She clutched her hands, her need, her want, her weakness, against herself, against the burning pulse of the arrow wound.

"You couldn't have stopped it," she said.

A flinch in Chaelus' eye answered her.

"I know why you had to go to him. I would have gone to him, too. In case you don't remember, I have done the same thing myself."

Chaelus glanced with her to where Michalas, her brother kept for her by the angels, finally slept, curled up beside a new fire that had only just been lit. "So you did."

She nodded.

"And still you can't find rest," Chaelus said.

She placed her hand upon his chest.

"Neither would you, even if you saved him."

Chaelus turned away to the surrounding white plain, looking somewhere beyond it, somewhere between the place from where he had just come, the white tower she had never seen, the seat from which he once ruled, where his brother still did and suffered for it, and another place, somewhere to the east, another place from his past where she knew he was fated still to go. She knew he looked between the two, hoping for the place where prophecy would finally let him be.

"Then tell me," Chaelus asked. "Where do you go when you cannot go forward and you cannot go back?"

She touched his face, cautious, not for her, but for him. Her own hesitation for him had already passed.

Chaelus' skin was taut from cold and weariness.

"You simply take the step that's in front of you," she said.

Chaelus reached up and took her hand. He clasped it between his. "You're eloquent. Though I fear in the end, any step I take will lead to both of them."

"Perhaps," she said. "Perhaps it will."

She slid her hand away.

"Or perhaps, in taking a step, something far greater will be allowed to take shape. Something not even prophecy, or you and I can tell."

She moved closer to him, wondering to which place he stared, to which fate he moved; for himself, for the Pale, and if she dared, even for her.

"When all hope fails," she said, "it is our faith in the end that carries us."

"Even for one who still doesn't believe?"

She smiled at the lack of faith of the one who would save them. "Even when he alone is awash in its glory?"

Chaelus feigned a smile. "Such are the machinations of prophecy."

Obidae walked up to them. The sharp odor of blood and fate and faith surrounded the Khaalish chieftain. He bowed his head to Chaelus, who stared back to the place from which he had come, to the vengeance he had left there upon the ones who tried to take their lives.

"But not the dead," Obidae muttered.

He released a fistful of red fletching like drops of blood across the snow, falling one by one as they were carried on the western wind.

"Shoa, it is time," Obidae said, his face lowered, in faith and in shame that he should ever be so bold. "We cannot stay here any longer."

Chaelus turned back from his vision and refuge, back to her.

"I know," he said. "I had to try. I had to see if my brother could still be saved. I was wrong."

She breathed in. Her breast filled, then released. She sagged with its waning, with all of its hope, and all of its loss, and every one of its moments that fell in between.

A gust of ice and snow blew up about them.

"Shabek," she whispered.

Obidae nodded. "The Dragon has taken the hearts of the east; it is in the hearts of the east and in the hearts of my people, where it must be defeated, not in hearts here. These Hunters will come again. I do not think we can stop them."

Chaelus turned and looked down toward the camp, past the reposing dead. He drew Sundengal, weighing her in his hand.

"Then let us bury the dead," he said. "And wake the hearts of the east from their slumber."

## Chapter Four: Shabek

Olivia sagged into the depths of the chair in the hollow of the small round chapel. A desperate moan defied her pressed lips. Tears welled around the corners of her eyes.

Amidst the flames and glowing coals of the cauldron, the shadows still lingered, passing each other among the flames, drifting between the horror of the vision she had just seen and the vain hope she still held against it. It was there, in that thin line, that moment in between, somewhere between the past and the future, that she had seen it. There, in that one dark moment of the present, waiting for them all, beyond the veil of safety of the Garden of Rua.

The truth of it terrified her.

She could still hear the cries from her vision, piercing between the flames; cries both of the soul and the flesh, cries from the Giver and from the twelve Servian knights she had sent to go with him.

It was hard to tell which cries lingered longer—those of the dying, or those who were left behind, rendered helpless by their vows and prophecy to save them.

Yet it was what she saw and heard after them, somewhere beneath the cries, that was the source of her terror; a whisper of something deeper than the shadows which hid it, in a place perhaps where even prophecy couldn't see or hear. Eleven cold, red flames, from eleven kings, turned eleven fallen Servian lords. Their whisper sounded like war.

Beyond them, beyond the fire, the darkened and dour bearded face of Al-Hoanar drew toward her. She sagged at the touch of the hand and one arm that his battles had left him.

"No," she muttered.

Al-Hoanar waited only the short desperate moment that his patience allowed.

"What did you see?" he asked.

"They've been away less than a day and the Hunters have already found them," she answered. Her voice trembled. "They're safe now, but they are not without loss. They are not without death."

She pushed herself up. She pressed her hands against the tears in her eyes, more this time than what usually came along with her visions; certainly more than any other time she could remember.

"Already, four of our knights have fallen," she said. "Al-Mariam was nearly among them. To arrowshot they perished. Only eight now remain. It seems our influence on prophecy has already been undone. The arrows were fletched with the blood feather of the Khaalish, but the Khaalish didn't shoot them. It was only made to look like they did, to feign a hazard against our alliance, against our trust, and against our faith."

"Hunters," Al-Hoanar growled.

"The Giver, and Obidae, found them first, but not soon enough. Not soon enough to stop them."

Al-Hoanar stepped away from the fire and back into the shadows. "I am glad they were the ones to find them. They do not suffer the same burden of faith that we do."

She reached her hand to the braided plaits of his bearded face.

Al-Hoanar pulled away this time.

"To never shed the blood of man," she whispered. "To
honor a promise made upon the death of the Giver to take
no man's life, as Chaelus' father Malius once took the life
of the Giver before; to make good a promise that was once
broken. It is no small matter. It is not without its significance,
Al-Hoanar."

"No, revered Mother, it is not, nor is it insignificant that
we will all die for it. And then, tell me: who will we serve?
Who is it that we will save?"

"Beware, Al-Hoanar. The seed of the Dragon, it grows
in fertile soil. Our testing isn't over yet, no. It has only just
begun. Though the Dragon may be threatened by the Giver's return, its eye has not and will never turn away from the
hearts and the promises of the very ones, the only ones, who
have ever stood against it."

Al-Hoanar stepped back into the dancing light of the
flames. "Too bad the Dragon doesn't know it no longer needs
to. It already has its eyes all around us. Very soon, and the
longer we stay here, the sooner it will see us all dead."

"No, Al-Hoanar, and, I'm afraid, yes. You were once
secure in Maedelous' council. You know what whisperers of
his are still among us."

Al-Hoanar pursed his lips as he bided his time to choose
his words. His grief-stricken stare struck her like a blow.

"Revered Mother," he said. "I was once in Maedelous' council. The beliefs that brought me there are no different than those shared by the ones who remain with him,
or even the beliefs I hold now. The only difference now is
that, whether by providence or prophecy, I was faced with a
choice that wouldn't let me remain with him."

"And that was?"

Al-Hoanar looked down and closed his eyes.

"Revered Mother, we looked to Maedelous and the others still look to him because we saw no hope."

Her breath escaped her, though she already knew what he said to be truth. She sank back into her seat, wondering if it would hold the sudden weight of her spirit.

"But I was there the day the Giver claimed Chaelus. I witnessed his divinity. But even that was not the choice I spoke of. It happened even before then."

Al-Hoanar's stare struck her just as before.

"It was from watching you, revered Mother; by watching your touch, ever gentle upon the threads that bound us all, never once claiming them as your own, but instead seeing the divinity in each of them, in each of us. Even in the frailest and the foulest amongst us, you found hope. And by watching you, so too did I."

"And what hope do you see in me now?"

"That, for the first time, at last, we are not alone."

She smiled, at the corners of her mouth. It was only a ghost, but she still felt her skin almost splinter.

And it felt good.

It felt like Rua. It felt like hope.

"No," she said. "We are not alone. No less so than we have ever been. Yet I think it is something that, perhaps, I had forgotten."

She reached out her hand.

Al-Hoanar clasped it in his.

She stood of her own accord.

"This hope," she said, "this time, we cannot, we shall not, I will not, stand idly by and wait for that hope to die."

The line of her mouth hardened again, but only near the surface. Beneath, it bathed in the warmth of stoked embers.

"Al-Hoanar, I thank you, my dear friend, for reminding me of this."

"Of what?"

"Of hope, of my own strength, and that I, that we, are not alone. But more than that is the simple truth that we never have been alone. Prophecy may guide us. But the Rua, it will, and has always protected us, in ways that even prophecy cannot foretell. The Dragon cannot defeat it. Not even its servants can.

"Please summon the knights to the synod, all of them. Then find Belloch. Please tell him to summon the Khaalish. Tell him we are in need of them as we prepare for war."

\*

Al-Aaron tossed in fever soaked madness beneath his furs. They clung across his limbs like a shroud. His chest felt like a hundred sordid stones. The wound in his belly burned with cold fire.

Across the ruins of the sacred tower, trumpets and men split the frozen air with calls of war, in this place where men had sworn to never shed the blood of man.

But that was war, wasn't it? Wasn't it madness?

The pallor of the knight surgeons who tended him belied their calm. The Mother's whisper to them had been urgent and swift. Her comforting of him had been even quicker, her departure hurried as the surgeons prepared their tools and salves to leave. Her instruction was plain.

Prepare the boy to leave the safety of the Garden and their exile.

But he couldn't be healed and he couldn't get away from what he suffered, and he never would.

With hastened care, they applied fresh linen to the blackened hole in his belly that had never quite scarred, where the ghost of his Teacher, Chaelus' father Malius, ran him through with his own blade a fortnight ago. But it had never been Malius, had it? It had never even been his ghost. It had always been the Dragon. And it still was.

He watched the old bandages, blackened with the Dragon's taint, burn upon the coals in the cauldron next to his bed. Its stench was foul and pressing and sweet, even beneath the fragrance of the hearth.

The numbing weight of his wound and his limbs kept him buried as if he were in the darkness of the cenotaph, like the one from which he had raised Chaelus, Roan Lord of the House of Malius, now vessel of the Giver reborn, from the dead.

But that was the veil of the Dragon, wasn't it? That was madness.

Even the older wound of his arm, where the Remnant blade had struck him, showed no sign of any restoration or healing. Though the black tendrils of shadow had receded, the weight of his sins that it carried still lingered within his flesh.

So he couldn't get away, not really, no matter where they went. No matter where prophecy, or the Mother, or even madness took him.

Even with all of the trumpets of war to protect him. Not even the wisdom of the Mother could save him. Not here, or there. Not even death, whose dark waters still waited just beyond his reach. Not even Chaelus, the vessel of the Giver reborn, or the quest upon which he had just left to save them all, to save the fallen Pale.

Not even that would save him.

So all he could do was stare back at the black gloved hand the dead man in the shadows offered him, the outstretched hand of a ghost.

The same ghost who had betrayed him, had all but killed him, the ghost of his Teacher, the ghost of Chaelus' father, the ghost of the fallen Servian lord, that had never really been a ghost at all.

Malius—no, the Dragon—smiled at him from the shadows.

*"You are so wise to fear me, my love."*

"I know what you are," Al-Aaron said. "I know how you deceived me. You will not do so again." His voice shook.

*"I'm not here to deceive you."*

"You are the Dragon and everything you say is a lie."

The Dragon, the face of Malius, smiled.

*"No, my dear, but you are wise to fear me because I speak the truth. You are wise to fear me because I have come back to save you, my love."*

\*

Wind, and ice, and freezing rain.

The boy, Login, drew his thin cloak even tighter, giving up all sense or reason to the vain hope that it would do him any good at all.

Maedelous, venerable and renounced Servian knight that he was, or had been, had commanded Login to wait for him here.

Beyond the meager protection of the narrow close in which he sheltered, the square descended in gradual terraces to the freezing wharf below. The ships stiffened and moaned as they waited in the cold, as the ice, just on the horizon, made its slow way south to entomb them. The sounds scraped like a funeral cry against his ears.

The sky lay low and dense above the city like a shroud.

Pitiful in their need, though not in their effort, the street people and vendors of Tulon still hawked their wares beneath the bright chafe of winter's first fall, but the hard edge of desperation sharpened and hurried their cries. The other townsfolk shuffled past them, their dark eyes cast downward, the bitter resolve of their desperation filling out the echo of their silence. It came from more than just the cold.

There was something else here.

Beyond them, across the square, four men in black cloaks stood with Maedelous in the shadows and low eaves of the shops, in relative shelter from curious eyes and the cold.

The shortest and fattest of the four was a city official of some sort. His badge of writ hung from his neck, somewhat hidden beneath his cloak.

The other three were not. They too bore the seal of Tulon, though more openly, like a ready excuse more than any real measure of merit. The weapons scattered across their bodies dispelled any further illusion that they were bureaucrats. They weren't even soldiers of the watch. No. They were entirely something else.

They were Hunters.

Maedelous leaned toward the bureaucrat.

The short fat man nodded to Maedelous and smiled. He smiled the coy smile of one who lies. The three Hunters hurried the bureaucrat away, eyes wary of the people around them.

Maedelous disappeared into the crowd.

Login receded deeper into the protection of the close, against the back of the wagon's hoardings.

Maedelous, once second only to the Mother in the Servian order, had come to Login when the Giver left to defeat the Dragon. Maedelous had come to him just when the grief of the loss of his mother, herself a knight of the order, overtook Login like a shadow. Maedelous had taken him under his care because he had no one else.

It was the loss of his father that drove his mother to her fall, and to her eventual sanctification as a Servian knight.

The Servian order had given his mother back to him, though.

Yet she hadn't come back the last time, when she left the sanctity of the Garden on whatever mission the Mother had sent her on. Hunters found her, and murdered her.

She would not have fought them, either. No, she would have kept her oath, her promise, her faith. Here, in Tulon, is where they said she had died, possibly by these very men.

And Maedelous had treated with them. Maedelous said they had come here for provisions, but Hunters weren't merchants.

The other twelve renounced knights, those Maedelous had taken with him, he had sent ahead to bring word of their arrival to the courts of the princes of Goarnn; to find friends, he said, and refuge for an order in exile now that the Dragon had been defeated and the former holds of most of the Servian lords, the white towers of the Evarun, had been abandoned.

They had left quickly, taking little with them for their journey, and Maedelous ignored Login's suggestion of seeking more anonymous help from a farmer's larder.

So why was Maedelous speaking with the very ones who hunted his former order? Maybe it had to do with the real reason why Maedelous had left. What other reason could there possibly be?

Maedelous darkened the open mouth of the close.

His scowl stretched to a thinner smile, like the one he seduced Login with a fortnight before, persuading Login to come with him, away from the safety of the Garden. Maedelous held out an armful of goods; sausage and bread and what looked like a small sack of grain, only the cold keeping them from the edge of damp and rot.

"Here are our provisions," Maedelous said. His fickle smile, just as it had before, left as if it had never been. "Put them well away. The road is long. It will be weary. It won't be long before we wonder where such sustenance has gone."

Login took the packages. Placing the loaf beneath his arm, he dropped the rest into the nearly empty satchel he already carried.

"Who was it you met with?" he asked, the question spoken before he realized its lack of wisdom.

Maedelous' eyes narrowed. He drew his hand up.

He reached to Login and placed the hand upon his brow.

Login stiffened at the chill of the old man's touch.

"You're holding fever, boy," Maedelous said. "I thought I told you to wait in the wagon."

"Who did you meet?"

Maedelous' smile receded.

"Get back to the wagon, boy. You're no good to me sick, or dead. Cover yourself up and get some rest. You're going to need every bit of it before we're through."

\*

Chaelus knelt down beside her.

Mariam, barely sleeping.

A subtle snow began to fall on the brittle cusp of night.

Half asleep, she lifted her face, her eyes still closed, to its winter kiss.

A Servian knight in service to the Giver reborn; in service to him.

And she had nearly died because of it, because of him.

And though he had tried, and though the care of the knights she served with had been enough for her wound, had he needed to, he couldn't have saved her. And not for want. It was the Giver's whim that had stood in his way, an omnipotent power that gave of itself, or kept itself from him as it willed. He had no say in any of it.

She had nearly died because of it, because of him, because prophecy had declined to help him anymore.

The remembered cries of the converted faithful from the day before danced upon the somber night air.

Or perhaps it was because the Giver knew him all too well, because the Giver had been a man like him once, too. Because the Giver knew he would have given away everything just to save her, just like he had tried to save Baelus only the day before. Because it knew that he couldn't, he wouldn't, ever withhold such a gift from someone he loved. Because he knew that the Giver had tried to do it once, too.

No matter what the cost, no matter how many died because of it.

If Mariam had only known that back when they first met, at his crossing of the Maddea, the veil which protected the Garden, back when she had tried to kill him. And that had only been the first time.

He gave a smile.

The beginning of one turned up the corner of her lips as if she could see him.

The light of picket fires blinked and fluttered around them. Khaalish warriors, summoned by their chieftain, Obidae, kept them safe at least until morning.

The light of their fires, and the one he tended next to her, warmed the color of her skin.

He passed his hand across her heated brow along the gentle edge of her pitch dark hair, but it was only the warmth of the fire. Fever hadn't claimed her yet. Hopefully, it wouldn't.

She leaned into his touch as if it were a salve.

Her eyes opened to him.

"We're leaving at first light," he whispered. "How are you feeling?"

"Fine," she answered, half asleep. A shiver claimed her. "Better."

He leaned over her. He drew her furs across to cover the bare shoulder of her gentle linen blouse.

She grasped his hand.

Her hand was warm. Her grip was strong.

Her stare glistened; half from tears awakened from her dreams, and half from a courage he had never seen or been touched by before, not before he met her.

Her lips opened to a silent speech.

"I should let you rest," he said.

"No."

With her other hand, she lifted the long edge of the fur cloak away from her. "You should stay."

## Chapter Five: Longing

"Tell me again," Al-Mariam whispered. Her breath rested upon the back of Chaelus' neck. His warm skin turned the color of soft morning. Her voice carried on the air with the hurried flutter of a dove. "Why must we go to the east?"

His scent filled her very soul as she breathed it back in.

She already knew his answer. To slay a dragon and win his kingdom back, he had once said, only to find that the dragon each must slay is his own, and the promises it whispers are never meant to come to pass. Who should know this better than he, Chaelus, once Lord of the House of Malius, and now vessel of the Giver reborn?

But he was also her lover now, too. He was still a man.

She nestled her chin against him. "And when you get there, tell me; whose dragon will you seek?"

The warmth of his skin diminished.

"Yours or somebody else's?" she asked.

"Whichever I am led to," Chaelus answered. "I will go wherever the blush of the Giver would have me be."

"Do you have a choice?"

"The Giver's voice is silent. I rarely hear him. But when he does speak to me, his answers come more often as questions. As for the rest of the time, when I can't hear him, I can only go to what my eyes see before me. I have no choice in either one, it seems. As for now, I can't hear or see him at all. I cannot help but wonder if he has abandoned me."

"What do your eyes see in the east?"

"To the east, Mariam, they see only death."

"Whose death do you see? Theirs? Ours? Yours?"

Chaelus stayed silent.

But she couldn't.

"What of her? What of the princess you left there when you came to your father's aid before your fall? What of Faerowyn? Will you go to her aid if she seeks you out?"

"Faerowyn is in the past," he answered.

"Isn't the past what you still seek? Or at least some end to it?"

Chaelus' shoulders stiffened.

"So at least it was with your kingdom, and your brother. I know you loved her once, as well."

Chaelus pulled away from her. He stood.

Around them, the camp prepared to leave. She could hear the sounds, but there was no joy in any of it.

She wondered if she had asked too much.

He turned to her. His face softened.

"To save her alone, I would go, if the Giver so moved me, or if there was no other path to go. But she is not my path, Mariam. She is not part of the past that still haunts me. But yes, if it were within my power to save her, I would."

She reached out to him, took his face in her hands.

"I know. That is why I love you."

She pressed her lips against his—soft, wet, warm against the cold. She stayed there, relishing the moment in between. It felt good.

The warmth of the morning sun fell in patches over them, around them, onto the place where Toman and the others had fallen the day before, their blood already swept away beneath the newly-fallen snow.

She pulled her cloak about her and pressed herself close to him, into his strength, into his warmth, into his promise, into his hope.

"But you must promise me, Chaelus, vessel of the Giver reborn, that if you do go to her, you won't go alone."

*

Michalas hung his head between the bouncing wooden slats of the slaver's wagon. The bandages which hid the mark of the angels felt tight upon his brow, but they softened the blows as the cart jolted over the frozen stones of the happas.

His tears felt cold upon his cheeks.

Tears.

They weren't from joy, or from sadness, though he felt plenty of both. Then again, perhaps that's exactly what they were, all of them at once, more feelings than he had ever known, feelings that tormented him ever since the angels had left him. Yet the fact that now he had started crying bothered him. It was messy, and harder to hide.

So many feelings pressed behind his eyes, like a second flesh that he couldn't touch, or cover up, or ever cause to go away.

At least they were his.

It was his only solace, if it even was one. At least the feelings were his, not something given to him. The angels had given him everything. He'd never had anything of his own before. But the angels were gone, and the feelings were his, even though they were uncomfortable and sometimes hurt unlike anything he had ever known.

He certainly didn't understand them.

He understood his feelings no more than he understood the Servian knights' plan to pose as slavers and merchants as they traveled east with the Giver. Why would they travel so willingly into the lands of the enemy? It certainly wasn't a comfortable decision for him, as one of the ones who had to pose as a slave, as his head bounced against the slats of the wagon.

Yet at least Obidae and the three Servian knights dressed in rags bounced along with him, though with far less misery. But then, they were Servian knights. He was just a boy.

All were knights, except for Obidae, the barbarian. Obidae even smiled at him once.

The three Servian knights, Al-Gogin, Al-Malice, and Al-Eliana, kept a reverent distance from him, their gossamer blades hidden amongst the rubbish of their rolling cage; tending to him but still unsure of him, of a boy who had been marked by angels, and of his role in the prophecy they served.

He wasn't sure of it yet himself, only that the angels had told him before they left that he had a part in this to play, and that he was to wait for it, and for them.

Al-Gogin stared at him from across the wagon. He was dour and dark of skin, once a trader of the seas before his fall. His eyes always seemed to be far-seeing, as if he still were.

Al-Malice and Al-Eliana, nearly sisters but for their salt and autumn hair, were strong and gentle both, just like his own sister. Just like the angels who used to tend him. One of them looked forward, to the east. The other looked back, to the far distance where they had come from.

Chaelus, the Giver, rode his gray mare beside them in silence, his spear at rest on his armored shoulder. The hem of his chainmail hauberk danced with the trot of the mare. His helmeted brow he kept bowed in shadow.

Chaelus' thoughts, his fears, and his feelings, he kept hidden to himself. At least he could. He'd certainly had more practice with them.

All Michalas could do was cry. Oh well. He smiled through his tears. He sang the words of prophecy that bound them all, that sounded constantly in his dreams, out loud softly.

*One who was but could not be*
*One who could not be but was*

*One to teach and One to save*
*The mark of the Dragon upon him*

*Born of Cradle, born of grave*
*Chosen from Forgotten Blood.*

Chaelus turned to him. Grief stood wreathed upon his brow more than the white runes of the Dragon, which mirrored Michalas' own.

"I still find it hard to sing of prophecy," Chaelus said.

"When you left for him, you knew you couldn't save him," Michalas said, wedging his face again between the slats. "But you tried anyway, because you think you brought this thing upon him. It's the only thing you can believe. It hurts less to believe that, than to believe the truth."

"And what truth is that, child who knows too much?" Chaelus asked. A smile turned his lips.

The cart jolted over rocks buried unseen beneath the snow.

Michalas winced. "That he was born with this shadow, just like you were. That he chose to stay in it too, just like you did. It's why you know you can't help him, not until he's ready."

"And what if he never is?"

"Then you will have to wait until it's time to take him home."

"You told me you used to speak with the angels that tended to you."

"I used to. But they went away, when you came. Now I can only wonder and wait, like you, I guess, and try to imagine what prophecy would want of me; a useless boy who can't quit crying." He wiped at his tears.

Chaelus' smile broadened. He turned back to the east, the direction in which they traveled. "Prophecy. It's the one thing upon which we're forced to depend, isn't it? But it's hard to believe in sometimes, when the very thing that saved you is the same thing that can cause you so much pain."

"Cause pain?" Michalas asked. "Is that what the Giver says to you?"

"Hmph. No. The ghost says nothing to me. Just like your angels."

"Has he left you?"

"I don't really know. I can only hear his silence."

"At least you're not alone." Michalas withdrew his head from the slats.

To keep the company of angels, and then to be without them, to be alone, hurt in ways he couldn't even begin to explain. He had been so long without their comfort; he could scarcely remember sometimes what it was like to be near them at all.

"And neither are you," Chaelus replied. He turned and stared at Mariam for a moment, riding ahead of them in splendor as their queen, in fine furs gathered over silks of gold and azure hue. "You should be grateful. The one you love has been returned to you."

"Do you love her? Do you love my sister?"

Chaelus turned back to him. His eyes softened, but held caution along their edges.

"You may have spoken with angels, but you are still too young to ask such things."

"I know that you've lain together."

Chaelus smiled.

"Or, perhaps you are not."

"She loves you, deeper than the others do. I know she does. She loves you for you, not for the things prophecy has made of you."

Chaelus turned away, his head down. Then he looked up again, past Mariam, toward the far eastern horizon.

"And I, her."

*

Al-Mariam spurred her mare through the loose-packed snow.

Queen Katrzyna, she reminded herself, returning with her stock of slaves and goods back to the city state of Karthesh.

She rode in golden splendor at the head of her mock guards and retinue, the men who served her, even the one she had given herself to last night.

She smiled.

The sun stood high in a clear sky. Its radiance filled her bones.

The frozen pine boughs passed overhead. They kept beat with her heart.

She felt her heart's rhythm as she pressed her nails into her palm. It distracted her from her heart's ache, an ache even greater than where the Hunter's arrow had pierced her.

It ached because she loved him, no matter how hard she had tried not to.

Chaelus, Roan Lord of the House of Malius, the vessel of the Giver reborn. His touch still lingered about her, within her, filling her, like a ghost. His scent, like a drug, even blessed the smell of pine and winter air about her.

Even as it terrified her.

Not him, but the thing of prophecy that made him, and the loss and suffering that would come to her, to all of them, because he served it, because they all did.

*Born to us to die for us*
*For only the fallen may rise.*

The cold whisper of prophecy whipped around her like a gale as the southern forest of Sanseveria drew away to make way for the vast expanse of the Kessel plain ahead.

It had whispered to her the night before, when the lust and the touch of their joining still lingered, and the sadness and the knowing of his eyes had already returned. She had heard it speak to her even as she held him; the thin blanket of furs only a small veil against the chill of winter surrounding them.

He had already died once. Now he was going to die again, at the hands of the Dragon and a past he had already defeated.

Or had he?

She knew now it was at least one reason why he felt he had to go there. It was why he had gone to his brother. He had hoped to save him, so he wouldn't have to go.

But prophecy had need of him still and she understood that he was powerless to stop it. They all were, as powerless as the four knights who had died next to her, and whom she had almost joined. And she knew that his death, when it came, would be the end of everything she had ever known. It was the way it had always been with anyone she had ever loved before.

The warmth of pain trickled between her fingers as her nails bit into her flesh.

She knew it as much as anyone.

She slipped away into the rush of pain that escaped her.

There are many different kinds of death.

*

Chaelus patted Idyliss' neck as he reined her in. The labored breath of a day's ride gathered in clouds around her flared nostrils. Sweat blanketed her flank.

The Servian knights disguised as merchant guards drew up behind him.

The wide expanse of the Kessel languished beneath them.

Across the distance that measured less than a day, the Vicarus sparkled in the last of the morning light; the eastern border of the Northern March, and the western borderlands of the Theocracy of the Pale.

Al-Vikitan, his mute spear, his coat of mail glistening, cantered up to him. He bowed his head. "Their eyes will soon be upon us."

"They already are," Chaelus replied, "along with those of the Hunters." The Servian knight would only use his spear for killing boar, not men. Chaelus knew that he alone, even with Obidae, could not, with only his steel, defend them all.

"And if they had chosen to, they could have killed us all by now. They failed once. They will not fail twice."

A shadow of the Dragon swept across the knight's face, full of doubt, full of anguish. "What will happen then?"

"There is something greater at work here that keeps them at bay. Something, some reason, prophecy or not, has allowed us the privilege of living another day."

The shadow of fear on the knight fled, the shadow of the Dragon. If only for that moment, his faith had been checked by a mere word.

"Then it is by your grace alone," Al-Vikitan offered.

"Perhaps, but I doubt it very much." He turned Idyliss away.

No one from Baelus' court had pursued him, either. He would have felt them. He would have felt the shadow within their presence, just as he felt the shadows of those eyes already upon him. Yet he doubted there were any of Baelus' men left that would, or could. Still, they had ridden hard, through the day and through the night. Because it was something else that pursued him, pursued them. It was the past. He had little left to use against it but to run, run from the guilt and the loss of all that it carried for him, run from one past to another.

Memories of the past swirled before him, like motes of cold dust and ash, like those stirred up in the sudden exodus of Maedelous' twelve Servian knights from the Mother's small chapel a fortnight ago. The once embers had floated then, filtering down across the morning sunlight let in by the small high window, like spring blossoms flung against winter's chill.

The Mother had simply stared at them as they left, slumped near the small and weary fire.

"It is unexpected," the Mother had said.

"Yet, then again, it isn't," he had replied.

"Not Maedelous' flight from us," the Mother said, her arms at rest within her lap. The tips of her fingers pressed toward each other, not quite touching but held there, where the moment in between could be forever held, until either patience or weariness gave it its way. "No. But the exodus of the knights who follow him, I did not predict."

The renounced and apostate knights had followed in the footsteps of Maedelous, once seneschal of the order, and now, it seemed, the very one who had betrayed them. The gossamer that had bound his blade, as well as that which had bound the blades of the twelve, had been neatly left behind, a symbol of their refusal of their vows and of their departure from the order.

"But he could."

"Yes," the Mother said. Her hands trembled, then fell against each other. "It would seem that he did."

He knew it was not so much the loss of the knights that troubled her as their number, and the words of prophecy that such a loss announced. He also knew he could not stay to help her. That would have to be another's task.

"I must go to him," he said, his words breaking across the silent chill. "I must go to my brother. The Dragon will only grow stronger in him the longer I wait. I have to try to save him."

"Yes," the Mother said. "But I wonder to what end."

He let his breath escape, the breath he didn't know he even held. The Mother did that to him, still.

He let himself smile as he remembered.

The Mother's frown had smoothed. "I wonder what end your own desire would bring."

"It would bring my brother back to me."

"No. Not even you can do that. He must do this on his own, or he must not. Your power, it is meant for something else, something far greater than your love for even him."

He felt his breath pull back. It bristled beneath his shoulders. She still did this to him, as well. "Do not speak to me now of higher purpose and prophecy. I know my fate all too well, and you know I have not refused it. I have defeated the Dragon once. I will do so again."

The Mother smiled. Its edges were soft, sad. "No. You haven't refused it, but you haven't surrendered to it either, even though you've been asked to take up a mantle no man should ever have to bear."

The Mother took up the length of her stave from beside her. With its blackened end, she stoked the dying embers. Brief tongues of flame spat up, flaring upon the air until they settled slow into the cold ash and dust of their brethren.

The Mother's smile evened somewhat, its corners a knife's edge. "I know you will fulfill your promise, Chaelus of the Roan House of Malius. But unless you are to fail, both yourself and the rest of the Pale as well, the vessel of the Giver reborn can place nothing before it, either."

Memory rarely beckons truth. It's too much like dust and ash.

He led Idyliss away from the waiting knights.

He led Idyliss up a hillock, through forest and between stones. Light was fading. The smell of pine and winter's loss filled his senses. It was from a ridge like this, higher in the mountains and farther to the west, and a different season, closer to his home, and several lifetimes ago, that he had first seen the arrival of Khaalish raiders as a boy. It was there, on that day, that his mother had died, and so had the soul of his father, holding her as she perished from a Khaalish arrow.

It was just like what had nearly happened to Al-Mariam but a few days before. Yet he had saved her. Or had he?

The ruin of Malius, his father, had come long before the ghosts of prophecy ever claimed Chaelus. So, too, had his own death. Perhaps all their fates were sealed to these patterns, this loss, long before.

All of them.

No matter who they were, or whom they loved. Whether it be Al-Aaron, who raised Chaelus from the dead, or the boy Michalas, who had been raised by angels, it was obvious that mercy, though granted, was just as often spared, and that prophecy would even claim a child.

No innocence was safe from it, neither purity nor sanctity.

What sin had any of them done, if prophecy had not first planned it for them? What loss of their own could they even begin to regret?

The plain of the Kessel stretched silent before him, like a promise, like a solemn warning, like a warding.

Chaelus took a deep breath and held it, holding to himself the moment in between. He waited as the cold air warmed in his chest. He remembered the warm touch of Mariam that still lingered upon his flesh.

The sun was a little higher; the shadows it cast, a little shorter.

There was still time.

There was still time for prophecy to take away everything. There was still time for it to save them, as well. Perhaps it would this time. Perhaps prophecy wouldn't feel the need to claim its price this day.

Perhaps, at the very least, it would give them just one more day.

## Chapter Six: Prophecy

Faerowyn trailed the palm of her hand along the polished marble sill. Tendrils of blue, purple and gold laced through the surface of the cold, blood-red stone. The morning light had yet to meet it. A chill swept through the thin pale azure of her sleeve as the gossamer dragged just beneath her fingers.

*One to teach and one to save.*

She whispered the words. The purr of her voice trembled beneath the soft crush of the veil upon her lips.

*The mark of the Dragon upon him.*

The mournful shadow of the tall white tower rippled to the west across the golden domes and lesser spires beneath her. The sun settled its fire across the sparkling water of the canals as they traced between and amidst the domes like golden fingers.

Watch-fires of the legion still burned throughout the city, the city from which the almost immortal Servian lord,

Ras Dalamas, had recently ruled until the will of prophecy and an assassin's blade had claimed him.

The morning, and mourning, silence had finally settled away from the darkness of the night. Even the darker places that still lingered—the places of shadow left between the shops and temples, the alleys and closes where Faerowyn once pretended to hide as a girl, always under the protective eye of her father's first spear—seemed brighter today. It was almost as if no shadow had ever settled there.

Perhaps there was a day, once upon a time, when none ever had.

Beyond all of it though, beyond the still shadow of the Sea of Beladun, the awakening light burned across the veiled slopes of the Albanjan peaks, breaching the solemn sanctum of its frozen summits and the farthest yet manifest reach of the Theocracy of the Pale. Beyond their gray haze, the western lands and their marches still waited in shadow, but only for now, only until her savior came to her. Then everything would change. The wheels of it were already in motion.

*One who was but could not be.*
*One who could not be but was.*

*One to rule and one to suffer.*
*The mark of the Dragon upon them.*

*Born to us to die for us.*
*For only the fallen may rule.*

*To tear the veil of shadowed Pale*
*So the Dragon will be revealed.*

She withdrew the small silken satchel from her bodice. She unclasped it and reached within. She drew out a single sprig of dried jasmine.

The somber coals of the brazier at the window's edge blistered and sputtered beneath the crumbled remains of it as she sprinkled it over them. The sweet fragrance of the smoke drifted over her and through her, an offering, a reminder of something, something old to be lost for something new. An offering made so that a promise that had once been lost to her could finally, at last, be returned.

She whispered again the words of prophecy.

*Born to us to die for us.*
*For only the Fallen may rise.*

"You look beautiful, my queen," the smooth tenor of Vas Ore greeted her from the shadows.

She eased her stare toward him.

In the room's farthest corner, before the small hollow of the servant's door, in the still cold shadows where the motes of the morning sun never had a chance to dance, the golden mask of Vas Ore sparkled from where he stood in the doorway. The strange light danced upon his vestigial crown as well; bits of black steel embroidering the silk cap set upon his brow.

The brightness of Vas Ore's small mask veiled his eyes alone; leaving all too exposed the dark, scarred flesh around his mouth. No matter how many times Faerowyn had stared upon the face of this man, if he even was one anymore, it still disturbed her.

The wizard high priest, one of the hands of the Taurate who had once served as her father's seneschal, was now hers;

at least in name. The tentacles he had already woven around her and throughout her life said something otherwise.

His shadow among the shadows, Vas Kael, waited in silence at his right hand. The pieces of his own shod bits of iron crown didn't glisten and he had no mask, instead he wore a brass chainmail veil that scarcely covered the scars of self-inflicted wounds upon his face; a sign of the wizard's devotion to his master.

She turned back to Vas Ore.

"Why do you still refuse to veil yourself?" she demanded.

In answer, the flesh cracked around Vas Ore's thin mouth as he smiled.

"I wouldn't dare to hide before such beauty as yours, my queen," he said. "I would let nothing stand between you and what simple truth my fragile lips might utter."

"It is no veil," she said, "but the seduction of the marsh queen that will beckon your truth from me. What did the old bitch say to you?"

"Your wariness of Bakassas is fruitless, my queen, as is your care that I would hold any devotion to her."

"I will have no other queen, no other god, before me."

"Once your promise is kept, know that you will be a god. And I assure you, there will be no other like you. Once your promise is kept, the Hands of the Taurate will only live to serve your purpose, my queen."

*Vows of prophecy.*

A prophecy for the Evarun. A prophecy for the Dragon.

*Vows of betrothal.*

All to have a kingdom, and to bring her lover back to her.

"What of your parley with her, then? Has it met with success?"

"She will continue to honor the treatise she made with your father. There will be no war from her."

"Good." Faerowyn's father, Mattea ex Laudus, Regulus of the Holy City of Paleos and First Princeps of the Theocratic CouncilFirst Prince, but never king—was now dead along with the rest of the Theocratic Council, their threat to her put down by the very hands of the wizard priests who stood before her now. It had been a long time since the council, or her father, had ever really ruled anyway.

"It is unfortunate," Vas Kael said. His voice was like gravel, his breath smelled like detritus. "The heresy and disillusion of the Theocratic Council, my queen. It is unfortunate that your father did not live to see his promise in you come to pass."

She pressed her fingers to her nose, still crisp with the scent of jasmine. It wasn't enough. "I assure you that I grieve for his loss, just as I'm sure you grieve for mine of him."

Vas Ore reached out his hand to her in feigned sympathy.

"As we all do, my queen, of course. He would have been proud of you," Vas Ore whispered, "to see you become what you've always desired, what he himself always desired for you." His whisper faded, the subtle promise of his invitation revealed as he stepped away from the small open door.

"Would he?"

"Trust me when I say that this was always what he wanted. He told me this himself, if not by word, than certainly by his deeds. He always knew that his greatest sacrifice would be for you."

She clutched the silk satchel close to her breast.

*Born to us to die for us.*

The voice of prophecy whispered from the shadows, the prophecy of the Dragon.
She held her breath.

*For only the fallen may rule.*

Vas Ore summoned her with his fingers.
"Come with us, my queen," he said. "It is time at last."
She released her breath.

*To tear the veil of shadowed Pale*

Vas Ore and Vas Kael ducked beneath the lintel of the servant's door.

*So the Dragon will be revealed.*

She followed them.
In the torchlight of the small spiraled stair, the wizards' shadows descended, past the halls and the chambers that ringed it, down beneath the palace that Ras Dalamas, first among the Servian Lords, had built over a century before around this bequeathed tower of the Evarun, to have a holy seat of his own from which his piety could rule. But that was before the Dragon had called him home, so the Servian knights had said, their assassin's sword dipped deep in his blood. Yet who knew anything anymore? Dalamas was dead. So was the whole of the Theocratic Council, and her father, who had feigned to govern beneath them all.

Only the wizards of the Taurate remained now, and her, and the empire over which she would rule.

She followed the two down even farther still, beneath where the pale stone of the tower's first making could still be seen before the light of the stone turned at last to shadow.

She had been here before. Too many times indeed, but never like this, never like it would be on this day, this day when everything would change.

Her wedding day.

Torches by the hundred score lined the cavern walls. There could never be enough of them, though. The darkness of this place bled from the stones like oil.

The low stone tombs of the cenotaph filled the ancient crypt. Their stone lids rested against them. Dark water filled them, the lights of the torches dancing like will-o'-the-wisps upon the water's surface.

Her father had brought her here once as a little girl, before her innocence was lost. But it was never like this. The tombs had never been opened, the dark tableau of both magic and gods laid out before her. Never quite like this.

The two Gorondian wizards waited for her beside the central well of the cenotaph. The other wizards, the whole of the Taurate it seemed, a hundred score, spread out like a shroud behind them. They swayed, chanting in their wizards' tongue, ecstatic that their prophecy was finally about to come true.

The Prophecy of the Dragon.

Before them, before her, between them, was the object of their rapture, and soon to be hers. The tip of a russet tentacle wavered just above the black water. The light from the hundred torches, and the shadows they created, danced across the shifting tremor and turmoil and lust of its flesh.

The Dragon.

Her betrothed.

The sepia water washed away from it over the rim of the cenotaph.

She stepped closer to it, to him.

She pressed her hands down over the gentle pleats of her gown. Her hips shifted in time with the sinuous wave of the Dragon's movement. It was like a talisman upon her. A spell. She watched herself, seduced, even as the Dragon's shadow and all of its dark power lifted like a miasma over her.

Beyond it, the soft whisper of Vas Ore and Vas Kael and all the other wizards of the Pale chanted just beneath their breath, concordant, like a dull, bitter scraping of iron.

She felt their words pulse within the stones beneath her feet, within her flesh and her bones. They were vows.

*Vows of prophecy.*
*Vows of betrothal.*

The black water from the cenotaph pooled around her feet, gathering there. It bled upward through the fabric of her pleated gown, like blood taken up by a bandage over an open wound. Its dampness clung across her like oil, binding the cloth of the gown to her flesh, the wedding gown in azure gossamer, once worn by her mother, a woman she never knew.

Her mother, whoever she was, whore or queen, never would have or could have ever dreamed of this, of how everything was about to be transformed. She never would have imagined how the one and only thing that ever really mattered to her daughter, the one thing she thought she had lost forever, could be given back to her today, simply because of this.

This one small sacrifice.

All to have her kingdom, and bring her love back to her.

The tip of the Dragon's tentacle leaned down to her face. It brushed against her lips. It smelled of musk and steel and the sweet taste of rotting things. Faerowyn caught her breath. Her veil clung to her lips as the Dragon pulled the cloth away from her.

The Dragon swayed before her, like a lover, like a king, like a god.

From a thin small seam at its tip, like a scar, its skin and flesh peeled away. The teeth of something more and less than either man or beast pressed out from its opened mouth. Its tongue tasted the air, tasted her breath. Its stench was foul and intoxicating, like a promise made to be broken.

Fear and arousal drove through her like a supple, tender knife, like she never could have imagined.

Desire, and power, and succor, the kinds of things that could only come from a god, quickly followed.

And it was, it was a god, this beast, this Dragon.

And very soon, so very soon, she would be one, too.

And she would have all of it.

The succor of the Dragon's breath caressed her and it covered her. It swallowed her soul. It consumed her will. It lit dark fires within her, unbridling her lust. Oil pulled the fabric of her wedding gown down away from her skin. Her limbs and her muscles twitched deep down in ecstasy, freed at last from the weight of it.

The head of the Dragon bent down farther. Its coarse wet skin brushed like agony against her neck.

She willed her weak flesh to stand. By her will and desire alone, she had to, if only for just a moment more. But she had so little of either left.

The Dragon lingered between her breasts.

Black bile dripped down her skin.

The wizards ceased their chanting. The noise of the waiting silence was palpable. It had a breath of its own and it pulsed against her ears, like her blood did within her veins.

*Vows of prophecy.*
*Vows of betrothal.*

Prophecy of the Evarun. Prophecy of the Dragon.

To have her kingdom, and bring her love back to her.

Yet in the end, she knew that neither prophecy would save her. Neither of them could. But she would make them both serve her. Let the wizards mutilate themselves for their prophecy and their faith. Let the servants of the Evarun sacrifice themselves for their prophet. Let them all think they could. Let their gods believe it, too. In the end, she would let them all die, because it would be her, and her alone, who would bring about her own destiny.

The head of the Dragon rubbed down around and against her hips.

"Now the only words left to be said are yours, my queen," Vas Ore said. "Then all will be as was promised to you."

"There is but one more thing I desire," Faerowyn said. Her voice sounded distant to her, as if it had already ceased to be hers.

It was finally time to reclaim what she had lost.

"You must only ask for it, my Queen."

The head of the Dragon nestled between her legs.

Desperately, she pressed herself against it, trying hard not to release herself too soon.

"I wish for the one they call savior to be brought before me," she gasped.

The world around her fluttered and blurred. The fire of pleasure burned through her like nothing she had ever known.

It was like death.

Just above the dancing shadows, Vas Ore smiled, his flesh cracking in the torchlight.

"It is already done. He already comes to you now."

\*

Chaelus, vessel of the Giver reborn, felt their arrival long before Al-Vikitan announced it.

"Riders!"

He had felt the long dark shadow of their coming even before he heard them as he descended the hillock, and even before then, as he had risked just one more vain hope against it.

Low dark clouds bore down across the plain. In the dead light beneath them, two columns of a Theocratic legion cohort rode along the happas that led up from the Kessel. Their crimson banners snapped in the wind. Still several leagues away, they made no secret of their approach. They didn't need to. The legions knew there was nothing the Servians would do, or could do, to stop them. Hunters rode about them, darting alongside their ranks like a pack of feral wolves.

A legion of men in unwitting service to the Dragon. Even if the Servian knights had numbered in the thousands, by their vow alone they were powerless against them, against these men. And so was Chaelus, because the voice of the Giver was silent within him.

He turned to the knight. "Tell everyone to be ready. I will do the talking." He spurred Idyliss away from the escarpment.

Mariam rode up to him.

Against the growing, looming darkness, she was still resplendent as a merchant queen, as if she had been born one. Beneath the gold coins adorning her brow, her stare was fierce, appropriate for her bearing. She unclasped her veil.

He met her stare until it softened.

"Not again," she pleaded.

He knew what she meant, and everything her words held back. No more death today.

He drew his mount alongside hers. He took her bandaged hand in his. It trembled at his touch.

"You should replace this with something finer," he said, holding the strength and weakness of her fingers, and her self-crucifixion that she bore. He smiled at her. "Your peasant bandages give us away too easily."

"What will they do?" Mariam asked.

"Nothing more than they've already done. Hunters ride with them, but only at the legion's convenience. The legion has writ over us now. If they wanted us dead we would already be so, whether you were to break your oath or not. You're safe, all of you. No Servian blood will be let here today."

"But what of you?"

"I am as safe as I will ever be. I'm quite sure Baelus has already sent riders east with word of my return and everything he has seen."

"He's not the only one who has. You and your deeds are no secret anymore."

"It is fine enough."

"That's why you won't try to stop them, either, isn't it? Because…"

He listened to the silence of the Giver.

"They would only send more," she finished.

Her hands were more relaxed now.

"They would," he said. "More than any army, or the Giver, could ever defend against. Everyone would die."

He looked into her, into the truth of her, deeper than her eyes or countenance could ever show, where only the Giver could see. Only love stared back at him.

"The promise of your oath isn't what will betray your order, Mariam. It's their reverence of me."

"For some of us," she took up his hand again, this time his in hers, "it is less by reverence than by choice."

"A fool only attracts fools."

Mariam smiled. She turned to the vastness before them, fastening back her veil.

"Then what kind of fools are they? For it seems you have attracted an army."

He smiled in reply.

The last song of daylight danced across her golden brow before the storm clouds and nightfall drew near.

"I think we should do our best to find out," he said, "shouldn't we, my noble if not gold-mongering queen?"

Mariam smiled behind her veil, wrapping a gentle slip of golden gossamer over her hands and the bandages they bore.

\*

Michalas clenched his eyes tighter. Fear gripped him, but at least it was his.

"Don't be afraid, little one," Al-Eliana whispered.

He jumped at her words.

Al-Eliana's auburn hair settled across her cheek. She pressed a soft cloth to the sides of his face where his tears had returned.

"I can tell you're afraid," she said. "Don't be ashamed of it. We all feel fear."

Beyond the slats of the wagon, down the slope of the rise, the lights of torches grew larger. They reminded him of the eyes of monsters from before, like the ones he had once imagined the campfires of the Khaalish to be when he had first met Chaelus a lifetime before, before the angels left him. This time, he was quite sure it wasn't his imagination.

"I remember once as a child," Al-Malice offered from the dark still corner of the wagon where she sat, her voice quiet, her long braids bright even in the shadows, "I remember once when I was afraid. Wolves had come down from the mountains, an entire pack of them. I remember my mother holding me in my bed as I listened to them call out to each other. I remember how she told me she had been afraid, too. I remember staring up at her and saying to her, "But you look so brave," and she brushed my hair away and told me simply that it was only because I was there with her, and my being with her reminded her that she didn't need to be afraid."

Al-Gogin smiled.

"It's the one great strength we have," he said, "it is the greatest strength. It's a greater strength than any man or legion alone can ever have."

"What is that?" Michalas wiped his nose upon his sleeve.

"Our need. Our lack of faith, our loss, and sometimes, even, I admit, our suffering." Al-Gogin stared past him to where the sounds of men and beasts, the rattling of arms of war, climbed toward them. "It's our weakness that makes us so strong. It's our humanness that allows us to come closest to, and eventually to know, the divine. Once you open yourself up to the divine, once you have been filled and sat still in the arms of Rua, anything is possible."

Obidae stirred from the shadow where he watched and waited and listened beside Al-Gogin.

Michalas stared back at the knight. His fear diminished. He smiled at him.

Obidae leaned over toward him. He pressed something small and hard and cold into Michalas' hand.

"He is right, child," Obidae said. "Do not forget."

Obidae kept his large hands wrapped around Michalas'.

No tears stained Obidae's cheeks.

Obidae even smelled brave. Like Michalas wanted to be.

"Take this. Keep it. Use it, and you will find out the difference between a vessel and a stone."

\*

Chaelus waited astride Idyliss at the edge of the escarpment, alongside the happas where it climbed from the Kessel to meet it, at the front of Mariam and the other Servian knights.

The first to surround them were the Hunters.

Haggard and lustful men in reach of their quarry, anticipating whatever prizes had been offered them, they circled around them in a clamor and chainmail and furs on horseback, with torches, sword and axe and spear and bow. They howled and jeered.

Chaelus and the Servians waited. The Hunters held back away from them.

Chaelus reined Idyliss before Mariam, his stare cautioning and encouraging the other knights waiting in the disguises of slaves and guards behind them, because that was all they had to protect them now; their disguise, their courage, and their faith. Hopefully prophecy, or the Giver, would lend a hand, too.

Legion cavalry soon flanked them. Beneath the dancing torchlight, their polished, banded lorica shimmered; their faces lost beneath the shadow of their chainmail veils.

But not their souls. No. He could see darkness within every one of them, writhing and twisted, the shadow of the Dragon reborn in legion.

Yet they were still men. Not Remnants. Not the Remnants from a lifetime before. Not the undead souls taken by the Dragon who had pursued him after he was raised. These weren't the soulless Remnants he had fought before. These were still men, because the Dragon's shadow still fed on them, because the Dragon succors the living. It doesn't suffer the dead.

And the Veil of the Dragon hid that fact from every one of them.

The rabble of Hunters bled away beneath the organized clamor of the legion as it closed in.

Chaelus brought Idyliss forward as mounted legionnaires sallied toward him. He palmed Sundengal's hilt.

"My name is Belos," Chaelus announced. "I'm captain of Queen Katrzyna's guard. I alone will speak for her, and demand you give us safe passage through to Karthesh."

Spears leveled at his chest, prodding his mail.

"The legion honors only one queen," one of the men snarled behind his armored veil, riding past him.

The legionnaire tore Mariam's veil away.

Mariam spat at him.

The legionnaire struck her across the brow.

Mariam turned her stare slowly back to the legionnaire who'd hit her. Her hand clutched Aela's hilt.

More men seized her. The legionnaire drew his sword.

Chaelus bellowed. He spurred Idyliss between them. He drew Sundengal in an arc against shaft and steel around him. He brought Sundengal down upon the legionnaire's sword hand.

The hand flew away in a spray of blood.

A spear slammed into him. A blur of azure hue crossed his vision. He fell over the side of Idyliss. The ground slammed against him, along with warmth and numbness that cloaked his side where the spear had pierced his mail.

But not his flesh.

He stood.

A dozen arms of legion foot soldiers seized him. Their swords pressed tight against his throat.

"Enough!" a voice boomed.

The commanding centurion of the cohort cantered toward them. He lowered one edge of his chainmail veil. Beneath his crested helmet, his face, eyes, the set of his jaw, were all carved deep from whatever fate had shaped him, deep into his soul, oddly like the lines on the face of the Mother.

The legionnaires kept their grips on Mariam and Chaelus. The spears and blades barely drew away. The wounded soldier was pulled away, screaming.

Chaelus looked to Mariam.

Her fierce gaze held his.

The voice of the Giver brushed against him, but it was wordless.

There was nothing he could say to her.

"Enough pretending," the commanding centurion said.

Chaelus turned back to him.

There was something different about the man, something different from the legionnaires who served beneath him. The shadow of the Dragon was no less within him than in they, but neither was it more so. Yet it should have been. To serve the Dragon as Chaelus presumed the Dragon would demand, it should have been.

The whisper of the Giver grew. It came without trumpets. It came without bells. It lingered in his ear, wordless but no less clear, with only the wash of azure hue to hold him back, and no flame to burn from his fingers or the edge of Sundengal's steel.

The Giver whispered the truth of the centurion to him, still wordless, but no less real; unveiling the man like a tableau before him.

All of him, including the part that wanted to be saved by him, by the Giver. But one word did the Giver whisper: his name.

The man named Gervasis removed his helm, placing it under his arm. He drew his mount close to Chaelus and leaned down. He sang a song of prophecy softly, the Prophecy of the Evarun.

> *One who was but could not be*
> *One who could not be but was.*
>
> *One to teach and One to save*
> *The mark of the Dragon upon him.*
>
> *Born of cradle, born of grave*
> *Chosen from forgotten blood.*
>
> *Born for us to die for us*
> *For only the fallen may rise.*
>
> *One to prepare the way*
> *Until the desert he will wait.*

*One to walk alone*
*He will raise twelve to show the way.*

*Neither spear nor shaft shall harm him*
*His symbol shall be his passage.*

*A Martyr by those who claim him*
*The Dragon's oath fulfilled.*

*Twelve to share the Gift*
*Twelve who did forget.*

*Herald the Dragon's return*
*As the Fallen they will rise.*

*To bring to fell the Shadowed Pale*
*When the Giver does return.*

*To lament the ones who will forget*
*The Dragon waits within.*

"Your name is Gervasis," Chaelus told the man, his voice even less, little more than a breath so that none other than the man before him would hear it.

Gervasis pursed his lips, the carved muscles of his face thoughtful, waiting, for something.

"I am," he said in an equally measured voice. Then Gervasis' voice boomed again, louder than it needed to be. "I am Gervasis ex Framea, First Spear of the First cohort of the Twelfth Theocratic Legion. And you, Chaelus, Roan Lord of the House of Malius, heretic and pretender to the title of Giver reborn, are my prisoner."

## Chapter Seven: Solace

Faerowyn stepped back, away from the window, away from the exultant cries and rapture of her people far beneath her.

She dabbed the fragile cloth against her lips.

A thin strand of bile went away with it, colored with blood and darker things; another piece of her soul.

It had only been a day, and already her throat burned with the loss of the pieces she had already spent. Her body ached with their ghosts and the threat of every payment she knew was still to come.

All to win a kingdom and regain the love she had lost.

She stared out the window, into the darkness, beyond the pulsing glow and ecstasy of the jeweled city beneath her, her capital, her throne. She stared out toward the west.

"When will you finally come to me?" she whispered.

Another wave passed through her, this time harder. She grimaced. She slumped to her knees.

Vas Ore's velvet gloved hand slipped over her shoulder.

"You've done well, my queen. Already, the people have begun to worship you, as our master grows within you."

His golden mask sparkled at the edge of her vision; the rusting light danced upon his vestigial crown, upon the bits of black steel embroidered in the silk cap on his brow—the mask that only veiled his eyes, exposing the dark and scarified flesh around his mouth.

Her vision blurred, as if there were two of him, but there weren't.

It was only his shadow, Vas Kael, who stood beside him.

Vas Kael's chainmail veil hung from his gilded cap, hiding his face only like rouge would a blistering scar. It did no better for the real wounds etched upon his face, the mark of the Gorondian wizards, the mark of the Taurate, their mark of the Dragon.

She caught her hand drifting to her womb.

"Tell him to leave," she commanded Vas Ore.

Vas Ore smiled. The flesh around his thin mouth cracked and bled.

No matter how many times she stared at the mouth of the man who had been her father's trusted friend, advisor, and murderer, it sickened her. Even now.

"Tell him," she winced.

Vas Ore's cracked lips smiled and bled. His tongue darted to clean them.

"No, my queen." Vas Ore's whisper caressed her skin, its ending as always as cruel as a whip. "We are the Hands of the Dragon. We are both here to help you through your sacrifice. Something to be lost for something gained. Soon, this will be over."

Another spasm came over her. She held her breath until the miasma passed through her.

"Tell me, then," she panted. "What is it that you gain from this?"

"Only the same as you," Vas Ore said. "Your desire is ours, my queen, to see the Prophecy of the Dragon fulfilled. While you must suffer for the moment the joy of being its mouth, we must suffer to wait as its Hands. Oh, but there is nothing more that could be desired, than to see the Prophecy of the Dragon fulfilled."

She waited, catching her shortened breath.

"Very soon, all of it will be over," Vas Ore said, the tenor of his voice lowered.

Vas Ore's hand lifted.

The miasma exploded past her gagging scream. Her body convulsed like the dead as she choked on the black secretion of the spawn within her.

Her breath came back to her in a ragged gasp. Like a false promise, one that was made to be broken. Like everything she had ever known or even loved, all so that a love she had lost could be regained.

Her hand trembled. She wiped the bile from her lips. She folded the cloth. It was stiff, but she persisted until she made it serve her.

She set the cloth upon the polished stone floor. The once gentle bit of fabric nearly disappeared against the purple and onyx veining, colored as it was with blood and flesh and darker things.

Come from her.

So he would come for her.

Chaelus, vessel of the Giver reborn.

Chaelus, her promise that never should have been broken.

The Gorondian wizards' soft steps drifted away, back into the long shadows like whispers in the dark.

She stood, careful, cautious as she did so, until she was sure the shadows would no longer move against her. The wizards had gone.

Beneath her, above the cries of the multitude who now worshiped her, the golden domes and lesser spires burned alive with the light of evening's fire. The shadow of the Sea of Beladun stretched beyond them to the darker silhouette of the Albanjan's frozen peaks, like a veil across the west.

It was from the west that he would come for her.

She withdrew the small silken satchel from her bodice. She unclasped it and reached within, drawing out a single sprig of dried jasmine.

The somber coals of the brazier at the window's edge blazed beneath it as she sprinkled it with a trembling hand. The sweet fragrance of the smoke drifted over her again, a last offering, so that a love once lost to her would at last be returned.

Because she needed him, because even before this, even before this sacrifice, she had always known she was to die like this. It was what she was born to do.

And only he could save her. Only he could raise the dead.

But only if he came soon.

He had to.

Because only Chaelus, once Roan Lord of the House of Malius, now vessel of the Giver reborn, the only man she had ever truly loved, the only one who could save her, had died like this once, too.

*

Login stared through the steam of his fevered breath, gathered just beyond the wagon's walls.

They had traveled inland and across the relative shelter of the western plain. Snow and ice had given way to a morass of mud and freezing rain.

It had been three days, with only fevered dreams to save him, through rolling fields and forest made gray by winter's first storm, and more dark clouds already starting to gather.

His dreams had long ceased to be dreams.

Just ahead, strange tall spires of pale white stone rose up from the landscape like ghosts, spiraled, broken, misshapen masses of things. They were little mountains shaped like pale flesh, washed black at their summits. They bled white as bone, starker and starker where they grew out of the gray and broken plain, stretching down into deep valleys where only desolate scrub could grow.

The smell of the grave drifted from the spires.

Tiny black sparrow-holes stared back at him like eyes from notches cut across the cliff faces; doors and windows, maybe, or something else.

The narrow path of the happas wound down into the valleys, winding between these macabre spires.

Clusters of steps bounded up the hillsides, smaller paths branching out away from them, to even steeper steps leading like ladders to the sparrow-holes, or doorways, if that's what they were, above them.

But there were no people.

The living, it seemed, had gone away.

Draperies of what looked like gossamer flowed between the spires. They shifted in the windless night and glowed as if they were bathed in moonlight. But there was no moon this night, and the glow was from neither moon nor star. Clouds blanketed the Pale like a shroud. The gentle drapery was like no cloth ever woven.

All was silent. There were no voices. Indeed, the living had surely gone.

Not even sparrows flew here.

The only sound was the methodic, staggered, swollen creak of the wagon, and Login's labored breath.

He tried to sit up. The rush of movement sent him stumbling back across the slick wood onto the jostling pallet in the wagon's rear.

Maedelous reached back to him. His touch was cold and void.

Login gasped.

"Damn you, boy," Maedelous said, pulling his hand away. He wiped it on his cloak. "You've been tossing for nearly three days and still your fever worsens. It may not be the Dragon's Sleep, but I bet you'll not live another three without shelter, and storms are coming. It'll be every bit of that and another three until were safe, as it were, within the walls of Essoris." His voice lessened, weary, his face turned out toward the darkness of the valley and the ghostly houses below.

Login eyed the spiraling cliffs nervously.

"What about here?" he murmured.

"Not wise," Maedelous answered. "Not wise at all. Only the dead find rest here in Osgarath." He waited. "This city once guarded the southern crossroads. It was the gateway between the Roan kingdoms of the north, the kingdoms of Goarnn to the south, and the Theocratic States to the east. But not anymore.

"And if you were wondering what happened..." Maedelous drew rein. The wagon slowed and jumped to a stop. "It died. If there was any way we could have gone around it, we would have."

Maedelous turned back to Login, then turned again to stare southward. The steam of his breath clung like a fever all of its own.

"So it doesn't bode well for either of us, wisdom or no, that it's the only refuge to be had from the accursed damp of these lambasted plains. The city itself stretches for leagues. The plains around are hopeless mires broken only by stone fissures that could swallow a man. There is no way around it, and with you sick, we can no longer sneak through."

"Thank you…," Login whispered.

"Don't thank me. It's the spirits of the dead that dwell here. They're kept in check by the Warders who dwell among them. But the Warders won't protect us from foolishness. Place what guards you have upon your mouth, your head, and most of all, your fevered heart. The appetites of the dead are ceaseless and will consume you quicker than you can know."

Maedelous paused again.

"There is a young blind king that still feigns to rule over the Warders of Osgarath. He is the last and the least of his lineage and his power is dwindling fast. Only his alliance with the dead keeps his usurpers away. Our arrival could be seen by him as a test. Under no circumstance let him know that a Servian knight seeks the benefit of his welfare."

"But you're not one anymore."

Maedelous studied him. A portion of a scowl moved across his face. Then it turned into the coldest of stares.

"Then, barring your mouth, you should do quite well here, child. For at least we know you're not afraid of death."

*

Olivia accepted the cloak from Al-Hoanar. She drew it, and his kindness, about her like a salve.

The first somber, mourning light of winter's day filtered down through the barren canopy of the sacred trees high

above. Never seeming to touch, the light surrounded everything in a glow gentle and harsh, hopeful and poignant, all of
it at once.

It was very much how she felt.

The sacred trees of the Garden, Sanseveria, the sacred
home of the Servian Order, the ancient Garden of Rua, spoke
amongst themselves in whispers, like solemn watchmen, like
giants, over the blanched stones of the ruined tower lying
mute beneath them on this holy ground where the prophets of
old once dwelled and saved.

But not anymore.

The days of the old prophets had passed.

On this morning, the eternally glowing coals of the
Waiting Fire offered the only real color, its stewarded flame
the only voice to lend hope that there would ever be something more here than the patient chill of loss. But the flame
too, was dying.

Beyond the ebbing fire, the grim faces of knight and
barbarian alike waited for her like ghosts, waiting for answers, for her to lead them, to tell them why it was she had
summoned them here, all together, like this.

It was the only way. She'd had to, or else choose to
watch what only faith and desire had held together fall blind-
ly and helplessly apart.

They sat apart now, just as they had lived for some time,
a score of days and nights at least, her knights and the Khaalish warriors who served them; the glisten of mail and the
stench of unwashed leather, the pallor of gossamer and the
harsh glare of sharpened steel.

The Khaalish, who had first come to them as their enemy, who had once hunted them, who, upon their conversion
by the Giver, had fought for them, and even after losing so
many of their own had then returned with the Giver to serve

them. The Servian knights' fragile alliance with them was now presumably one of faith, but she already knew too well, after the betrayal by Maedelous and his disciples, the limitations that faith alone, or even prophecy, can bring.

The fact that their chieftain, Obidae, had gone with the Giver on his quest to confront the Dragon in the east, leaving his blood second, Belloch, in his stead, left certain aspects of the relationship all the more questionable.

The three Tenders in their rust-colored robes stewarded the Waiting Fire as they were eternally tasked to. They pressed their skills upon its still-burning embers. The small flames soon flickered then swelled back into a promise once again.

The Tenders turned their own knowing stare on her, gray and solemn, as they backed away once more into the shadows.

Belloch's cruel visage wasted no time in rising beyond the burgeoning fire's edge, his barren eyes seeming to float behind the pale jagged scar that stretched down his face; a dead stripe struck down across his bronzed and hardened skin.

Then he smiled. It was as shrill as a smile could be.

Al-Hoanar bristled beside her.

She gently held his hand where it rested on the spiked hilt of his gossamer-bound spagot."How may we serve you, Revered Mother?" Belloch asked.

His voice slid across her like paste across sand. The blood of Obidae perhaps ran through the man, but his soul belonged to another; to what or whom, she didn't yet know. The Dragon concealed itself in many ways. Either way, she knew she could not trust him.

"The Hunters of the Theocracy have been set upon us," she said. "Already they gather in greater numbers along the forest's edge. Soon, they will lay siege to the Garden of Rua itself, and though most of them will not survive their trial through it, we cannot assume they will all fail either, not anymore. I've come to believe we must assume that enough of them, enough to do what they've been sent to do, will succeed. It would take only a few."

"Is that not why we are here, Revered Mother, to protect you?" Belloch asked.

She waited for courage. She waited for faith.

"I do not doubt the courage and the faith of you and your warriors, or even the sharpness of your steel, but there are many different kinds of death, and from most of them we are no longer safe here, even if you did defeat all of our enemies. Our refuge here has been lost. We must leave the sanctuary of the Garden. It is time for us to leave Sanseveria."

"Where would we go?" came the baffled but consistent reply from among the gathered Servian knights. "Where will we go?"

The Khaalish and their erstwhile chieftain kept their silence.

"We will go to the east," she replied. "Past the reach and the lands of the Theocracy." The weight of everything she had ever known and watched so many suffer for descended at last upon her. "We will go back to our spiritual homeland. We will go to my home. We will go and we will find safety, in the land of the Evarun."

All of the knights grew silent as well.

Because they knew it wasn't their home, even though it may have been hers once so many lifetimes ago.

To most of them, Evarun was nothing but a legend, and a tomb.

To most of them, who understood the purpose of the life that had been given to them; to save the Pale from the Dragon's Sleep, not to hide away and die in their own.

She slid the small prayer stone hanging from her neck back and forth between her fingers, straightening herself in her chair.

"Belloch," she summoned. "To honor the promise of your master, Obidae, I would ask you and your warriors to serve as our corporeal protectors until we reach it."

Belloch turned his head, cracking the bone and sinew beneath. He waited. He breathed in the moment before him, the moment that lay in between. For that moment, he seemed larger than he should be.

"Our blood for the safety of yours?" he asked. "To shed your enemy's blood, so you don't have to."

Beyond the words she had just spoken, there was no other word she least wanted to say, to ask, of anyone, least of all the Khaalish who had already shed so much blood of their own for them. Yet not even for that, but for the hypocrisy it meant. Because Belloch was right. She wanted the Khaalish to kill and die for them so her knights didn't have to.

And the breath of it, the very truth of it, along with all the hypocrisy and deceit it contained, fumbled out like a sigh as it escaped her lips.

"Yes," she said. "That is correct. That is what I wish."

Belloch smiled again. It was just as shrill as before.

"Rest assured, Revered Mother, as Obidae is my blood and my master, any promise he made to you will no less be my own."

*

The day's last light was no less mournful. It mingled closely with the early stars above. Snow clouds gathered and waited beneath.

Olivia paused as she climbed the narrow stair, her breath taken away from her as much by the sight above her as the realization of the truth that was still settling through her.

But there was nothing else left for them to do, and no more promises to be made.

She forced herself to climb the rest of the stair.

Al-Aaron leaned against the broken arch of the window, opened long ago to the sky above. Wrapped in heavy furs, he shivered. Will-o'-the-wisps of glowing snow descended around him.

"You shouldn't be up, child," she said. "You can scarcely even stand."

"I keep thinking I should be better by now," Al-Aaron murmured.

"You have scarcely seen the passing of a moon since your return. Your wounds are deep. Your healing, it will take time."

"The snows are already deep. Winter has come early."

Olivia put her thin arms around the boy, his arms even thinner than hers. She pulled her cloak around them both.

She held him until such warmth as he had grew, and then at last her own did as well.

Beyond the broken arch, camp fires sparked across the valley as the knights and what was left of the barbarian horde prepared themselves for their journey, for their flight.

Funny, how once upon a time she had never meant for any of them to stay here.

She had never meant for so many things to happen, yet they still had though.

"Surgeon!" she called out, her voice shrill yet strangely strong against the stones and the cold.

"It's time you returned to your bed before you take a chill," she whispered. "We will leave early on the morrow. You will need your rest before then."

*Before you catch fever, for fever is the Dragon's call. Isn't that what brought us here, child, when you left us to save him, to go and raise a king from the dead, because his dead father had told you to? And oh, how it has cost you.*

"I can't sleep," he replied, "and I will not be dragged in a litter."

"No," she brushed his hair with her fingers, "I wouldn't think so."

*No. You didn't bring us here, child. I had already done that. I alone did that when I brought us to this sacred place that was only intended to be our rest. Instead, it has turned out to be our prison. But I won't let us die here. Not like this. At least in Evarun, beyond its sacred veil, perhaps there still may be found some hope. At least, I can hope that this time will be different. Perhaps this time, perhaps there, there will be someone left we can save.*

*Perhaps this time, we can start by saving them. Perhaps we can start even by saving ourselves.*

Isn't that what each of them had done, Al-Aaron, Al-Mariam, and even Chaelus—broken their promise to save someone they loved? And though Chaelus had failed, perhaps it didn't mean he was wrong.

"Where do you think he is now?" Al-Aaron stared up at her.

Dark shadows still plagued his eyes, eyes that had seen too much, far more than any child's should. But they were his, and she loved him for them.

"Where is the Giver now?" he said.

But they were darker today than they were yesterday. Something had changed in him.

She turned her face up to the blanketing sky.

Will-o'-the-wisps spiraled downward.

She watched them until all sense of direction was lost. It felt nice, perhaps, even better this way, to surrender, to let things go.

To accept the things she could not change—to let prophecy, or fate, unfold.

To lay claim at last to the only thing that remained. Hope.

She pulled the child closer to her. "I would expect he's already a prisoner of the Theocracy by now, just like he was always intended to be."

## Chapter Eight: Summons

Chaelus let the legionnaire yank his bound wrists above his head, pressing his face against the rough-hewn post.

More visible than shadow, the rot of the Dragon had already begun to claim the legionnaire. It showed beneath the forced intimacy of the torchlight. Very soon, the shadow would claim the man completely.

The legionnaire jerked Chaelus' arms above him again, making sure the rope over the spike was secure.

Rot of the man's flesh. Rot of the man's soul, small bits, just the beginning, until only fear remains. Almost no more than what war and weather and lust can do to a man, but just beneath the cuts and the scabs lurked traces of things too dark to be seen unless you wanted to see them. But most wouldn't want to, they couldn't want to; certainly not this man. Like most, he didn't seem to care either way.

For anyone else to see it, they would have to have seen their own. And most, like him, wouldn't want to, couldn't want to. The other legionnaires didn't want to. The same was already happening to them.

The Dragon's Sleep would soon come to claim them all.

The legionnaire spat in his face.

The legionnaire laughed, his rotten crooked teeth, his fetid breath, no worse than the rest of him, inside and out.

"You're no god," the legionnaire mocked. He pulled one more time at the ropes binding Chaelus' wrists above him.

Chaelus turned to the ugly visage of the man who would never know anything else, no light, only the shadow of the Dragon that had already begun to claim him, and soon would consume them all. He could only stare, though. With only the silence of the Giver before him, and no more holy fire to burn through him, he could only wait.

He stared past the legionnaire and the Dragon to the circle of pits being dug around him by those he loved beneath the crack of whip and rod. He stared at each one of them, the ones who served him and the ones who had saved him; and at the one he loved most of all.

Until she stared back at him.

It was hers, it was Mariam's stare, stripped down from her golden ruse and clothed in beggar's cloth. It was her stare that bore down on him and cut through him, until, all too quickly, there was nothing left for him to bear it with.

Because, once more, there was nothing he could do to save her, because of a prophecy and a dead prophet that wouldn't let him, that left him only the silence of the Giver and no azure flame to save her. One more time, he was left to fail her again.

"Tell me, why do you fear me?" Chaelus asked the legionnaire.

The legionnaire grimaced.

The legionnaire's fist struck his brow, slamming his forehead against the post.

Blood and truth clouded his vision.

But still no azure glow. No warm blush of the Giver to lean into, or even listen to. No blue fire to help him to save, or punish.

Only silence.

And the brutal intimacy of torchlight.

And the short, succinct, crack and blinding pain of the flail against his back.

That's when the screams came from the ones he loved. That's when they cried out. Not at their suffering, but at his, because they could do nothing to save him. One after the other, their cries came until soon only the pain left any sound, and the cries of all the ones he loved fell mute beneath it.

*

Michalas shivered in the wet dark and pressed his aching, bleeding body against the muddy wall of the pit he had been forced to dig. It was shallow and narrow, and he could scarcely do more than lay down within it. It was little more than a grave. Perhaps that's just what it was.

He didn't care.

At least it was dark here. At least it was silent here. At least there was no screaming here. But even the logs and earth above couldn't blot out everything, certainly not the sights and sounds that still lingered. Nothing could make those go away. They kept coming back to him.

Like the terror-filled sound of dirt thrown across the logs above him.

Like the gray of the morning when they had first reached the legion camp, its palisade a perfect circle around a perfect rings of tents, with the whipping post at its center.

He remembered Chaelus' tortured stare as the soldiers hung him there and took turns at beating him.

He remembered the tortured face of his sister as Chaelus' flesh gave way. He remembered the sorrow in her eyes when he couldn't turn to face her anymore.

He remembered how the soldiers had whipped and beat them all.

He remembered the faces of Al-Gogin, Al-Malice, and Al-Eliana and the other knights as they each were forced to dig their pits, how each of them kept watch over him, giving him courage with their stares, even after their own had already been lost. And they did give him courage, just as if they were angels.

Even if they weren't, they could have been.

He remembered Obidae and how he had kept watch on the soldiers around them. With his glaring stare alone, Obidae had brought their whips and clubs upon himself, so that few guards were left to keep watch over and torture a mere boy.

The barbarian was an angel, too.

But he was still so afraid. The fear, it still pressed against the backs of his eyes and stiffened deep in his legs. It nestled in the burning wounds left by the whip upon his back. He pressed himself tighter against the mud wall of his pit, his cell, his tomb. Its coolness eased the pain. Bits of earth and damp dark things dripped across his eyes.

He remembered that it was a bright night by the time they had finished digging the pits. Obidae had scarcely been able to stand beneath his bleeding flesh. Snow had just started to fall again. It was so cold.

He remembered Chaelus' beaten and bleeding husk, left to hang, naked, still under guard by a dozen or more legion spears.

He felt the small round stone still in his belt, the one Obidae had given him. He reached for it, sliding it out. He slipped it between his trembling fingers, careful not to let it fall. The small stone was smooth, but not polished. He held it up to his nose. It still smelled of musk and living things.

His thumb rubbed against it. His fingernail scratched against its surface. It was his.

The smallest of slivers fell from it.

\*

It was the faintest blush. But it was there. An azure glimpse captured for a moment against a storm-wrought sky.

Like a drink of water for the dying.

Chaelus rolled his head up with all the weight and the pain of the living. The torture of his flesh clawed through him. The weight of it pulled against his broken wrists held high above his head.

The light washed over everything. It settled across the world like a fiery halo. But it didn't burn.

It settled like a dove across the spears and veils of the soldiers, legionnaires who would soon cease to be men. Their heads bowed beneath it into slumber. It settled over the covered pits of the ones he loved. The grief within them grew still. It settled across the blood-covered dirt beneath his feet. It settled across the post from which he hung. He lifted his face up to it as if it were a draft of cool water.

And it was.

He waited until the figure of the man appeared before him: Talus, the vessel of the Giver before him.

The storm clouds closed. The darkness of the legion encampment returned. The light still washed over the ghost of the man who possessed him.

"Why have you abandoned me?" Chaelus murmured.

Talus, the vessel of the Giver before him, stepped toward him, between and through the log-covered pits around him, where the ones he loved suffered; past the sleeping sentries who, when woken on the morrow, would surely die for their failure. At least they would die as men.

Talus still walked with his staff, his hand still resting upon his bloodied side where Sundengal had once pierced him at the hand of Chaelus' father. He appeared just as he had when the Giver first came to Chaelus, not so long ago, and consumed him wholly in body and spirit, making him who he was today.

Chaelus, the vessel of the Giver reborn.

The Giver's coarse brown hair and pale skin still framed shadowed eyes of the grayest blue.

"I haven't abandoned you," Talus replied. A chime still carried upon his voice. "I am still here. I stand before you now, and I was no less here, and no less real, the moment before you saw me. You are not alone."

Talus stepped closer, his sandaled feet carried just over and sometimes beneath the sand. "That is what you fail to see, Chaelus. It's what you continue to fail to see, and it is why you've turned away from me."

"I haven't turned away," Chaelus moaned. "I see your silence. I see your impotence for me."

"Then you've forgotten what I promised you. That my blood is your blood and that it alone shall protect you; that my path is your path, and that my fate will always be your fate. My strength, it will always be yours to wield."

"For what?" Chaelus said. "Your strength? Your power? I have seen it and I have wielded it before. But your gift, it seems, is only by your whim, and it is only to help those I care nothing about. For those I love, you give me nothing, and no help with which to save them."

Talus let his staff fall.

He reached up to touch Chaelus' cheek, his hand red with his blood.

Chaelus pulled away from the warmth as if it were a chill.

"Then it is your love that is misplaced," Talus said. "It is why you've turned away, and it is the one thing I cannot force you to see. I am so sorry. I was no different. My love was once misplaced, too."

Talus cupped Chaelus' face with his hands. The warmth of the Giver's blood surged through him. "But I love you now, just as Rua does, so I will tell you my promise once again."

Chaelus struggled against it, against the Giver's touch, and his words.

"My blood is your blood," Talus said. "It alone shall protect you. And my path is still your path. My fate will always be your fate. My strength, it will always be yours."

Talus released him.

"For me, it was my son. He died, killed by the Dragon's own hand, but the Dragon led me to believe it was by mine, that it was my hand that killed him. Suffering is sometimes so much more desirable than the truth, and so it was that the Dragon used this against me. To keep me from the purpose for which I'd already been chosen."

"And what purpose was that?"

Talus backed away.

"To save others. To save a world. To save you."

"But not your son."

"No. Not my son." Talus turned away. "His purpose was not for me to decide, or govern. Only to love."

Talus reached down and picked up his staff.

"His purpose was for something far greater than me. It still is."

Talus leaned his forehead against his staff.

"But now, know that the Dragon seeks to deceive you, just as it did to me. You will be tested. You have already defeated the Dragon once, but don't let that fool you. Now it wants you even more. It needs you in a way that only you will unfortunately soon understand. Not yet, but soon. To the Dragon, you are like a lover who was lost. But do not let it have you, no matter what desires it puts before you. There are so many veils it can use against you. Let each one of them pass. Do not let them deceive you. No matter what their horror may be, no matter their joy. No matter their beauty."

"And what then can I do for the ones I love?"

"You must let them all go, so they may fulfill the purpose prophecy has woven for them. Prophecy, you must remember, was never meant for you or me to weave. Even the prophet is no more than a vessel. So it is and must be."

Talus stopped beside the pit in which the child of prophecy, Michalas, suffered alone. He knelt down beside it, gathering his robe, reaching over the soil-covered beams, his hand almost blessing, but more than that; reaching.

"My son has a greater purpose planned for him than even I could have imagined. And sometimes it is still so hard for me to let him go, even now. At least in this, Chaelus, know that you do not suffer alone."

Talus stood. The storm clouds rent open above him. Azure flame bathed him and shrouded him in its glow.

"I know all too well what you grieve for, Chaelus. But know this: you cannot love for fear of loss." A sad smile crept onto Talus' lips. "To truly serve, you must love, instead, for the desire to give."

Talus' voice lingered as his light and form faded.

"And please, remember, for me, that there is another who still suffers with you."

*

Al-Mariam fought against eyes that wanted to open, that wanted to see, that wanted to live. Yet the dim hope of sunlight still found its way through to her. It burned between the posts above like blood and loss against her frail sight.

She clutched the rigid slip of rough cloth she wore tight against her.

Her swollen mouth and cheek throbbed where the legionnaires had beaten her. She parted her lips against the pain, past the thick swelling of her throat, to a lament she remembered. The words came to her un-beckoned, a verse that her mother had once sung to her when she was a little girl, on the day her father passed away from them.

*When blood dyes crimson*
*The virgin skein of wool*
*So too must die*
*My heart, my love, my soul*

*Such is the parlay*
*We all must make*
*To fall in love*
*Our heart indeed must break*

*So go young nobles*
*And prepare your fall.*
*The blood of the innocents*
*Awaits your call.*

And now, she would soon be with her mother and father both, and Michalas would be with her as well. At least they would still be together, all of them.

Her life, and her love for the Giver, for Chaelus, was already lost to her after only just a glimpse. But would she get to see him there, after the bower of death had taken them? Or would he be swept away from her there as well, aloft and alone upon the solemn, bitter wings of prophecy?

And what would her death be for? What noble sacrifice would it serve? What parlay?

For what quest were they all sent to die, everyone, alone like this, in a dirty hole in the ground, where no other voice could be heard or felt but the empty and even colder voice of prophecy? A prophecy, it seemed, that was meant for nothing.

But it couldn't be. Could it?

Her sight dim, still frail, she reached her fingers up until the warmth of the sunlight touched them. Chill had gathered around her fingers, matting the blood of her torn and battered skin where she had beat her fists against wood and earth. She had never thought she could escape, but at least she knew she had tried. She had failed, but at least she had tried.

Anger filled her.

Prophecy had put her here, the one that possessed the heart and mind of the man she loved, and now it would do nothing to save him.

Chaelus, the man she loved, who was powerless against all of it, a pawn of prophecy unable to save himself.

He was no longer simply the barbarian lord and king, just beyond the sharpened edge of her own blade, who more than once swayed her with only a word, then with a kiss, from a desperate and foolish pride that had already forced her away from everything she held dear; even the oath, her promise she had made to the Mother, and to her order.

No longer was he just a man. No. Prophecy had made him more. More than he had ever wanted to be.

The warmth of the gentle light spread like wildfire across her bitter skin as she understood.

Her still tender wound pulsed just beneath her breast.

Because she knew he would save her if he could. She knew at least that much. If not for the prophecy from which they all had to suffer. She remembered his grief at being denied by prophecy before, denied saving her, saving his brother.

But he had still saved her even then, hadn't he?

She couldn't help but sigh from the pain that awoke within her heart, just above the still healing scar where the arrow had pierced her.

She trembled beneath the fragile hope of the morning sun, as tears, at last, finally drew over her.

Perhaps he still would save them all.

## Chapter Nine: Vessel

Chaelus awoke beneath the soft touch of a woman's hand, his head cradled against her body on a warm bed of furs.

A wet sponge pushed against his lips.

"Drink," the woman said.

Chaelus opened his mouth to answer.

A draft of cool water eased his broken flesh.

Long fair hair hung over the woman's face and over the leather slave collar wrapped around her neck. A meager, pale robe only just covered her, her skin trembling beneath it as she pulled a heavy fur around him.

Beyond her, the long shadows of morning drew out like knives across the carpeted floor of the tent. The cries and calls of men and beast and the din of rough steel echoed beyond it. The marshalling calls of war.

Inside the tent, around him, the warmth of fires and the supple scent of jasmine fended away the sounds, and the chill.

"You have no fever," she whispered in amazement. "Just like your wounds that have already healed. You have healed yourself. Rua has healed you!"

He pushed himself upright, away from her. His arms trembled.

The mordant wounds upon his back and the pain that should accompany them felt like distant ghosts. Only the memory of the whip and the sticks remained, and the suffering cries inflicted on the ones he loved.

Beneath the woman's fair hair, her blue eyes continued to widen.

"They left you there all night. You . . . you should be dead. But Rua has healed you." She bowed her head in a rush, hiding her eyes from him. "You are the Giver!"

Her name came to him like a whisper bathed in azure flame, but just her name. And the flame was cold around her. She didn't see it. He knew at once the Giver wouldn't let him save her. The Giver wouldn't let him save any of them. He would only tell him their names.

"Ona," he said.

He reached up to touch her face. He lifted her chin.

Ona froze, her eyes fearful, hopeful. The Dragon's shadow within her, still small, writhed beneath his touch.

"Are you . . ." Ona trembled. "You are . . ."

"Enough," a rough voice commanded.

Ona, the slave girl, slunk back in fear, withdrawing beneath the sputtering jasmine-filled shadows.

Chaelus struggled, naked, to his feet.

Gervasis stood across the tent from him. He wore a simple robe with azure trim. His lorica hung cleaned and polished and dressed on a rack in the corner behind him, his gray hair was cut in the patrician style. He reminded Chaelus in many ways also of Thinnius, the Servian knight who had sacrificed himself not so long ago, to save them all.

A banquet table spread lay between them, platters of quail and fruit arranged across it fit for a king. More chamber fires burned around them. The chill had already begun to diminish.

"Tell me," Gervasis asked, "why have you come to me?"

Gervasis' expression was stoic, unmoving. The Dragon's shadow within him billowed beneath an azure cloak, like a flaming mantle.

"It's not for you that I've come," he answered.

"Then for what? Just to die, crucified upon the prostrate cross as a heretic? Surely you must have known it would come to this, and for every one of your Servian knights as well."

"Release us."

"You could have kept yourself from me, you know, from my legion, quite easily, but you didn't. The blood of the divine, I believe it is said, flows through your veins. You could have run from me. Or you could have destroyed me just as well. But you didn't do either. And now what? Will you strike me down? Because I can't let you go, not now that I have you. Or is it, perhaps, your destiny to die here?"

"You can let us go. I know what it is you want from me."

"I'm not sure you do. I certainly don't. Not yet. Prophecy can be such a vague and fickle thing, can it not? My matron often described it to me as something of a quilt that is never fully woven." Gervasis selected a pear from the table and bit from it. "But you know, when I first saw you, and even before then, when I first heard of you, I knew that at least the weaving of our passing would share a common thread."

Gervasis strode past him to stare, his back toward Chaelus, out into the legion camp beyond.

"So what is it, then? What thread could it be? It is like a force, or a vision, inside me. Something I cannot deny. It's as if there is some debt I have yet to repay you for," Gervasis said, "for a sacrifice you have yet to make."

"And what sacrifice is that? What debt?"

"I was hoping you would tell me," Gervasis smiled. "Are you not said to be the vessel of the Giver reborn?"

"You would have me save you, but you have scourged me for heresy. You have beaten and tortured the ones I love."

"Those are the charges, and the punishment for those charges that have been placed against you. I had no choice."

"Release us."

"I cannot. The master I serve will not allow it."

Beneath Gervasis, beneath the husk of him, beneath his flesh, beneath Gervasis ex Framea, First Spear of the First cohort of the Twelfth Theocratic Legion, the shadow of the Dragon struggled against the azure flame. But the Giver would show no more from beyond its veil.

"I can only save you if you release me from my master," Gervasis smiled.

"From what master? From the Dragon?"

Gervasis' smile faded. He gestured to the table and its setting. "Almost. That would almost be easier, I think, but break bread with me and I'll show you."

Gervasis sat on one of the long benches and leaned forward, his chin in the crux of his folded, hardened hands. A silver goblet sat before him, engraved with dragons around its rim. A dagger, the same motif etched upon its pommel and guard, sat with its blade sunk deep into the table.

Both flickered with the golden light from the chamber fires.

Chaelus sat down opposite Gervasis.

"Thank you," Gervasis said.

"I have little choice," Chaelus replied.

Gervasis lifted a thin loaf. He broke it in two. He handed one half to Chaelus.

"So say we all. But you, in fact, do. Like I said, I have heard the stories of your miracles. Strike me down. Strike down my camp, my men. Burn me with your pale fire until my sin melts from my very bones. Burn all of this legion, all of it, and then take your friends and walk away from here. It might be better than the alternative that has been thrust upon you."

"And what if prophecy won't let me?" he whispered.

Gervasis rolled his eyes. He bit into the bread.

"Then still, there's something I would show you." He held up his forearm and snapped his fingers.

Another slave, a boy, entered through the back flap of the tent. He carried a small engraved wooden chest. He placed it on the table before Gervasis.

Gervasis pulled the dagger from the tabletop. He flicked open the clasp of the chest and pushed it over. "Because I know who you've come for."

Gold coins, auras, bright with their own flame in the light of the fire and in their sound, cascaded and rolled across the surface of the table. They were new and unmarred, their edges and the face of the woman marked upon them crisp, the familiar face of an, until now, unknown queen.

A rolling coin shivered to a stop before Chaelus.

The face of the queen was one he already knew.

Upon the coin, the queen's face stared in profile. Beneath her crown, her eyes still beckoned him from beyond her veil, just as they had so many years ago, long before either the Dragon or the Giver had claimed him, when they had said goodbye to him so long ago beneath the mottled light of the morning sun.

Faerowyn.

"Faerowyn is queen," he whispered as he picked it up.

On the back of the coin, the stamp of a dragon flew.

"Empress, actually," Gervasis said, a slight smile upon his lips. He raised the goblet to them. "Only just made."

Chaelus closed his mouth from the words he hadn't realized he had spoken.

"It's a point of technicality, though," Gervasis said. "But you would do well to remember it when I bring you as tribute before her, once we arrive in the Holy City of Paleos a fortnight from now. Let me show you something else."

Gervasis reached down beside him. He lifted up Sundengal, still in her scabbard. He set her upon the table, across the gold auras bearing Faerowyn's image. The shifting light of the tent danced upon all.

"Your father's sword, I presume, now yours." Gervasis stopped himself. "No, mine, actually. A bit of a symbol, as it were, of the life you gave away."

"It isn't my life anymore," Chaelus answered, though it wasn't a question.

"No. Instead, you traded it for this."

Gervasis lifted and dropped a leather whip atop the gold coins and Sundengal. The strands of the flail were still dark with dried flesh and blood.

His flesh. His blood.

"Now tell me, how does that bit of prophecy go?" Gervasis asked.

*One to walk alone*
*He will raise twelve to show the way.*

*Neither spear nor shaft shall harm him*
*His symbol shall be his passage.*

Gervasis lowered his gaze to the table.

"But it seems that whips do, sort of, at least until you heal yourself or prophecy does it for you. The same, of course, cannot be said for my amputated trooper. But if the world doesn't end before, perhaps an early retirement might suit him.

"But not you. The slave girl's no fool. Few of us really are. And I am sorry for your and your company's punishment, but my orders left me little choice." He rubbed his head and lifted his stare to Chaelus. "You must understand there's no way my queen would ever let me bring an unrepentant prophet back. And if not her, then certainly not the new master she serves."

Gervasis stood. He gestured.

"Please, stand."

Gervasis nodded to the slave girl, Ona.

Chaelus stood.

Ona carefully placed the fur around his shoulders. Her hands were gentle, almost reverent upon him. She knelt down before him and tied a rope around his waist.

"I can't let anyone wonder who you've come to raise from the dead," Gervasis said. "The Theocratic Council is no more. Faerowyn's father is dead, put to death by his own daughter, murdered by the Taurate he served. Faerowyn is no longer the girl she was, but I know she loved you once. Perhaps she still does. Perhaps there's still something left in her that you can save."

He rapped the dagger on the table three times.

Two sentries came in. They seized Chaelus by the arms.

"Remember what I have told you, prophet," Gervasis said. "And forgive me again, for the same reasons I've already said, but some of the ones you love, your knights who follow you, won't be coming with us."

*

Login stared in awe at the vision sprawled out beneath the storm-wrought sky.

Osgarath, the City of the Dead. No gates stood to protect it. None were needed. No walls surrounded its haunted spires. Broken carts and empty stalls lined its streets. Empty wicker baskets blew among them. None who still walked here were left among the living. There were not even birds to take wing from its sparrow-holes. Not even ravens or crows.

The happas broadened as it descended into the city hollowed out from stone. It stretched for leagues. Now, before an empty square, a pair of obelisks stood watch. Beyond them, the face of either a palace or a tomb stood out against the pale gray stone. Colonnades of pillars and windows and statues adorned it. The runes of a spell, or a warding, were written across the pale stone of all of them.

But not all the stones were dead, and apparently, neither were the living.

Maedelous jerked the cart to a stop before the paired pale obelisks.

Login held onto the wagon's hoarding. He staggered to his feet. Fever burned against his brow and behind his eyes.

Beneath the runes, stories covered the obelisks, great stories of men and deeds, of trade and even of conquest. The stories unfolded, wrapping the obelisks all the way up to their summit.

The runes had been carved on them crudely after, like a sad ending.

Two men, guards, their armor and their cloaks, even their faces and even their spears painted white like alabaster, kept watch on either side of great carved wooden doors of black oak, their spears crossed between them.

"They guard against nothing," Maedelous whispered. "All the traders, even the people are gone. No coin has passed between men here for some time, and coin is why men stay, or blood."

Maedelous climbed down with trembling hands. "Pay attention to my words, boy, and do exactly as I say, for only death lives here and it has no need for either patience or fools."

Login sagged down from the cart after Maedelous, stumbling under the weight of his fever.

On the great black doors, the carvings showed the same scenes, beneath the same runes as on the stone.

The painted-faced guards lifted their spears as if they had been waiting here for them. Their stare they kept forward. No words. No challenge. They opened the doors for them to a darkened hall.

Login followed Maedelous past them.

In the darkness beyond, three gray-cloaked men waited, bearing torches and wearing masks of alabaster each adorned with the face of a child. Smaller, dull and unpolished, bronze doors waited beyond them. The torchlight spread a muted gray amber across them both.

"Welcome to Osgarath," the center man said, his voice cool. "And to the welcoming hearth of Aeofyn, king."

The smart musk of decay filled the air.

Maedelous drew his staff close to him.

"We only seek refuge for the night," Maedelous said. He seized Login by the shoulder. "Only for one night. My companion is sick with fever. Without shelter, he will not last through the coming storm."

The center man stepped toward them.

"So few come. Even fewer stay." He bowed toward them. "Please, come with us."

The two behind him opened the bronze doors. A narrow passage opened up beyond them into a larger hall of somber light.

Small high windows, seven of them, washed the sculpted ceiling in a glow, draping the hall in a gradually descending shadow, ending in a darkness that surrounded the pale stone of the throne at the farthest end.

By twos, darker robed men gathered into the small hall, stark against the whiteness. They whispered among the shadows surrounding the throne.

A blind boy walked in, no older than Login.

King Aeofyn surely; again, as if he had been waiting for them.

Gossamer covered the king's eyes, wrapped around his head over dark circles and pallor.

The same pallor and sightlessness filled the air. It settled over the sculpted pale of the cavern hall, breathing life away from the living rock itself.

There was nothing to see here but a sullen whisper.

It carried upon the breath and stares of the guards and scribes and the courtesans that surrounded them. It whispered to and fro amongst the gauze tapestries blowing between the spiraling cliffs that made up this kingdom. Beyond it, within it, only the eyes of the souls of the dead could see. And they stared through everything.

While the living, while the boy king, it seemed, stared at nothing.

A hawkish gray cur slunk down at the king's feet.

A man, one of the ones dressed in gray, perhaps one of the Warders that Maedelous had mentioned, inclined his head toward them. The man grimaced as he whispered something into Aeofyn's ear.

Aeofyn's weak lips parted.

His hand draped down. His fingers brushed the top of the cur's head.

"It is said that our compassion to travelers," Aeofyn said, his voice a rivulet, "is above renown. Is this why you've come to us?"

"We seek only your briefest compassion," Maedelous said. "My escort has taken ill with fever. He requires shelter and I, I cannot travel alone without him. Without your grace, I fear neither of us will survive our passage home."

"And where is home?" Aeofyn asked.

"Essoris," Maedelous said, "my lord. I am a trader from the northern reach of Goarnn."

The Warder whispered something once more.

"You come from Tulon?" the king asked. "Along the border of the Roan March, do you not?"

Maedelous hesitated. "We do."

"I only guess this for there is no other place a trader could come from, is there? Only barbarians and proselytizers, say you not. But then I would ask of you, what word do you bring me of them, of the Roan kings and our Servian brothers there?"

Maedelous stammered. "No, no word, sire. My trade wasn't with them. Surely, for the Theocracy holds writ against their order, and even contempt of the Roan kings it would seem, yes?"

"And indeed it does, yes, on both accounts. But you also know we are not a part of the Theocracy, and neither are the Goarnn kingdoms. So why would we care?"

Aeofyn plucked at the cur's hair.

"So why do you care what writ the Theocracy holds while you are well within the borders of my kingdom?"

"I only wish to assure you of the truth of my words, sire."

"Which is how I know you are lying to me. In fact, I would go so far as to say that even your pity for your dying friend here is false."

Maedelous sighed.

"But the question to be asked is why do you come here and weave such a poisonous thread among us, here where it is known that the dead see everything?"

"Because he's afraid."

Login spoke before he knew the words had even come from his mouth, or why.

Maedelous seized his arm again.

"Don't be a fool," Maedelous spat, a shock against Login's neck. "You're going to get us both killed."

Aeofyn pressed his lips and his blind eyes together, wearier shadows painted clouds around them.

Login wrestled his arm free of Maedelous. The room swam about him.

Aeofyn held up his hand.

The room ceased to spin.

"But you, young dying one, you are not afraid, are you?" Aeofyn whispered.

The hawkish-faced cur sat upright.

"Tell me why?" Aeofyn asked.

The answer was simple.

"Because I have nothing left to lose," Login answered. "Everything I had has already been taken from me."

Aeofyn clapped his hands once.

Six knights in whitewashed mail stepped out of the darkness around them, their painted white hands at the hilts of their swords.

Maedelous turned pale.

Aeofyn slumped into his throne. "Then we are not so different, you and I. We are not so different from those that dwell here. I pray that you and your companion will indeed stay with us, and may the spirits of the dead watch over you both."

## Chapter Ten: Oblation

Faerowyn slid back into the deep velvet seat of her throne, its shining arms laced with glittering golden filigree and jewels, dragons wrought upon dragons coiling around themselves in shimmering fire. She leaned back against the radiant spires that crowned her like the rays of the rising sun.

She, Faerowyn, the Dragon Queen.

Or was she even her? Had she become the Dragon already?

She wiped at the blood still upon her face. The taste of it burned deep inside her throat.

She wasn't really sure which one she was anymore. Even so soon after, even after only two days. It had only been seven days since the Dragon had taken her, since she had given herself to it, her body and her soul.

*Vows of prophecy.*
*Vows of betrothal.*

*A martyr of the Dragon's veil*
*Will be chosen to be queen.*

*To rule the Pale beyond the veil.*

*Brought down on bended knee.*

*A broken promise she must keep*
*To bear the Dragon's seed.*

Already, its seed was growing within her. Already its hunger within her grew. Already, she knew she would soon be no more.

But not yet. For now, at least, she still knew who and what she was. She still knew how much she had given up to have this, this one last chance to make everything right. Surely that meant at least there was some of her left. Surely, something, anything, enough perhaps still to be saved by the time her savior finally came for her.

Chaelus was coming. He had already crossed the border of the Theocracy. Her Gervasis had already captured him for her. Her first spear would bring him to her.

He was finally coming, her savior, for her.

The second of the two messengers reached the far end of the pillared and pearlescent hall, his hurried, frantic footfalls fading.

The gathered courtesans and the hanging scribes still stood some distance away, safely among the shadows, watching her from behind their veils. The wizard priests of the Taurate whispered among them, bleeding through the shadows between them, so that among the colored veils of her court, all their eyes would remain veiled as well.

She looked down to the first of the two messengers who had come to her, the one she had asked to whisper his treaty to her, slumped now against her feet and only barely breathing. She ran her bloodied fingers through his hair.

His eyes had darkened, somewhat misty.

He had trembled at first, when she took him in her arms, not knowing what would happen to him, what his new queen would do to him.

But then, she had trembled too, hadn't she? Neither had she been able to stop it, and neither could he, stop the Dragon once it finally overcame her, possessed her, bore through her and consumed her like no lover she had ever known, pouring out from deep beneath her skin, its eyes set deep inside hers, its taste and hunger let loose upon her tongue.

And oh, how it had hungered.

To feed its growing seed within her.

So at her command, the poor man had whispered his message to her, fear upon his voice. He had whispered in her ear just as she commanded him, so that she could have him closer, so she wouldn't fail the Dragon, her lover, when it claimed him.

His bright doe-like eyes had glistened as she framed his gentle trembling face within her hands; so trusting, so fearful, of his queen. And as he spoke those words, that the heretic, her savior, would soon be here, would soon be brought before her, she scarcely was able to keep the Dragon at bay. The messenger, the poor young man, had screamed terribly as she closed her lips over his. He had known it was much more than a kiss.

He screamed until she tore herself from him, blood and darker things trailing from his lips, dripping from hers.

It still drained now down her throat. It still wetted her lips.

And she knew she couldn't save him.

Nor could anyone else, not anymore.

The gathered courtesans and scribes and the wizards who whispered had watched her from the solace and safety of the shadows of the pillared hall, while the wizards whispered to them so they wouldn't run, so they wouldn't flee.

The Dragon within her had pulled the young man back to her, seizing him with her hands, and as her mouth closed upon his again, she could only listen to his distant, muffled cries.

But it wasn't her, anymore, was it?

His screams had rattled to the barest of whimpers, a whisper really. There they ended, finally, just as her own cries had not so very long before. But he would never sit on a throne like she did. And no one would ever come to save him, like her savior was coming soon to save her.

The only thing the messenger could do now, the only hope he had left, was to dream, to fall into the Dragon's Sleep until even that hope drained away from him, until all will was gone from him and the remnant of his husk was resurrected anew to serve the Dragon's will.

She touched her growing womb. It pressed up from beneath her dress, already, after only seven days.

The man's eyes stared up at her from somewhere beyond, where he cradled himself at her feet. The stain of blood and darker things colored his chin, his face, his chest. Black tendrils had begun to lace across his pale skin.

Soon, the Dragon's Sleep would take him.

Soon, the Dragon's Sleep would take them all.

Even the one she had just let go.

Even her lover who was coming for her, for she knew it was the only way he could save her.

The clangor of the closing doors bathed in mother of pearl rippled across the hall to her.

The messenger who remained stayed there trembling; his blood and sepia-stained lips fumbled upon themselves, seeking a word, a plea. She couldn't discern the sound of it.

But she understood it, because she had whispered the same thing when the Dragon had taken her, when she had given herself up to it.

At least her plea had been answered.

She couldn't answer this man's plea, not in the way he would have hoped, if he even had hope left.

No.

The thin black tendrils laced across and through his flesh like serpents, like wyrms, like dragons.

She slipped down to him from the seat of her golden throne. She cradled her arms around him. She placed her wet, hungry lips over his. It was just a kiss

He trembled.

She tasted him.

The pulse of the Dragon quickened within her veins. It stretched across her growing womb.

At least she could do this much for him.

At least she could help him so that he no longer cared.

*

Some moments last longer than others, longer perhaps than any moment should, and some memories last even longer still.

Olivia had barely been able to stare into the eyes of the Servian knight before her, dark sad mournful eyes they were, shaped by the bitterness of loss and hardened by the kind of fear that can only ever end in hate. She could only stare beneath them past the harsh light of eleven cold red flames.

Flames that had no veil this time to hide behind.

The Servian knight's blade, a dagger, hovered like a ghost, lingering upon the edge of her vision like a word escaping, or a prophecy still to be unveiled; a dark prophecy, the kind that can only be voiced in shadow and flame.

The soft glow of the moon above their second night's encampment danced on the dagger's quivering edge.

Hate.

She couldn't even remember his name, and she couldn't find her voice, to call out, to call for help, or even to pray.

Her voice had been lost beneath all the other voices it seemed, lost beneath the trampling of the hundredfold around her preparing for the next day's march, who knew nothing about the man, the Servian knight, who was preparing to kill her.

The only moment that lasted longer than this was the one when her nameless assassin fell.

The sound of a sharp retort. The crunch of steel and bone and skin.

The man's crying grunt that faded to a whisper when his dark, startled, scared, all too knowing eyes softened at the sudden truth flashing before him.

Only then did she remember his name.

It was Al-Cannan.

His name rang inside her as the chime of his long dagger danced out and spun across the rocky ground.

The haggard stare of Al-Hoanar came into view behind him, the long hilt of his spagot, his short stabbing blade with the spike at its pommel, gripped within his hand; his eyes a meld of something, somewhere, between the living and the dead.

Then the silence came, and the whispers, and the cries of the Servian knights who called out around them as some of them finally heard, and finally saw, what had happened. One of their own had tried to kill the Mother. One of their own had struck him down.

Al-Hoanar gripped her hand as he rode beside her, bringing her back to the present.

She winced. The memory faded beneath blowing snow and the bright glare of a winter sun.

Al-Hoanar led her mare beside his own.

His face stiffened with care. "Do not do this. Please stop suffering for what you think I've done."

The long train of knights and Khaalish warriors stretched before and behind them. So many of them, knight and barbarian alike, fixed their stares on either her or the menace of the fading forest and growing hilltops around them. The sanctity and the safety of the Garden, of Sanseveria, was already two days past.

"And what did you do?" she asked, her words hollow and shaking, useless against the pallor of the Servian knight who had fallen at her feet. "When you struck him down?"

"I did nothing against my vows." Al-Hoanar's voice trembled. "My promise isn't dead, and neither is he, at least not yet, and certainly not by my hand. But you already know this."

He urged his mare with his boot, leading hers beside him.

She did know it, and she sagged beneath the strange burden that the man, her knight, her assassin, still lived. She sagged beneath the burden that it troubled her so.

"I know," she said. "And I am grateful to you for both."

Al-Hoanar tapped his finger across the steel spike at the end of his spagot and smiled. "There are times when a point is better made with a cudgel than a blade."

His smile faded. "The traitorous coward waited until after we had left the Garden, so that once he killed you, he could run to the safety of his master."

"But who is his master?"

"Hunters? Maedelous? The Dragon itself? I don't know. I don't care. But they will find him. We left him behind so they would. We left him like a traitor should be, tied to a prostrate cross. At least this way, when they do find him, they and their master will know they haven't won this. At least, they haven't won it yet."

His smile returned. "And when they're done with him, so too will he."

She sighed.

"Then his death will be lost, for they were never his master."

## Chapter Eleven: Crucifixion

Chaelus bowed his head against the bouncing slats of the slavers' wagon, his hands bound in chains above his head, watching the once-verdant fields of the Theocracy pass by him in shadow and rot as the wagon trembled south across the worn and weary stones of the happas.

It was all he could do. It was all there was left for him to do.

He could still see them, all of them. He could still see the knights' faces staring back at him with their dead eyes, staring back at him from the edge of the encampment; seven of them, each of them with arms and legs flayed out upon a prostrate cross, staring back at him, staring through him long after they had passed from his sight.

At least their deaths had already passed, and quickly, for a death such as theirs.

But not their purpose, their corpses left on the cross as a message to the Servian order, and to the whole of the west, that the Theocratic legion, and the dragon queen, had finally come.

Seven Servian knights crucified on the order of Gervasis ex Framea, First Spear of the First Cohort of the Twelfth Theocratic Legion, to send a message from his queen, his empress, Faerowyn, once true love of Chaelus, the vessel of the Giver reborn.

Yet they hadn't died because of any of those things, had they? No. They had died because of *him*. That was why, three days later, the ghosts of their faces still stared back at him.

Their azure flame burned bright beneath the dark water of their death.

Chaelus slumped from the chains holding his hands over his head. He fell away from the slats of the slaver's wagon that had been nothing but a foolish ruse.

How could they, how could he, have been so wrong, to think he could fool prophecy itself, or even a legion? No more could he save his brother and win a kingdom back.

He stared past his ghosts to the ones he loved and who still lived, the ones he loved most of all, marching behind him to the whips and drums and chant of a legion.

Mariam, Michalas and Obidae stumbled bound, with bleeding feet, behind the wagon. The First Cohort of the Twelfth Theocratic Legion marched in rank behind them.

There was nothing now from him, not even the admonition of the Giver, that could save them.

*You love for fear of loss.*
*You must love, instead, for the desire to give.*

But there was nothing left for him to give them, was there?

He so wanted to call to her, to Mariam, to Michalas, to Obidae, to the ones he loved who still lived, to give them hope. But he had no hope to offer them. Even his love for them was a curse.

The whisper of Mariam's lips upon his skin, and the strength he felt while lying with her, at least this memory still stayed with him. It still pulled at him. It still summoned him. It was the only strength he had since the Giver left, because of a blaze of azure flame and the condemned souls of another legion half a world and another lifetime away.

All to save his brother and win his kingdom back. To be freed from his past. It was him. It had always been him. It is always the vessel, never the drink.

To the south, a cry sounded upon the broken hills. It broke across the scattered pines. Wind billowed. Melting snow flew about them like rain.

The shouts of the soldiers, of a legion, rang out around him.

But the whispers beneath, the whispers of their shadows were louder.

Their shadows whispered in awe, they whispered in fear.

*Dragon.*

They whispered this until the legion whips of the centurions sounded across the backs of their own men, and the ones Chaelus loved most. They must hurry to the beat of a drum, to the forced march of a legion, of the Dragon.

Gervasis reined in beside the wagon. His guards held rank behind him.

The shadow of the Dragon within him was strangely still; only a pale shadow within him.

"You don't eat," Gervasis said.

"Do not do this," Chaelus said.

"I do as I must, for the queen who commands me. A slave is still a slave no matter who his master is."

"That is why you hurry to her call."

Gervasis looked up to the blowing tempest that called to them.

"The queen alone is my master. I do not serve hers."

"Then why did you do this? Why did you crucify those knights?"

"Because I had to, because I am only a man, and men must do the things that prophecy would never dare; because there is no spirit of the Giver who whispers truths to me. There is no holy fire at my hand by which I could protect and defend. There was once a time when Chaelus, Roan Lord of the House of Malius, would have done the same."

Chaelus stood up. He had only his hands, and they were bound. He had no fire. He had no steel. He had nothing to help him strike the man riding next to him, the man who kept him prisoner, who tortured his friends, his lover, and who had just executed seven Servian knights.

But it wasn't Gervasis, and he wouldn't kill him even if he could, and not because the Giver waited mute inside him, or that his holy fire wouldn't burn. It wasn't even because of the chains that bound him, or kept Sundengal from him. No. It was because what Gervasis said was true. He would have done no different. He had done worse, long before the Giver or prophecy claimed him.

And if it was by prophecy, or the Giver, that because of him all who loved him would die, than they were no better.

"I did it because I have something greater to defend," Gervasis said. "As for my debt, I pray your master speaks to you before mine has her way with you. Otherwise, you will have no choice but to die like your friends."

Gervasis' voice lowered as he reined his horse away.

"We will reach the Imperial capital of Paleos in less than a fortnight. You should eat before then. For what it's worth, I made sure the death of your knights went quick for them, and for their part, know that they died willingly and without fear, for you."

Michalas rubbed his thumb against the gentle hollow of the stone, careful to keep it hidden from the soldiers around him. His thumb grew warm against it.

He took strength from it, just as he took his strength from the towering presence of Obidae behind him, just as he took strength from the sight of his sister in front of him, even if she thought she had none left to give him as she stared lost at the empty husk of the Giver kept in chains before her.

He took it just as he took it still from the death and memory of Al-Malice, Al-Eliana, and Al-Gogin, and the other Servian knights. He took it because he knew he needed all of it. He knew he needed all of them, as much as he had ever needed the angels before them, even if he had only just met them.

They all did, they all needed each other, even the Giver who hung like a broken man, already crucified before them. Mostly he needed it, mostly Chaelus did.

They had all lost so much of it already, and not just strength, but something else. They had lost their hope.

He absently wiped his arm across his eyes.

But there were no more tears. The feelings were still there, all of them, still all mixed up together so he couldn't even tell them apart. But they were a little farther back now, a little farther away, a little more distant.

He felt almost safer.

Almost like when the angels used to come.

Yet the memory of the dead, the ghosts of Al-Malice, Al-Eliana and Al-Gogin, still floated before him, their faces exactly how they had been when they died; staring back at him, staring into him, giving him their strength, the strength of the dead, the strength of the dying. It was the same look they gave to the ones who killed them. And they hadn't cried at all.

None of them did. Not even Obidae, or his sister, or even himself, watching them die. That was when he realized it was the end of the moment in between. That was the first time he hadn't cried since the angels left him.

Ahead of them, a flock of ravens took wing from a dead man who had fallen beside the road, along the edge of rotting fields left from the last season. The corpse was putrid. The man had been dead for a long time.

Michalas had grown used to seeing them now, in every field and every village, outside the high ramparts of every city they passed. The corpses, they always stayed silent against the sound of terror and dancing inside the walls. The dead, at least they were safe.

Obidae's shadow drew over him like a warm mantle.

Obidae whispered to him. His voice grated from his wounds. But still he kept it to a whisper.

"Nothing is without meaning, child. Not even death. Not even theirs. Remember what's been given to you, and always remember why."

*

Al-Mariam stumbled, her feet cut and bleeding against the stones of the happas. The meltwaters flowed past her in a gully alongside them, but her limbs were still cold. She pulled the thin hard cloth tighter around her.

It was her heart and soul that broke and froze and shattered with every step, because, still, even after everything, after endless leagues, she still hadn't seen Chaelus set his stare upon her. Whether he couldn't, or he wouldn't, whether he was even Chaelus, or the Giver, either one, she really didn't even care anymore. She just wanted him. She needed him. She needed to look once more into the crystal mirror of his eyes. Even if it meant she could never again feel the touch of his skin.

Just his look would be enough for her. It would be enough at least to tell her why. But she knew why, didn't she?

She placed her hand to the healing wound beneath her breast. It still helped help her to remember, to remember him, but the truth seemed farther and more distant with every southward league they marched.

Another bestial cry broke free from there, from the southern horizon, where the city of Paleos and the Dragon Queen waited for them. That fact beat as much upon her heart and mind as it did upon on the wind. Real or imagined, the cries had become more and more frequent. They were a part of things. Like the wind, like shadows.

She looked up to him.

Then it was there. What she had wanted. Chaelus' stare lifted up to hers.

It held her in place, her legs frozen upon the bleeding stones.

But his stare was empty. It was a void. It was broken. It didn't have strength. It didn't have hope. It didn't even have tears.

"Why?" she screamed at him in a whisper. But she already knew the answer.

The shouting filth of the guards beat at her. They shoved her. Their labored curses echoed behind their chainmail veils.

Obidae's hand pressed against her back. She heard his urgent gentle plea beneath the rising crack of a whip, beneath the breaking cry of her heart.

Then, all of them at once, Chaelus, or the vessel of the Giver reborn, or the man she had sworn once loved her back—or was it just the man who perhaps survived one death too many, one sacrifice too much, the Roan Lord of the House of Malius—either way, his stare fled away from her like a ghost, but like it was a part of things; like wind, like shadows, like the phantom cries of dragons.

*

Login slumped against the wall of the cell.

"You fool of a boy," Maedelous said. "It's been days now since we were left here to rot. It will mean more than just death for the two of us. You have no idea what's at stake, or what price our failure will bring."

Login pushed himself upright against the wall of the cell, trying to stand, but he couldn't.

The old man glared at him but it wasn't anger in his eyes, it was fear.

"Perhaps I was wrong," Maedelous whispered. "Perhaps I was wrong about you all along."

Maedelous' hands shook. He wiped spittle from the corner of his mouth. He crumpled to the floor across from Login.

Maedelous turned to the small square window high up on the wall. Muted light broke through it, settling upon the motes of dust that drifted in the air around them.

"That window isn't there to bring light for us, boy. And it isn't for sparrows, either. It's for the dead, and when they come, boy, pray they'll be quick with us, for mercy they forgot along with their lives long, long ago. At least that will be some mercy."

"Who is there to suffer other than us?" Login asked.

"More than you could know."

"Are any of the dead here, are they Servian? Are any of the dead the ones you betrayed?"

Maedelous looked at him, a sad line written across his aged and brittle face.

"And tell me, what would you know of that, boy?"

The drum of footsteps ascended beyond the door toward them.

Maedelous scrambled to his feet.

The tangled clank of steel as the lock turned.

Four knights in alabaster rushed in. One with a torch, the other three held drawn swords pointed toward Maedelous.

Maedelous backed up against the wall as much as he could, but he stood straight with his chin raised.

"I see you finally remembered us," he sneered.

King Aeofyn's hand felt out the doorway as he led himself in.

The guards held themselves in a firm ring around Maedelous.

The blind king tilted his head, listening. He walked past Maedelous toward Login on the whisper of sandaled feet.

Whatever strength Login had left fled away.

Aeofyn crouched down. He held out his hand to him.

"Come with me."

Login stared back at the king, uncertain.

"Please," Aeofyn said.

He took Aeofyn's hand. It was cool against his fevered flesh.

The blind king helped him up. Effortlessly, he led them alone out into the unlit passage.

"Where are you taking him?" Maedelous shouted behind him, but the pale stone swallowed his cry.

Login clutched King Aeofyn's small hand. Gossamer-bound, like the boy's eyes. His thin fingers, though, were quick, and his other hand fluttered before him, responding to everything, even the air.

Aeofyn led them down sightless halls and unseen steps. The only sound was their breath and the whisper of their footsteps. With no words, only his breath and his touch, the blind boy king led them deftly downward into the bright night of an open courtyard hewn from the living stone.

The mantle of night waited just above the layered memories of the passing day, already struck in blood across the sky, even as what must be the first whispers of the dead called out, already twisting among the pallid spires. Shimmers of azure and of a deeper blue danced among the ghosts' pale strands.

The tiny windows, the sparrow-holes, looked out over the court all around them. Too little and too high to offer any view, with no candlelight revealing the living still here, they really were more like passages of the dead, as from the tombs of old, than they were any window of the living.

Perhaps that is all they ever were.

Aside from the whispers of the dead, though, the palace of young King Aeofyn was still, and it was silent. It was as it should be. It was as silent as a tomb.

Only the soft scrape of stone and the broken hush of grass beneath their feet spoke anything for the living. Too few of them could be seen or heard, or even found here.

Only the dead.

"The dead," Login whispered. "Do they speak, my lord?"

"They do," Aeofyn said. "They speak always to those, to anyone, who will listen."

"What do they say?"

"Mostly, they sing. They sing songs. They sing songs because no one else will sing to them."

"What kind of songs?"

"Only laments, anymore, though once their songs were filled with joy."

"Then why do they stay here?"

"They stay because they have nowhere else to go. The spheres are at war. They stay because they have no home. They are like refugees while they wait for prophecy to unfold. So we've given them a place where at least some of them can find solace."

"And where are the living? I've seen none but your court since we arrived. No traders. No children. How do the living live here?"

"The living left because they were too afraid of the dead. They think it is the dead that won't suffer them, but it is the other way around. They are afraid of the dead who whisper their love songs to them. The dead, who can still see the ones they love, but cannot be with them."

Aeofyn paused.

"Those of us who tend to them, we have learned to do without many things, too. I am sorry I could not come for you sooner."

A lump rose in Login's throat.

"Can they see you? The ghosts?"

Aeofyn's face brightened, just a shade.

"Oh yes, they can. The dead can see everything. They know everything, everything about you. Even more than you dare know yourself. The dead are wise. They are far wiser than you or me. They are no longer hindered by the ignorance of this mortal coil."

"Will they hurt you?" Login asked.

"No. But they will show you things, sometimes things you wish you had never been made to see, the kind of things only a trusted friend would dare to share with you, the kind you would dare to listen to."

"I would not want to, I think, see these things."

"Yet sometimes they are things we must know anyway." Aeofyn turned. He seized Login's other hand, his expression earnest. "Will you trust me?"

"You are a king."

"But will you trust what the dead say to me?"

Login thought.

"It cannot be any worse than lies of the living, I suppose."

Aeofyn gave a sad smile.

"The one you travel with, he intends to use you. He has brought you as parlay to one of the Goarnn princes, to treat with him for an alliance, to help him raise an army. This one prince in particular is known for his love of boys, as well as bloodshed."

Login stammered. His stomach tightened.

Aeofyn squeezed his hands and let him go. He walked a short way then stooped and brushed the back of his bound hand across the grass.

"The ghosts, they tell me sometimes of their regrets too, of the things they wish they had known, and done, in life. Do you have regrets, Login? Tell me, have you ever loved and lost?"

Login stepped toward him. A river of sudden fear threatened to consume him.

"Maedelous," he answered. "I didn't know anyone else to turn to. My mother, my father, everyone else I have ever loved was gone. I was afraid. I didn't want to be alone anymore."

Aeofyn turned back to him. Sadness and understanding and a smile danced beneath the shadows of his gossamer-bound eyes.

"And he offered you solace. He offered you guidance, like a father would."

Aeofyn held up his hand to him.

"Maedelous believes the Servian knights have failed in their oath to see the prophecy fulfilled, but more than that, he believes they have failed in their oath to prevent the return of the Dragon. Or even to try to defend against it. Perhaps he's right. But he has forgotten that this was never their oath to begin with. They were only ever meant to warn. Yet, like the dead, no one would listen to them."

Login took his hand.

Aeofyn pulled himself back up. Then, even for a blind boy king, his stare grew distant.

"Prophecy says the Dragon must return. Prophecy has prepared a way to stand against it— a prophet, or two it seems to be— to serve as an example for the rest of us. But truth and ghosts aside, Maedelous never believed in prophecy and he will not suffer his will, or the Pale, to depend upon the two that prophecy has chosen; at least, not on them alone. That is why he has chosen you."

"He chose me for what?"

"I don't know, and strangely, neither do the dead. But I think it is more than I have told you. It makes me believe that even he doesn't know, not yet. I can only tell you that he chose you, and you alone, for a reason. He believes that you alone can save what will soon be forever lost."

"But you said I was to be a sacrifice."

Aeofyn smiled. "There are many different types of death. You will be sacrificed. We all are. And I am afraid you will die, just as we all must. But what kind of death that will be, well, that is the part that is always, I think, left up to us."

Aeofyn's blind stare returned to him.

"Maedelous' faith isn't entirely dead yet. But he's lost. He's been deceived by his own wisdom and his own devices, or possibly, by the veil of the Dragon itself. But I think, I believe—no, I hope—that there is something, a power greater than prophecy, at work here. Either way, Maedelous' pride will be his undoing, and yours too, I'm afraid, if you're not careful.

"Maedelous knows that the hope of prophecy has left him. His betrayal of his promise and the ones he loved won't be buried, and not even the Dragon's veil can offer him solace. He treads the thinnest of lines, a balancing act that he believes has been thrust upon him, and he knows he must be wary, and he knows he must be afraid, because he knows both the Dragon and the angels are watching him, and both will always come to claim their own."

Login stepped away from the boy king, his feet a faded whisper in the grass beneath the growing lament of the dead above him. Even his fever, it seemed, had almost burned the flesh of another.

"What do I do?"

"Sleep this night. Let Rua bless you. Then let the dead protect your dreams. Your fever is gone. Go with him on the morrow. Accept your fate. Make it your own. And don't be afraid, Login. The dead have assured me. They told me you're not alone anymore. They've told me you never really were. They talk to each other, you know, the dead. They tell me that a prophecy must always unfold, and that there's a reason why it's always called prophecy instead of truth."

*

"Oh no," Olivia whispered.

But she already knew that it was. She had already seen it. She had already felt it. She had already felt the first ghost-like touch of the legion nails driving through her own wrists a few nights ago. She could still feel it, its sore burning pulse just beneath the blush of her skin.

But it was their wrists, not hers, her children, her Servian knights, seven of them, who stared down at her now with their dead eyes, their frozen skin, their mutilated flesh half-eaten by crows as they thawed briefly each midday, crucified for their faith and for hers upon the prostate cross.

Al-Gogin, Al-Malice, Al-Eliana, Al-Turin, Al-Solan, Al-Vikitan, and Al-Borak were their names. She knew their names. She had selected them for their faith. She had sentenced them to death for it.

But her pain was only a ghost of what theirs had been. Her faith was likewise only a glimmer of theirs. Her death, when it finally came, would only ever be but a shadow of theirs.

A mote of prophecy she had hoped would never, ever, be meant for them drifted through her mind.

*Born to us to die for us.*
*For only the fallen may rise.*

But then again, perhaps it always was meant to be like this, for all of them, even her. Eleven out of twelve of the knights she sent were already dead.

Eleven.

Olivia shook the beginning of the thought from her head.

These were her martyrs. Of the twelve, only Al-Mariam still remained in this life. Only she remained a living servant of prophecy, a martyr all to herself.

Al-Hoanar wept openly. But it was not from fear, or even from the suffering of their loss. No. He already knew the face of death too well. No. He wept from the all too bitter truth of the sacrifice of the dead knights before him, of the tragedy of their faith, and of the tragedy of his own. And perhaps, even of its loss as well.

And she understood it all too well.

His anguish sounded out against the winding and watchful river Vicarus. The seven times mark of the prostrate cross above it.

It was nearly midday and the crows started to descend again.

"Take them down," she pleaded.

Their Khaalish guards glared at her and at Al-Hoanar as they kept watch across the river, and the plain, and the hills surrounding them. But the frozen arc of the Vicarus that flowed beneath them, and the plain, and the hillocks around them, and the abandoned legion encampment at their feet, didn't seem to care.

It was already too late.

The Theocratic Legion had left them its warning. They were hunting for them. No, better, they were waiting for them. They were watching for them. And there was nowhere left for them to hide. They would take them when they pleased. They already had as their prisoner the only one who could save them.

The very one she had sent to them.

Chaelus, the vessel of the Giver reborn.

Al-Aaron watched her just as he watched all of them, from some distance away, alone as he always was; his expression a void. But then he wasn't really alone, was he, not with the ghost he still kept with him. For some, their demons can only come out through prayer and by fasting, and by waiting.

Belloch and the Khaalish spears he now led for her, the ones who had taken the burden of their protection, numbered only a few more than two hundred. Her Servian knights, who by their oaths would sooner give their lives than take another's, numbered not even four score.

They had left behind the refuge and the sanctity of the Garden, the only solace her knights had ever known and could touch with their hands. Now it was legions that hunted for them.

The exposed barren plain of the Kessel and the dangers it possessed stretched beyond their sight to the east, between them and whatever hope was left in the lands of the Evarun.

Yet was it even hope they would find there? Was there any hope to be found with those who had left it so long ago? Or would the machinations of the Dragon and eleven who still served it find them first? Had it already?

Olivia clutched at her sister's prayer stone hanging around her neck. Its smooth, cool comfort sank beneath her trembling touch. The cold bite of winter, and the suffering and loss before her, and all that was still to come, had drunk up what little strength and hope she had left.

The harsh stench of her dubious protector was no encouragement when it came.

"What is it, Belloch?" she whispered.

"Scouts have returned," he growled. "You are being hunted again. They are closer this time. Either stupid or bold, I do not know."

"What did they see?"

A dull pair of thumps sounded in the snow.

"Ask them yourself."

Al-Hoanar ran toward them at the sight.

Two severed heads stared back at her, their cold blood like clotted sand scattered across the snow. Their condemning stare wouldn't let her go.

Olivia staggered back. There was no more strength to help her. No more hope.

Al-Hoanar threw his arm around her, holding her up.

Belloch sniffed. He nodded toward his offering. "They have been trailing you since you left. I stopped them."

"Why did you do this?" she begged.

Al-Hoanar looked at Belloch, then back at her, his face afire with grief, rage, and understanding.

"They left you a message." Belloch looked at the crucified knights and then back at her. "So we left one for them."

"They were only watching us," she said. "They could not have attacked. You were too many for them."

Belloch stepped back. He nodded toward Al-Hoanar.

"Then I do not understand. Does it bother you to see such deeds done, or would you prefer to only hear of it after? Because, Revered Mother, your would-be assassin is no less dead by now. What we did was no less than what your own knight did to him, his own Servian brother, when he left him tied upon a cross little more than a week ago."

## Chapter Twelve: Languish

In the dark, Michalas rolled the tiny stone within his palm, hidden against his chest as he lay. His hands were still bound. The soldiers slept in their ordered encampment around him. The stone was smaller now, smoother, the small hollow he had made finally becoming the shape of something, like a vessel.

Nearly a fortnight had passed, beaten beneath the sharp break of a whip and the forced march of a Theocratic legion.

He took a bite of the bread he had saved from the evening meal. Beaten, yet still fed bread and stew.

The shadows of men glanced at them from shadows along the happas as they passed, from village and vale, past the rotting corpses of cattle and fetid fields that grew more and more common with every passing league. The shadows of men had nothing to eat, but they didn't seem to care. Once their glances passed, they always turned back, to stare southward.

The guards' stares drew more frequently to the southern horizon as well, along with the darkening skies above them.

At least it was getting warmer; even the nights, a little bit.

The snow blanket had gone. More than either the drums

or the whips, the warmth of the spring thaw settled with their passage south, bringing with it the cracking of ice and the dripping of water, and a cadence that brought a strange solace to their passage.

"The strength of the Albanj still protects us," Obidae muttered through his broken lip nearby. "It cares little for the western winter winds. Even this far south, in the western marches, winter would be deep upon us."

"Which means we're getting closer, aren't we? We'll be in Paleos soon," Mariam murmured.

It was only in the dark that they spoke now, while the soldiers slept, though not the sentries. But they didn't listen. They listened to the night. The night had sounds all of its own. From the soldiers' whispers, it was the sound of dragons.

Only the three of them spoke. Chaelus had said nothing to them for the passing of a fortnight.

"We will see the sun rise on the holy city of Paleos tomorrow," Obidae said. "Even though it is no longer holy, and hasn't been so for nearly an age."

"And what then?" Michalas asked.

The furtive crack of frozen limbs sounded in the woods about them, and the deliberate tread of hunted things.

"I don't know," his sister answered. "I don't know."

"We will be led in tribute through the city," Obidae whispered. "We will be taken before their people. They will mock us and they will spit upon us. They will throw their stones upon us. Then we will be taken before their queen."

"I've listened to the soldiers. Her name is Faerowyn," Mariam said. "She was Chaelus' lover once, before prophecy took him from her."

Obidae shrugged.

Stones from something, something fleeing and hidden,

cascaded down the wooded slope in the wash below.

The sentries stirred. Their cries sounded into the dark.

Obidae closed his eyes.

"Then, I think, we will find out indeed whether or not prophecy has abandoned us."

*

Al-Mariam held her breath.

The domed city of Paleos beneath them, gilded and bejeweled like a virgin bridesmaid, reclined along the languid shore of the Sea of Beladun like a glittering whore.

Its domes sparkled against the morning sun. Its light burned against her brow. But it was the stench that held her most.

Even from here, more than a league away, you could smell the foul perfume that the entire city wore. Its scent languished like the stench of death.

If only her hands weren't tied together she could stifle it, or turn away and run. She could plug her ears so she wouldn't have to listen to the lamenting cries of the lost souls who suffered there, the lament that drifted just above the drum beat of the legion bringing their mistress her prize. They sounded like beasts.

Al- Mariam turned away. She stumbled over the callous stones of the happas descending toward the city from the surrounding windswept hills.

Another whip crack sounded against Obidae's back behind her, but no cry came from Obidae. He offered nothing to reward the men who beat him.

In front of him, Michalas was silent as well, like a ghost. His dark eyes had turned far seeing. No tears had marked his cheeks in a fortnight. If it weren't for his eyes, she would have thought him dead. But she knew the angels hadn't returned to him either, only that something else within him had changed.

Ahead of her, Chaelus, her lover, the Giver reborn, the source of their hope, might as well have been dead.

Alone in the darkness of his own malaise, he suffered nothing from the wounds that should have killed him, but from the something darker that had possessed his soul. No spear or shaft would harm him. Prophecy said so. But something greater would; something darker could. It had already begun to claim him. His stare looked nowhere now, alone and impotent; an all too willing subject in the wheeled cage of his captors.

With no other word or glance or solace coming from him, nothing offered from him to her, to tell her anything else, nothing for a fortnight, she could only assume that this is was how he wanted it to be. Because he, Chaelus, the Giver reborn, her savior, had done nothing to stop it.

She had seen him stop it before. At the very least, she had seen him try. Even if he had failed, he had tried.

But not this time. This time, he had done nothing to stop anything. He had done nothing to save them, to save her, not even the seven Servian knights left crucified behind them. He had not even done anything to save himself.

And he could have. If not for them, if not for her, at least for prophecy.

*One to teach and one to save.*

But he didn't, she could only guess, because of what prophecy had done to him.

*Born for us to die for us.*

Or what he had chosen to take from it.

So let him be. So let prophecy be, beneath the crack of a whip and the beat of a drum.

She swallowed the sickness in her throat and glanced back at her brother and the barbarian chief. She stared at the legion marching behind them.

They would take care of each other, Obidae, Michalas and she. It would seem they were all they had left. It would be enough. It had to be.

Behind them, the thousand spears of the Twelfth Theocratic Legion marched them to their doom, beneath the drumbeat and snapping blood-red banners of dragons.

She turned back to the reclining city, the whore that it was. She wouldn't turn away from it anymore.

Behind the slaver's wagon, before her fate, the callous stones tore at her already wounded feet.

She spat upon the invitation written in her own blood across them, and staggered toward whatever fate prophecy had prepared for her.

*

Michalas stumbled before the crowds, lost in the sharp beat of the drum and the harsh glare of trumpets and the screams.

His feet were numb, distant, and bleeding. But all he could feel was the drumbeat of the strange joyful lament of the dying that filled the city streets.

He felt it even more than he felt their hurled stones, and rotted food, and the bloodcurdling cries, from where they gathered and danced alongside the broad width of the happas. Even the little boys and girls in tattered gowns threw their stones at him.

He could feel the Dragon in every one of them. He could see it in the eyes of the dancing dead that they were. None of them knew it though, that they were all going to die. They wouldn't even begin to know before it was already too late. And it already was.

He couldn't cry for them. He wanted to, but he couldn't. It was as if all his tears were gone, and he wasn't sure they were ever coming back. Perhaps he didn't need them anymore. Perhaps they had already taught him everything they were supposed to teach him. His tears and the stone, both.

So he staggered in step behind Chaelus' wagon, behind his sister, and before Obidae, and lost himself in the cool touch of that tiny stone between his fingers, and the gentle hollow he had dug there and where his thumb now rested.

It was a small, shallow, gentle space, a place in between. It was the place where he had been waiting.

And then one more reason occurred to him, perhaps, why it was he had stopped crying, why he couldn't cry anymore for the sadness laid out before him. Perhaps it was because his tears would do nothing to help the dying, and tears for the living weren't needed anymore.

\*

Chaelus sank deeper to a place inside himself. It was the only place where he could hide, the only place left that was safe.

The long shadow of the tower fell across him, built here long ago by the Evarun, just like his own built in the western land from which he had once ruled. The shadow of it overtook the shimmer of Paleos around him, like a promise already denied. It was like a requiem, and it was because of him. He had brought the shadow with him.

Without even steel or holy fire to blame, he still brought death and scourging upon the ones in this place, upon these people, even as he delivered the ones he loved to it.

Mariam: who loved him back and who had let him love her, slowly, before his lips had even met hers, beneath the warmth under that cold sky; whom he never should have allowed to follow him, even if he could have stopped her.

A bloodcurdling scream split the air, like the ghosts of dragon cries that had followed them here. But this death cry was real, and a dwindling tremor of the dying soon followed it.

At least it wasn't someone he loved. Not yet. It was just one of the souls of the city that were already damned, left to rot and die in the halls and tunnels beneath and the shadows of the alleys above, where no one was there who could ever see, or hear.

The Dragon was already here. Just in time to feed upon one of the damned souls Chaelus had been sent here to save. There was no escape left for them, none that he could offer, not from the Dragon they had already sacrificed themselves to.

The only thing he could do for them, the only thing he could see that was left for him to do, the only thing that hadn't already been taken away from him, was what so many others had already been willing to do, had already done, what *he* had already done for prophecy. It was to give himself, to die himself, just like he had already done so many other times before. Just this one last time, if only it could be just that.

The wagon shuddered to a stop. Legionnaires dragged him from it by the chains that bound his wrists.

The glittering walls of the palace surrounded and

climbed up the white tower's base like a fallen shroud, its stones as bright as the city they ruled over. Its golden domes glittered more than the ancient pillar of the Evarun they courted, jewels among jewels lording over a city lost in its own demise.

Chaelus stumbled before the guards. They followed Gervasis, who marched before him, leading them up wide steps to tall doors adorned in mother of pearl.

The men's shadows, those of Gervasis' retinue, the small portion of his legion he had taken with them within the city walls, the shadow of the Dragon, billowed and plumed around them. Their fearful stares darted to the dead stares of the guards who flanked the doors, slumped and twitching, their spears leaning, their crimson cloaks only half hanging from their shoulders, the bodies of the dead and dying left sprawled upon the steps before them.

These were not like the men of Baelus' hall. These were not like those who had marched him here. Of those who still breathed, the Dragon's shadow cloaked them completely, not unlike the Remnants, the demons he had faced so many months, so many lifetimes before.

The Dragon was here. The Dragon had already returned.

Gervasis marched past them all, his own shadow trembling, his pale light unflinching. Gervasis' men followed their leader, pushing Chaelus with them.

The doors slammed shut behind them.

Against the darkness, marble columns shimmered like albescent pearls, each wider than even a pair of men could ever reach their arms around, towering like gods to where the ceiling disappeared beyond the glowing wash of clerestory light high above.

The columns marched in rows down the length of the massive hall, shaping a hundred smaller halls in between;

secret places, each of them, where the eyes of one would never meet those of another, only their whispers.

Chaelus doubted there were any secrets whispered by men here anymore. The only whispers here were certainly the Dragon's own. The Dragon's shadow filled the hall like the water of a tomb.

Between and beneath the columns, the dark pools of cenotaphs, cauldrons for the dead, vessels for those summoned to the Dragon's Sleep, had already been built. The cenotaphs filled the darkest reaches of the shimmering hall, an erstwhile audience of the dead for the golden throne glittering like a sun at the hall's farthest end.

The scent of jasmine braced the air. It scarcely covered the stench of death.

Yet still, it held him like a stone, along with the sight of the woman reclining on the throne.

The legionnaires pushed him toward her.

Faerowyn, the woman he had once loved and who now was queen, waited there in languor. Long, pale gossamer dressed her ivory flesh, the supple heave of her resting breasts framed beneath her sable hair.

Her parted red lips were only a promise behind an azure veil.

There was no shadow about her.

The legionnaires forced Chaelus to his knees. Their boots pressed down against his spine.

Gervasis stepped aside, his head bowed, still with only the ghost of a shadow drifting around him.

Faerowyn's mouth drew down in a sad smile at its edges. She stood. Her robes softly rustled as she gathered her long train about her.

With a deliberate pause at each step, Faerowyn descended the glittering dais toward him.

"They said you would come to me," she said. "To strike me down with holy fire, they said, quickened from the temple of your very own flesh."

She stopped before him. For an instant, black tendrils of the Dragon's shadow billowed across her eyes and quickened across her flesh. "But I think you are no danger to me, Chaelus, my lover."

The air thickened around her. The Dragon's shadow spread out from her like wings. Her eyes descended to the full depth of sepia wells.

She turned to Gervasis. "You have done well." Her voice deepened. The mouth of the Dragon spoke through her. "Leave us."

The rap of Gervasis' fist upon his armored chest echoed across the hall. He remained there for a moment. His shadow quickened. Then he left. His men followed him.

The malevolent shadow of the Dragon in Faerowyn withdrew, concealed itself somehow again, even from him.

Faerowyn walked in a slow circle around him.

"They've tried to hurt you," she said.

Chaelus stared past her, to the frozen rapture of her golden throne, inscribed like a rising sun.

"I've often thought of you," she said, "of us. Often have I thought of what we were, of what we could have become, Chaelus, Roan Lord of the House of Malius."

She drew behind him, close to him. Her nearness to him quickened his senses, awakened his blood, like spreading cracks upon a frozen sea, no matter the presence of the Dragon within her.

"I've missed you," Faerowyn said.

"I'm no longer him," Chaelus said.

The nail of Faerowyn's finger pressed down his spine.

"No," she said. "You're not. And I should not forget

that now you are called savior, as well."

Faerowyn continued her circle around him. "It suits you, though. But know that my heart, my soul, they've been dim for their loss of you."

She ended with her back to him, its gentle turning no less a spell.

"You have always gotten what you wanted," Chaelus said. "I see you have again. You are a queen now, an Empress. It is more than your father could have ever dreamt for you. The men of nations will bow down in fear before you."

"It is my sacrifice," Faerowyn said, a brush of lament across her voice.

"As long as I have known you," Chaelus said, "I have never taken you for a martyr."

"Then perhaps you don't know me as well as you think you do."

Faerowyn turned to him. The gaiety of her eyes matched the smile draped across her veiled lips.

"But if not me, then," she said, "the only martyr left here is you."

Faerowyn held out her gloved hand, her palm downward, for him to take.

He didn't, but he stood.

"Come with me," she said.

Her smile still feigned sadness as she led him gently toward a bright doorway.

The memory of the Dragon's shadow within her diminished beneath the radiance of a verdant morning. Bird song took wing as they stepped upon a greensward. The garden was vast and it was lush and it crawled like nymphs up the chaste marble buttresses of the palace walls.

Faerowyn trailed her fingertips along a polished stone wall edging the path. The trail of her sleeve whispered beneath them. Its sound mingled with her scent like the unrepentant pull of a wave.

It was an ocean of tired and weary need that Chaelus felt returning to him. Like a glass of cool water. Its tow summoned him.

Faerowyn stared at him from beyond her veil in silence. Waiting. Tempting.

"What do you want from me?" Chaelus asked.

Faerowyn's hand brushed against his wrist, like a kiss.

"I only want what you've already given to so many others," she said. "It should be nothing for you to do this for me."

Her touch quickened upon Chaelus' wrist. With her other hand, she unclasped the corner of her veil. It descended from her face like a ghost. Beneath it smiled the face Chaelus remembered, before his death, before his rebirth, before everything; a girl's face with fervent lips. But only for a moment.

Long traces of shadow quickened beneath her skin. The deep wells of her eyes consumed what light landed within their returning shadow.

The shadow of the Dragon consumed her again. Its black eyes stared back at him.

"And what would you ask?" he said. "Faerowyn, dragon queen."

Faerowyn's smile faded to nothing.

"I would have you save me," she said.

*Chapter Thirteen: Consecration*

Login drew his hood against the falling snow.

Only Maedelous' thin mouth showed beneath the darkness of his. A shrewd smile danced across his lips.

The small wagon pitched and swayed but stayed atop the rutted track, weighted down as it was with the provisions King Aeofyn had given them for their short journey of three days south to Goarnn.

Three more days to find his fate, to be bought and sold for the sake of prophecy—or something else.

He and Maedelous had said little to each other. But now Maedelous stirred.

"Do you think you're wise, boy?" Maedelous asked, surprising him. "Do you think you know? Do you think you know what it means to have a king favor you so, even a blind one, and a boy king at that?" He flicked the bay mare's reins. "You are nothing but a pawn. And you're lucky you're not dead."

"Isn't that what you want?" Login replied. "Isn't that why you brought me with you?"

Maedelous' smile receded to a frown.

The last of the ghost spires had already fallen behind them that morning, pale against the darkness of the storm-wrought sky; the last rites of a long-dead kingdom. The broken land swayed into hillocks again to the south.

The songs of the dead still pursued them, but they weren't fearful; more like the comforting song of a mother. Perhaps even his.

"I will tell you what I want. A prince named Oarn Dur has taken up to rule from one of the ivory towers of the Eva-run that rest on Goarnn's northern border. He claims to be a king, but he's nothing like one. He's a fiend and a warlord and not our friend at all. But there is something we need from him."

"We? Isn't he the one you plan to give me to as parlay? Is that how you plan to get what you want?"

Maedelous' smile returned.

"So young King Aeofyn has indeed found a friend. A friend with whom he can share the babbling lies of the dead."

The gentle song upon the wind died. You could hear its breath escape. The only thing louder was the void that re-placed it.

"He told me enough. If not that, then why else did you bring me with you?"

Maedelous' smile broadened and softened.

"When you're old, a young man can help you with a great many things, things you would have otherwise gladly done yourself when vigor and chance were still with you. Age is not unlike a veil. It changes the way you look at things. It has changed a great many things in me."

"Why would the king lie to me?"

"He lives with the dead, boy. That is what the dead do. And he is a king. Lying is what kings do. But don't worry; I don't plan on giving you away to anyone. You're far too im-portant to me for that."

"Then what of the Hunters in Tulon? What was your parley with them?"

Maedelous' eyes brightened and sharpened as the shadow over him lifted away from the truth, away from something more dangerous even than the lie that hid it.

"You're quick," he said. "I tried to right a wrong. One of the other things you'll discover as you get older is that life is full of things, full of mistakes, that never should have been made; promises, sometimes, that never should have been broken."

Ravens swarmed just beyond the horizon of broken hills.

Login reined in the nag.

"Well, go on," Maedelous said. His eyes narrowed. "Don't stop now; let us see what the birds of the dead are up to."

Login got the nag going again. The happas wound eastward up the slopes of the hills before turning back again near their summit.

The raven cries grew louder, only just above the cacophony of their wings. There were no other sounds. Not even the din of the wagon's wheels.

Beyond the ridge, in the valley beneath, twelve corpses hung impaled upon spears.

The spears had been thrust between their legs and exited from their mouths. They had been dead for several days, some a day more or less than the others. Their deaths had been so fearfully executed that they hadn't died quickly. You could tell by the way their rotting hands still clutched the ends of the spears above them.

Each one's death had been terrible, and long. They had been deliberately kept alive like this. Their swords had been thrust into the ground just beneath their reach.

Maedelous jumped off the wagon's seat. He staggered up the hill toward them, waving his arms. The ravens scattered with bitter cries.

A rent sky of dusk spread out like a tapestry above the valley, behind the stony ridge. Streaks of sepia cloud painted red by the setting sun looked like torn and tattered and bleeding cloth; like bloodied gossamer.

"No. No. No. No. No!"

His last utterance a gurgled scream, the wracked cry of an old and broken man, Maedelous slumped to the ground on his knees beneath them, and wept.

*

Al-Mariam waited: she waited until the boot steps of the guards drew away above her. She slid her aching body down to the stone floor of her pit, her cell, her tomb.

A thin line of pallid light cut across the floor. The air it showed was thick with dust; each mote like its own memory of loss, like a ghost, like a promise, like a will-o'-the-wisp, as the memory of the dead came over her with all the chill of a winter storm.

She whispered their names.

Al-Toman.

Al-Maxus.

Al-Nokius.

Al-Evan.

Al-Gogin.

Al-Malice.

Al-Eliana.

Al-Turin.

Al-Solan.

Al-Vikitan.

Al-Borak.

Every one of them.

Her shoulders shook as she wept for their loss, as she wept for her own, her brothers and sisters. She wept for her blood, Michalas, and for Obidae, her friend. She wept for Chaelus, whom she knew was already dead. She wept until she knew she couldn't stop. She wept because beneath the weight of each of their names was her own name, because of all of them, only her own name was the one she had left to speak.

It made no sense to her. What purpose could there be for any of them to suffer all this loss? Surely there had to be one. If not for her, then at least for Obidae, and Michalas, the ones who still suffered with her.

A stone tapping echoed through the rock from the pit beside her. Michalas. Michalas and his little stone.

She wiped the tears from her eyes.

At least she could be grateful that, unlike Chaelus, he didn't, and she didn't, have to suffer alone, whatever the purpose of their suffering. And whatever purpose it was, at least she knew a way to get there.

She would wait with them. She would hope. No less so for weeping.

In the moment that rests in between.

Shabek.

*

Michalas stared up at the narrow, tender slivers of gray light coming through the trapdoor above.

The harsh clip of boots drew toward it, then silence, and the subtle creak of leather.

Whoever it was leaned down to the trapdoor. His voice sounded terse and broken.

"I need you to help me, child. I know you are one of the two who are paired by prophecy. So I must have you tell me something."

He waited while the man paused.

"Tell me," the man asked. "Do you know what damnation is?"

Michalas' tongue thickened and he couldn't speak, even if he had dared to.

The man's breath languished as he waited.

"I was thinking you might know, given the mark the angels placed upon your brow. Or perhaps you're still too young to know this, prophecy or no."

Michalas winced, because he did. He knew it well.

"Perhaps, then, I should tell you what I know," the man said, "at least so far as I can guess. I suppose I know because I have suffered long enough myself." He paused. "I will tell you what damnation is. It is having known grace, having known her mercy, having known her hope, but then having her taken away from you all at once, and knowing you will never get to see her again."

Michalas wanted to speak; he wanted to speak to the man about the loss of the angels. He wanted to ask the man about his own loss. He wanted to tell him how strange it was that he would find this here.

"But the real question is," the man continued, "having known grace, and having lost her, do you still try to seek her again? Or do you simply watch her wither from afar, safe in the anguish of her loss, until it consumes you and everything else about you?"

The gray light burned bright like a halo above him, for a moment. For a moment, the trapdoor seemed to disappear beneath it.

"So tell me," the man asked, "what would you do, young prophet, if you found you actually had a choice?"

The man waited for him.

The weight of Michalas' tongue fell away. The sound of his own voice surprised him as it crackled past his lips. "I know what damnation is. It is fear that keeps us there."

The man stood.

"And so it is," he whispered. "Thank you."

Michalas stood and waited until the clip of the man's boot steps faded away. He smiled.

Suddenly, he remembered; he remembered what it sounded like. He smiled.

Grace. It sounded like angels.

It sounded like the gentle slip of a bolt removed and a trapdoor being sprung open, even if it wasn't the one above him. It didn't matter. He knew what it felt like. Grace. Like weakness made whole. Like a vessel made from stone.

He whispered to the ghost of the man who had just set him free. "Damnation feels like the loss of angels. Grace is being reminded that they never left."

He raised his voice to his sister in her nearby cell.

"Mariam?"

"Michalas?" The sound of hope colored her voice.

"Thank you for saving me."

*

Chaelus breathed to calm his anguish. The night air in the garden smelled like jasmine. The smell of death lurked just underneath here, too. The sounds of death though, had nothing to veil them.

He listened to the rapturous cries of the city beyond the palace walls mingle with the painful lament of the dying. Because they were, some more so than others, each to their own glorious call of their queen, of the Dragon, all of them blind to the suffering around them, blind to their own, blind behind the veil of the Dragon that had descended upon every one of them so many ages ago.

The Dragon had blinded him also, once. Just as prophecy did with him now, leaving him to wait alone in the Garden, without solace, with her.

He watched the shadow of the Dragon linger over Faerowyn's face, the face of the woman he had once loved but who wasn't her anymore, perhaps; like one loves a memory, because that was all she was now. A memory, a memory of something, of just one more thing he had already lost.

The Dragon still tried to hide its shadow within her but he could see it clearly now, like the dawn of night against day.

Faerowyn drew close to him. She parted her lips in expectation, subtly concealed behind her partially open veil.

"How can you ask me to save you?" he said, stepping back from her. "All while you crucify the ones I love."

"Love," she mused. "Love is why I called for you." She reached out to him, her hand resting soft, cautious, testing, upon his chest. "Isn't love why you came to me?"

Above her veil, dark tears edged her eyes, but they were tears of the Dragon.

"It was prophecy that sent me here," he answered.

"And those who claim to follow it? I tell you that love is not the reason they sent you here. You are, as you always were to them, a sacrifice."

"It is my sacrifice," he returned.

Faerowyn pulled her hand away. The shadow of the Dragon darkened her eyes.

"And as long as I have known you, you have always been the martyr. It seems fitting that anyone who loved you should be one, too. Perhaps that's what I am. And isn't that what they wanted anyway, to give their lives for you? To die themselves as martyrs? If so, then perhaps I've done them a favor."

"At what point did you sell your soul? What promise did the Dragon whisper to you in shadow? Surely it was for more than just to be queen."

Faerowyn lifted her finger to his lips. A sad smile danced across her own.

"There are so many things you couldn't understand, my love; things that I don't even know how to tell you. Or perhaps you do? Your wisdom, it already knows the truth. It sees, I can tell. This is nothing that I have done. It is something that has happened to me. The Taurate, the wizards, my father. I have been nothing but a pawn in all of this, I swear. To be queen means nothing to me. My desire has only and always been to be with you."

"But it is your choice now. It's the death you have chosen. It's the coin you have been paid in, and that you pay your people. It's what you're about to deliver in debt across the rest of the suffering Pale."

Faerowyn's fingers dropped again to his chest.

"Death. For the city around us, yes. For my people I couldn't save. But not for you. Not for me. Not for anyone else. It doesn't have to be. And as for your friends, not all of them are dead yet, either," she whispered. "Have I not saved the ones you love most among them?"

"Only to hold me captive here."

"No. I saved them because I love you, because I want you to be my king."

"You have already chosen your king, and it is shadow. There is no more love left in you. You have shown this plainly enough."

"That's where you're wrong! Your loved ones still live because I listened to your heart from even this far away. I did it to show you that I need you, that not all of the Pale, not all of me is lost; perhaps not even all the love we once shared. If only you knew how much I have suffered to bring you home to me."

Faerowyn drew her face up to his.

He tried to back away.

The spell of jasmine, of her, though, it held him.

"I need you, Chaelus. I need you, my love. And yes, I am a martyr, too. And this was my sacrifice, to die myself, so that I could live long enough to have you. Because it was the only way I could. And a thousand more deaths I've already died since then, all so I could see you, touch you, tell you. It was the only way I knew to bring you here, to me. Please don't make me die another. I need you more than you can know."

A breath, a moment away.

"I need you to save me," Faerowyn whispered.

His very heart and flesh trembled as the ocean of her washed against his feet.

"I cannot save you from yourself," he said. "I can't save you from the things you have done. I don't know when the Dragon first whispered itself to you, but it has already consumed you. It flows beneath your very skin. It is the blood in your very veins and its death has become your very breath."

Faerowyn's hand traced across his chest to his heart. "No."

"It is true, Faerowyn, and I have already failed too much, failed to save too many, and have damned too many in doing so. You don't understand. I do not get to choose."

Faerowyn unclasped the rest of her veil. It shimmered as it fell. Her rouge lips opened up to him.

The shadow of the Dragon turned beneath her skin like a forgotten ghost.

The Giver stayed silent within him.

Tears gathered in Faerowyn's eyes. She placed her hands around his face. The chill of the Dragon drew through them.

The waves of her dark ocean crashed over him. The shadow of the Dragon billowed beneath them.

"If only I could save you, Faerowyn, I would," he said. "I swear to you."

Faerowyn's hands tightened upon his face.

Her lips brushed against his. Her scent consumed him. The soft touch of her skin on his neck wrapped around him, summoning him deeper with the warm caress of her other hand.

"But you can save me. You already are, even if I do have to die. There is nothing else you have to do. Just stay. I couldn't stop what they've done to me. I had little choice in it. But I can do this. Perhaps, now that I am queen, perhaps I can do this much, at least. Perhaps now, at last, I can stop this. I just . . . I just can't do it alone."

Faerowyn's lips closed over his.

For one breath, for one lingering moment, a whisper.

"Not without you."

## Chapter Fourteen: Sacrifice

Login watched the moonlight dance across the graves in the rain.

Mud, lots of mud, had made the digging of the graves that much easier, but still they were only shallow, covered by stones. The dead knights' swords had been buried with them.

Twelve former Servian knights sent before them to parley with a king. Twelve former Servian knights left for them as a warning by the same. Twelve apostates. Twelve martyrs for Maedelous.

Maedelous probed at the coals of their small, hidden fire.

A narrow crevasse with a small cave gave them shelter from watching eyes, and from the rain that had suddenly started again as if it had never stopped, that seemed as if it never would again; the same rain that drowned out the sounds of whatever was abroad in the night around them. Even the moonlight had nearly gone away.

"No man should die like that," Maedelous said. "Certainly not those men." He wept. "They were good men."

"What of the other Servian knights who are hunted?"

Maedelous sighed. "Still you ask."

"Because you will not answer me."

"Do you know why your mother and father died?" Mae-delous asked.

Login glared back at him. "You know how! They were murdered. They were murdered by Hunters. The very ones you treated with, likely. So why do you mock me?"

"I don't mock you, child. And I didn't ask you how they died. I asked you why."

"I didn't know they had to have a reason to be murdered."

Maedelous threw a small stick into the fire.

"No. No, they didn't. But every choice we make has an effect. Every cast stone has its ripples. And when we all cast stones, it is sometimes hard to tell where or from which stone such ripples come."

"You lied to me when my mother died. I trusted you when there was no one else left for me to trust. You used me, and you betrayed me."

Maedelous sighed.

"Then let me start over with you, boy." Maedelous re-moved his poker, a long stick now glowing red. "Please, let me at least do that."

Login waited for Maedelous in silence.

"Do you know why I left the Servian order?"

"Because you betrayed them, it would seem."

Maedelous blew on the stick. A small flame erupted and danced upon its end.

"Well, truth be told, which I think is where we are at, I left in large part because of your parents. You see, I knew them both quite well, and in their lives, and in each of their deaths, they taught me something. When I brought you into my protection, I did so at your mother's request. I never told you these things. She knew what fate awaited her outside the safety of the Garden, but she believed in the promise she made for her faith even more. So much so that she was willing to die for it. And she did. That is why she died. That is why they both died: for faith.

"You see, long ago, Olivia, the Mother of the order, made a promise to take the Servian knights to safety. The schism between the Servian lords and the Servian knights was at hand. The Servian lords had already killed far too many of our own. They'd broken their vow long before, and the Servian knights, they — we—were defenseless against them.

"There were only two places that offered us safety from forsaking our vows. Evarun, our spiritual home, and the Garden where Col Durath, the watchtower, waits. Evarun is a land far away. It is where our people fled once long before, abandoning the Pale for sake of their piety. Knowing this, and knowing the day of the Dragon was coming, the Mother chose to wait instead, and keep watch over the Pale from the safety of the Garden."

The flame at the end of the poker flickered away.

"So you would blame her?" Login asked. "You would blame the Mother for all of this?"

"No. I blame myself, because I did not stand against her decision."

"So you send the Hunters against her now."

"No. Still you don't listen. I sent the Hunters against no one. I merely parleyed with them to try to buy the Mother time so that perhaps fewer of the order might meet your parents' fate. It is what I should have argued for then, but now it is too late. And in that sense, she was right. You can't treat with those the Dragon has already claimed, and I was not as successful with it as I would have liked."

Maedelous tucked the stick back into the fire.

"We live in a world, boy, that hunts us down and kills us like animals, and we let them. So when the Dragon comes, tell me, boy: Who will be left to save the world?"

"You would rather she had abandoned the world?"

Maedelous stood up slowly, holding onto the rock face.

"No. But there comes a time when there is nowhere left to run. There comes a time when every man must fight. The schism that exiled us was never about our vows. It was only about power. Our vows—they never should have been."

Maedelous turned and looked out into the unseen night, toward the rock-covered graves of the twelve former Servian knights.

"I picked them myself, you see, all of them. They were good men, and they had, each of them, come to believe as I do. But they should never have died like that. I am glad to know they fought back, and well. They are cruel, but the Goarnn never leave the arms of cowards with them when they die."

"What do you mean?"

"I have to smile for them just a little bit, imagining how many of Oarn Dur's men it must have taken to finally bring them down alive."

Maedelous paused. His breath thickened.

"Al-Rumen."

"Al-Maldoren."

"Al-Dar."

"Al-Soma."

"Al-Ronin."

"Al-Cambin."

"Al-Robert."

"Al-Chael."

"Al-Got."

"Al-Simondin."

"Al-Dorn."

"Al-Bertram."

Maedelous' voice choked on the last name.

"They were like my sons. They were like my brothers. They were not apostates. I buried these men. I loved them."

Login stood.

"I know. You used their surnames because you knew you were still burying Servian knights."

*

Chaelus sat up on the edge of the bed. He lifted his face to the bright mantle of the morning sun, descending through the open tower window.

It danced over everything. Polished stone transcended to soft cloth beneath it. Silken sheets became as taut as stone.

His flesh and his vigor pulsed harder than bone.

A supple tremor seduced his skin, just underneath it. It ran down the length of his arm. His muscles quickened beneath its touch. His hairs stood on edge. His old wounds awakened to it, letting their memories of glory blood and shield days unfold like a tapestry before him.

Like something that had been undone, or a trap that had been set free.

He gripped Sundengal's hilt where it hung from the bedpost beside him. His legs swung down to polished stone. His breath filled him as it had never done before.

He drew Sundengal slowly. Her chime and her blade burned as bright as a promise, a promise once broken but now remade. It would never be broken again. The subtle chime of her steel rang like the clarion call of a church bell.

Like a dream.

Outside the window, a clear sky beckoned over the joyous rabble of his people in the imperial capital of Paleos beneath him.

He looked down from his white tower, one of the twelve of the Evarun, the ones the Servian lords had claimed. Ras Dalamas had ruled here, just like his father, Ras Malius, had ruled from his.

But Ras Dalamas, just like his father and the rest of the Fallen Ones, hadn't ruled anything for an age. They hid instead, like cowards, from their failures and from their broken promises. Ras Malius hid in his shame. Ras Dalamas hid in his pride, both while the Theocratic Council and the Taurate ruled in their stead.

The fates of the Servian lords were all as one: the same whisper, the same death.

But it wouldn't be his death. Not anymore. He wouldn't hide, not from anyone or anything, not even prophecy. Not ever again.

He strode to the intricate woven stone of the balustrade that seemed to float along the window's edge.

The Holy City of Paleos sprawled out beneath him. Domes of gold and spires of silver glittered beneath their halos. Their church bells began to ring. A call to worship her, Faerowyn, the Dragon queen, the woman he had loved before. The woman he had lost. Now she wanted him to save her. To repay him, she would make him king again.

To save her and win his kingdom back.

Her touch came up like a thought beside him. Her mere presence was a drug.

"Do you remember," Faerowyn asked, "when we used to hide together beneath the Losson halls? Do you remember when you told me that parchment and prophecy would wither, but your love for me would never die?"

"Before your father called you home." Chaelus turned to her.

Passion fell from her like a raiment, like a chorus. Her morning dress trailed across the stones like a kiss. Her skin shone like ivory beneath it.

Her lips parted. "Before your father called you back to yours." She traced her fingers across his chest.

She took Sundengal from his grasp. She slid the long steel blade back into its scabbard. She let it fall to the floor.

And a door, unseen, slammed shut inside him, a door to something he couldn't remember.

She pressed herself against him, her head just over his heart. The supple feel of her flesh beneath his hands, the liquid feel of her touch upon his skin intoxicated him. Her dress slipped away from her shoulders. It fell to the floor with in verdant crush of lace.

"But now, at last, we're together again," she said, "with nothing between us, and nothing that could ever tear us apart."

And the door, the one inside him, creaked; like one that shuts but never closes; like one does beneath a draft of wind that swirls and beats you until it takes hold of your heart and never lets go.

His chest tightened.

He could almost remember where the door went; almost. Perhaps it went to somewhere or something he had left behind. Some sort of promise. A promise never meant to be broken. But he couldn't remember what promise it was.

Her hands poured over him. Her breath poured through him, upon his ear, against his lips.

But the something he had forgotten behind the door held him back from her. He hesitated.

"I think there's something I've forgotten," he stammered.

Her hands, her breath, stopped. She laughed.

Her hands moved over him again, slower, more deliberate, more precise. "When you become king," she said, slipping down to her knees. Her mouth opened to him, her tongue drew wet across her lips, like a promise. "Tell me, what will it matter?"

## Chapter Fifteen: Regret

"Leave him to me!" Faerowyn screamed. "Do not touch him with your foul hands."

She struggled to sit upright upon her throne. Her womb burned.

"Very well," Vas Ore scoffed. He dragged the toe of his slipper across Chaelus' limp and naked form where it sprawled pallid across the rotting rush-covered steps beneath her. "Yet I can't help but wonder why you waste your time with a dead prophet. What promise could you possibly hope to gain?"

The long shadows of the morning had already passed. The muted light cast ill shadows across Vas Ore's golden mask. The hanging bits of steel of his crown rattled like detritus upon his brow. His cracked lips pulled back in a sneer.

Vas Kael stood in the shadows beside him.

"What promise indeed?" Vas Kael echoed.

Vas Ore stepped back, clutching up his robe like he would from a foul spill. His eyes never left Chaelus. "Chaelus, once vessel of the Giver reborn."

"Of what imagined use could he possibly still be to her?" Vas Kael finished.

Faerowyn glared at them. She wiped the blood from the corner of her mouth. Chaelus' blood. Her blood.

Chaelus murmured something from beneath the veil of the Dragon's Sleep. His breath and voice drew in short sharp bursts, the babbling of one near death, but not so near as anyone else would be for he was chosen, and she knew that, somewhere, his soul was still safe. There was time yet.

The Dragon's bile drained from Chaelus' lips.

Just as it drained from hers.

But with no fabled glow of the prophet yet to save her, save her from the beast growing within her and the Dragon which sought to possess her.

Awake, he could do nothing to protect her or save her, and she knew she could do nothing to let him. But in his dreams, in his dreams he was hers alone.

He wasn't, though. Something was holding him back from her even there in the Dragon's Sleep, where there should be no one but her. Something still kept him from her.

There was still time, though. There had to be.

"I will be done with him when I am done. Now leave me."

"He will never be yours," Vas Ore said. "Prophecy and the Dragon have already claimed him, just as they have claimed you. They have used him to their fill. Now his usefulness to them is over."

Another coughing spasm took her, taking a bit more bile from her this time.

Vas Ore waited, just away from her, as she reclaimed herself. He reached over and traced his fingers through her matted hair.

She flinched.

"But I know how you loved him once. Such suffering it must be to want him still, knowing you can never have him. Such a sacrifice it must be for you. Such a hell."

"What would a wizard know of such things?" she sneered.

"Everything," Vas Ore said.

Vas Kael smiled, a grotesque mockery painted beneath his lusterless visage. "But a queen, a lover, a mother, she would know this most of all, wouldn't she?"

Vas Ore traced his fingers down her hair, between her breasts, and drew circles across her womb. "A fallen prophet is never mourned. If only the blood of the father had been the blood of the son. Such great things he could have been."

Vas Kael reached up beneath his golden veil with brass-armored fingers. With the blade of one of its nails, he cut into his cheek. A thin red line opened up amongst the scars. A shallow gasp of ecstasy escaped his lips. He withdrew his hand from behind his veil and licked the blood from his fingertip. "But his seed, that is another thing."

Vas Ore's voice deepened. "Already, the twelfth is made whole."

"It grows strong within you," Vas Kael finished.

Her womb stretched out to Vas Ore's touch.

She quivered beneath it.

"I am exultant for it," she said. Her voice trembled.

"I'm quite certain you are," Vas Ore cooed. "Is it not what we've all been waiting for?"

"What we've all been promised?" Vas Kael said.

There was still time for him to save her. There had to be. He had to. He had to because he loved her.

"And oh, what ecstasy it will be to know," Vas Ore said, "that as the Pale around you burns, and the tortured souls lament in rapture beneath your sandaled feet, it will all be because of you, my queen, vessel of the Dragon reborn."

"Must it all end in suffering?" Faerowyn whispered. "Must it all end in death?"

Vas Ore stood. The iron shards of his crown grew still. His scared face drew pale. He whispered back.

"You cannot see the shadow without the flame."

Vas Kael's ecstasy faded. His stare receded.

"Snuff out the flame. You forget the darkness."

*

"Why must we go so far south?" the Mother asked.

The darkness was absolute but for the light of the camp fires. Even their warmth did little to settle the chill already resting deep within her bones.

Spits of scrawny meat roasted over the flames, fowls her knights had brought down that day as they marched. The meat crackled and simmered, but hunger wasn't what plagued her.

"We have to," Al-Hoanar said. "But no farther than here, I promise you, no farther than is safe. We will stay well north of the city state of Harloth, but to go farther north would bring us too close to the haunted ruins of Galadash. That city has been dead for far too long."

"But this still takes us deep into the Theocracy."

"I know. But it is a path the Khaalish know well." He bit a piece of meat from his spit. "It's the path they take when they raid the western lands."

"Though we don't light campfires on the way when we do," Belloch said, walking toward them. "Should we invite the legion to sup with us, too?"

"Hmph," Al-Hoanar muttered. He wiped his mouth on the stump of his other arm. "That's because by the very first raid you've already let them know you're here."

Belloch smiled and squatted with them.

"Either way, fires or not, secrecy or not, I am sorry to say I do not think we will make it much farther without trouble."

"Excuse me?" Olivia said.

"The Hunters who follow you will not let you leave the Kessel. You are such easy prey for them here. The Kessel is wide and vast and open. There is no place for you to hide from them here."

"But isn't this where you cross? Do the legions of the west not hinder you?"

"No."

"Why do they not?"

"Because, as Al-Hoanar said, they fear us." Belloch shrugged. "You, they hunt."

"Are you not our protection?"

"Against Hunters, yes, but against a legion, we are too few. But I think at least you are safe tonight. The Hunters, they will watch and they will wait. They know now that they can't come too close. But they will watch just the same. They will wait until your hope draws nearest. Then they will call. And a legion, it is waiting in the city of Harloth only for their word to summon them."

"So what do we do?"

Belloch took a spit from above the fire and tore a bite from it.

"What do we do?" she repeated.

"Do what you do best, Revered Mother, and pray. Otherwise, by steel alone, you will never make it to Evarun."

\*

Al-Aaron listened.

He listened to the Mother, to Al-Hoanar and to Belloch, the Khaalish chieftain. And he listened to the ghost of Malius, who he once thought was his Teacher. He listened to the whisper of the Dragon.

He listened beneath the bright mantle of a winter's night, where the storm was only just coming to pass, just beyond the edge of the campfire light, just beyond the promise of the Tender's sacred fire they carried with them; here, where the ghost who whispered to him always managed to find him alone. It was the place he always managed to find himself, the only place where, somewhere between the darkness and the light, he could at least listen to the whisper of small things.

Like the rattle of chains and the oiled creak of leather, the crumpled rustling of broken leaves upon the wind, or sometimes, like now, just a whisper.

If only it wasn't this one.

Malius' black-gloved fingers caressed the flat of the blade of one of the swords taken from the Hunters Belloch had beheaded.

Al-Aaron withdrew into his furs. He drew them tight around his body in a hopeless shield. The never-healing wound in his belly, where Malius had once run him through, felt colder now than even the sky above.

*"Do you hear it?"* Malius asked. *"Do you hear the songs of war that they sing?"*

"There isn't any war," Al-Aaron countered. "Not yet."

*"You will hear it, not yet. Very soon, every soul will hear it. And very soon, everyone you love will die upon its song."*

Khaalish warriors walked past. They nodded their respect to him as they laughed, unseeing, unaware, blind to the enemy, the ghost, in their midst.

He nodded back. He wondered if they saw a floating sword before them, or was that just part of the vision, too. His head swooned.

"And the Giver will defeat you, Dragon, this time as well," he whispered back. "So leave me be."

Malius, the Dragon, returned the sword to where the Khaalish arms were stacked.

*"You know I can never do that. I am you and you are me. I am every bit a part of you now, my love."*

Al-Aaron drew his furs, his shield, closer, knowing he couldn't, knowing it wouldn't do him any good at all.

"But I do not want you."

*"Only death can take you away from me now, my love. But I won't let that happen to you. No, I am here to protect you, and even, I daresay, protect the ones you love. And you wouldn't want that anyway, to die. Because if you were dead, I wonder who would save them?"*

"Save them from what?"

*"Why, from the war they are bringing upon themselves, a war that is already being started by one of your own. The one who has left to gather an army. His army. And if he gets his army, I wonder who he intends to use it on first?"*

"Maedelous."

Malius smiled.

"Younger."

The rough voice of Belloch barked from behind him.

Al-Aaron jumped.

Malius slowly faded to the night.

"Who are you speaking to?" Belloch asked.

Al-Aaron settled back and stared up at him. He kept one hand across the chill of his wound. "Nobody."

Belloch's scarred face smiled. "Hmm."

Belloch walked around him to where Malius had only just been. He picked up the same sword Malius had just held in his gloved hand. He ran his thumb along the long sharp edge of the blade.

"The Revered Mother is worried," Belloch said. "She doesn't understand some things that she should."

"She's afraid."

"She leads you to your doom."

"She leads us by her faith."

"Faith can die here, too, out upon the cauldron plain. For many, it does; for most. I have seen it. I have made it happen to them."

"Then why do you serve her?"

"I do not serve her. I serve my word to Obidae. And I believe that Obidae will die soon. He and your Giver, whom he serves."

Belloch threw the sword back onto the others with a clangor. The sound filled the night. "I know he will."

Al-Aaron could only stare back at him.

"I know," Belloch continued, "because I too can speak with the ghosts."

## Chapter Sixteen: Shield Maiden

The vengeful tip of the Khaalish horde shattered like a wave upon rock beneath the force of his golden legion. It splintered beneath Sundengal's blood-covered arc in his hand. The red feathers of the barbarian horde dissolved beneath the long spears of his bright army; a golden storm cloud forged in the fire of destiny and will.

His will. Chaelus smiled. His army.

Chaelus, Holy Emperor of the Pale.

Idyliss danced beneath him. Her hooves thundered over the dead and the dying, across the whole blood-soaked plain of the Kessel. And there was nothing left that could stand against him, him and his bright and holy legion, a glory fire of brazen white and holy light and trumpet sounds, nothing; nothing from the east and nothing left from the west. Nothing, not even prophecy could defeat him. Not on this day.

"They will be routed soon, my lord," his princeps announced beside him, pulling his gladius free from the neck of a barbarian's twitching corpse.

"Good," Chaelus replied. "Then we will finish them off in good order as we crush them against the Albanjan spine."

A distant trumpet call sounded.

Idyliss reared up.

His vanguard drew in close to him.

Another charge of Roan cavalry rode at them from across the plain, from the west. But they were beleaguered. They were staggering, empty of will. They had to be. Their forces had already been beaten. They knew they would soon die in sundered mail and shattered shield. They came now only to offer themselves beneath the shattering trumpets of war.

They, and the remnants of the Khaalish barbarians who had been so bold as to rally the few remaining Roan Lords of the west, who had come to actually challenge the peace he had brought them, would soon be nothing but memory. The past would finally be left to the past, and the past would be nothing but burnt ash.

"Tell me more of Baelus and his legion."

"They are still held back against the arch of the Vicar-us. They are nearly routed as well, my lord." His princeps sneered. "Only his own mercenary cohort remains."

Chaelus smiled. He reined Idyliss in.

"Good. Let my brother's army bleed out slowly. Make them pay. But let no spear or arrow claim him. Let him wait for his end. Let him wonder why. I want to be there for it my-self. I want to be there myself, to see him down on his knees with a legion boot on his back when he begs for mercy for the treason he's laid against me."

*

Chaelus fisted Baelus' hair. He lifted his brother's face closer.

Baelus' bloodied stare, his dark eyes, glared back at him. Baelus clutched at the wound in his abdomen, a sword thrust in the same place where their father had wounded him as a boy. A legionnaire kept his boot against his spine.

The trumpet cries of war blared around them, against the sharp beat of a drum, and the doom of prophecy made to come full circle.

"There was once a time, Baelus, when you could have had a seat at my side," Chaelus said. "But you tried to supplant me instead. You left me for dead. You took your pleasure from it. You took your joy. You took my throne. You tried to take my destiny. But now look at you. You don't even know, you can't even see, that even after all of that, I still tried to save you."

Baelus glared at him through shredded black hair. His eyes grew darker still, like pools of black oil. Baelus spat at him.

"You couldn't save anyone, brother. You couldn't even save our father. You couldn't even save yourself. What made you think you could possibly save me? Or that I even wanted you to."

The cries of war drew out like a march against the sudden alarmed calls of his bright legion.

"You don't even realize that it's still you," Baelus said, "that it's always been you who needs saving."

A stammering request from his princeps sounded behind him.

"What is it?" he asked.

"My lord," the princeps said, his face ghostly, "another Roan army comes from the west. It's another legion. We have only your vanguard with us. The rest of the legion is still pursuing the rout."

There they were, another bright army, formed up against him.

"Tell the men to form ranks. Shield wall."

"We're not enough to hold them. The men have marched too far to get here."

"They will hold."

Baelus smiled. He spoke but he said no words, his challenge lost deep beneath the trumpet cries of war. A cry of war so deafening, only silence can remain.

But not reason.

For a moment, Baelus' face changed, his stare softened. He looked afraid. Tears welled in his eyes. He looked like another boy, whose sister Chaelus once knew.

\*

Arrows fell like rain. Chaelus staggered beneath their weight, on his shield and from those that found their way past; two in his leg, one beneath his chest where he had faltered. Blood pumped around the shaft where his heart should be.

*But neither spear nor shaft shall harm him.*

The memory of prophecy came to him as the surprise of blood drained from his lips, and around broken, red-feathered shafts.

Sundengal slipped from his grasp to the cries of the remains of his dying bright legion, and the gentle calling of bells.

He collapsed to the torched grasses and broken, bloodied stones of the plain.

Then the darkness of war fled beneath an azure flame.

The supple arm of a woman reached down from it to help him.

Her face was veiled by the glow, but it was framed by sable hair. Her voice carried like a dove above the now distant sounds of death.

"Come to me," she said.

She held a great shield, pierced by red-feathered arrows and scored, like a ward over them both, just above her armored breast. Golden scales covered her. A scabbarded blade hung from her waist.

Around him, of his men, of his bright legion, his vanguard, his shield guard, only a few score still stood, fighting against the enemy only to survive, only to have hope for another day. He didn't know them. He didn't know these men. He had never seen their faces. He had never forged those bonds that war and comradeship bring between men. He didn't know what field of war this was. There had been too many.

Beyond her shield, the missiles, the arrows, which had only just filled the sky like black rain, were gone, like a dream.

Only the shield maiden still stood above him, reaching down to him. Azure skies stretched above her.

Chaelus struggled to speak. "Who are you?"

Her chin lifted with all of, and only, the dignity an angel could possibly bear. There was nothing else she could be.

She withdrew her hand. She drew her blade forth, silver in sound and light, its sparkle like a halo.

With its tip, she pushed Sundengal across the bloody grass and gore and stone until it was within his reach.

She knelt down before him and wrapped his hand around its hilt.

A wry smile dressed her lips behind the illumination of her holy veil.

"I'm your shield maiden," she answered. "Chaelus, vessel of the Giver reborn, be glad, for I'm here to save you. For too long the Dragon has hid you from me. But you are hidden no more. Now you must rise. Your fight here is far from over."

*

Gervasis waited before her like a stone.

"You don't believe in me," Faerowyn said, "do you."

Her hands trembled. The thin black tendrils laced beneath her skin. No veil or sleeve would cover them. The small coffer she held trembled with her. Its lid slipped free, snapping shut.

Small things sound loud in the night. Like terror. Like a tomb. Louder even than the lamenting cries of rapture in the city beneath them. The sound brought tears to her eyes, like the smoke from the fires burning freely among the shops and the homes and the temples should have but did not.

It had already begun.

The small shriveled sprig of jasmine, her last one, trembled in her other hand. She held it up to her face. She breathed it in, all of it. Even stale, the ghost of its magic poured through her like a drug, a salve, an antidote, a promise. It was the only thing that burned against the scent of death that followed her everywhere now, clinging to her very skin and waiting, just pressing behind her eyes. It pressed from within her womb. The scent was the only thing she had left that reminded her of him, her savior, Chaelus, Roan Lord of the House of Malius, vessel of the Giver reborn, the one who had yet to save her.

"Do you."

Gervasis stood before, waiting on her word, just like he always did, unmoving. His face seemed paler than usual though, this time. He seemed older too, in only his tunic and robe, pleated in humble silver instead of gold, his armor polished and put away, more like her father now than her soldier but just like he had always been to her, the father she had never had, for all the many years he'd served her.

He looked humble and strong in silver moonlight.

"I serve you now, my queen," Gervasis said, "as I have served you ever since you were a child, just as your father asked me to."

"Was that why you stayed with me? Is that why you stay with me now?"

"I have no choice but to stay, my queen."

"I don't doubt your loyalty, Gervasis. I never have. I've never had to threaten you for it, unlike some, something my father never understood."

"Your father understood it all too well. He understood many things. That is why he's dead."

"But still you don't answer me."

Gervasis' gray eyes stared just past her. He stared toward her savior, hung naked upon the wall behind her throne.

Did Gervasis know what she sought from him? Did he wonder? Because he didn't stare at Chaelus, he stared at something deeper, something just beyond, something farther inward, something just within himself that even to her, he wouldn't yield.

Gervasis' eyes were not unlike his eyes, her savior's eyes. Like Chaelus' eyes, they were deeper, somehow, and in some strange way, they were the same.

"It wasn't a question," Gervasis answered.

She smiled at him, even if he hadn't meant for her to, the same man who had stalwartly kept her safe from a thousand different kinds of death, all except this one. Whether it be by an assassin's blade, or by poison, or by her own words or deed, or even her father's, he had kept her safe, just as he had promised her father.

So that she could be this.

Within her bloated womb, the beast she bore cried out in hunger. It shook her. Clutching her womb, she stumbled back as her gorge rose.

She dropped the coffer and it smashed on the floor.

"Then I will make it one," she gasped. "Do. You?"

Slowly, inexorably, unexplainably, he relaxed. Or was it pity?

"Do I believe in you?" Gervasis asked.

She straightened as the tremor passed. Perhaps it was.

Gervasis turned to her. His eyes held her, like her father's once did. His voice was just as calm and just as severe.

"I do, my dear Faerowyn. I always have. I can't not. I raised you from a little girl, and to see you grow into womanhood was the closest thing to grace I have ever known."

Gervasis paused.

"And now your father is dead, and you are my queen. You are the Holy Empress of the Pale. The whole of it will soon bow down before you. They will fear you. They will worship you and the demon you now hold in your womb. But what you have become, it is not the girl I raised. I only hope that there is still some of her left in you."

She wiped blood and bile from her chin with her sleeve.

Straightening her gown, she stumbled toward him, tripping over the drained husk of the legionnaire that lay between them, one of his men she had sent to bring him to her.

She caught her balance with her trembling hand upon his unmoving chest.

For a moment, the price of everything she had done, even the death of the soldier beneath her, fell away.

"Perhaps she still is," she whispered. She wiped a strand of hair away from her face. "But it's of no matter now. And I will never doubt your loyalty, Gervasis, no matter what your answer is, because of who you are. You are a good man. Of all the men in my life, you are the only one who has never abandoned me. You are the only one who has never left."

Her hand slipped away from his chest.

"But for everything you have done for me, and for all that I am about to do, I really think now, that you should."

\*

Chaelus opened his eyes from dreams to the light of a single flame, but no azure hue. Numbing pain crawled behind his eyes and through his flesh and down into his very bones.

His throat and insides burned.

Iron shackles pulled at his wrists above him. Cold polished stone pressed against his back. He hung naked, chained to the wall behind a golden throne, its radiance set ablaze with the light from fires beyond the darkness of Faerowyn's hall.

Faerowyn, and the Dragon's Sleep, had claimed him.

It was where the pain was absent that he felt it most, an empty place that no amount of pain would ever fill. He remembered where he had gone. He remembered the Dragon's Sleep where Faerowyn, where the Dragon, had taken him.

Despite everything that had been returned to him and given to him anew, some part of him had wanted it too. It was this fact that burned within him the most, the greatest pain from the coldest of flames.

Beyond the warmth of the single flame, from the single candle held before him, the stone cut face of Gervasis emerged, like a whisper in the dark.

"Gervasis," he croaked, unsure if this man, this vision, was even real, unsure if anything was anymore, of what was, and wasn't a dream.

"You have lasted longer with her than I feared, and more than I had hoped."

"Why have you come to me?"

"Because you came to me. Because you are the vessel of the Giver reborn, and I am taking you from this place."

"Your queen won't let you. She won't let me. Not even in my dreams."

Gervasis hesitated, pain for the first time etched upon his brow. His shadow, for a moment, quickened.

"And I cannot save you either," Chaelus said. "For I am already lost."

"But you've already saved me. I've already watched you turn away the will of the Dragon in Faerowyn, my queen. I have watched its shadow splinter upon the rock of your faith."

"My faith is nothing. If it were greater, I wouldn't be here."

"Tell me what I must do for you."

"Bring me water."

"There is only wine."

"Then I will take wine, and I would ask you a question, centurion."

"Of course, Teacher."

"Tell me, why did you hide your legion from her?"

"What?"

"You left them far beyond the city walls. You knew that those few who passed beneath would soon die by her. The city burns and the land for hundreds of leagues is barren. But your men, the men who marched us here, they still had bread. So too did we. Why?"

"I know too well the shadow that claims this place, that claims her."

"The Dragon's Sleep. It is why you saved your men, for fear of it. It's why you came back to her. It's why you brought me here, to save her. You know it, because once it claimed you."

"Forgive me, Teacher. My legion, such as is left of it, is camped less than a day's march to the north. They are not the Servian knights who follow you, but they still remain men. The Dragon hasn't claimed all of them yet. They wait for my command. Just ask me, and I will call them here. I will set you free."

"No."

"I could unlock these chains and cast them away from you. You could be free, free from the Dragon, free from her. But you wouldn't go, would you?"

"No. Because you would be dead within a day along with everyone you know, including your men." He smiled. "And I would be bound here again within two."

"And you would let her take you."

"I would."

"For prophecy?"

"No, for love. But not for Faerowyn, queen. There is something else I had forgotten, or I hadn't yet learned. Only by my sacrifice can I save the ones I love from her. It is the only way I have left. To give for the sake of giving, with no thought of return. So I must stay here. I must stay here so that I can save the living from the dead. It is all I can do."

Gervasis stepped back from him.

Chaelus closed his eyes. "But there is someone I need you to save for me."

"The woman who posed as a queen?"

"Her name is Mariam. She is my heart, though my heart does not deserve her. She is my shield maiden. Save her, the boy, and the Khaalish. At least they can still finish what they came for."

"I will do as you ask."

Gervasis reached up and kissed his cheek. "The Dragon has claimed my queen, but it has tried and it has failed against you. It will try to take you again. I pray it will not succeed. But either way, know that Faerowyn, queen, and all who remain within these walls, will die by tomorrow's morning."

## Chapter Seventeen: Truth

Chaelus reined Idyliss in on a broken hilltop overlooking the vigor and cries of war, a bitter, weary sound that he suddenly realized would never leave him.

Faerowyn drew her armored roan beside him.

A golden crown adorned her brow, like a rising sun over the sepia night of her tresses. Golden raiment cascaded from it across her face and brow. Her lips, like always, summoned him like a fire set deep within his blood. They summoned his shame and reminded him of his weariness as well.

He removed his helm at the sight of his young lover, his queen.

"The second Roan army has been beaten back," he said. "The bulk of the Khaalish tribes as well."

"I thought you said you had already defeated them."

"I did. And I will defeat them easily enough again, I promise you."

"I know you will."

She hesitated.

"I saw that you fell. I was afraid. Tell me, who was it that came to you?"

A storm of arrows, and an angel who had left him just as she had come to him, like a dream. He had not seen her since.

"I don't know," he answered. "She was a ghost."

"You don't remember?"

Like someone he had once known before. Like a swinging door that never really closes.

"I don't know. Only that she was familiar to me."

Faerowyn smiled. "Then I will comb through the ranks until I find her. I would like to speak to her. I would like to repay her for what she has done for you."

She was a ghost, his shield maiden, like a promise, but one that didn't yet know. There was something else about her, something she wanted, something he didn't trust, like a payment for a debt he had yet to take.

The roan stallion pranced restless beneath Faerowyn's thighs, full of vigor and promise as she reined him away, a promise made to be broken.

"But if you see her first, do tell her you won't be needing her anymore, for I've brought you another legion. I will care for your every need. Your victory is assured, my love. The end of your war is near."

Darkness passed over her.

The field of war changed before him.

Now, Chaelus struggled to stand as he waited. He weighed the heavy spear in his shaking hand, ready to throw it, ready to pierce it through the very heart of the thing, whatever beast it was, that stood before him.

He knew he couldn't stand much longer.

Crows swirled above them both, he and his enemy, swooping down upon the flesh of the already vanquished between them. All beneath a war sky, with a settling sun, above a battlefield torn asunder.

Yet it was still his, but for this one opponent left, this one final enemy of his glory, still defiant across the blood-soaked, broken plain, this field of war that would never go away.

Black wings of leather and bone spread out from the beast, then closed, a single silhouette against the blood-soaked sky, this beast, this dragon. His dragon.

Then, like a snowdrop against the night, a figure of white, a woman strode toward him from beneath its shadow.

Her white gown drew blood from the field along its hem as she walked, like a bandage on a wound. She made her way amongst the corpses and broken spears, unmoved but for her stare fixed upon him, pleading with him.

Faerowyn.

Her stare was so cold, so lonely, so desperate.

"Look!" she said as she neared. Her arms gestured around her. "Look at what she has done to us!"

Behind Faerowyn, in the place where the dragon had been, the shield maiden who had saved him stood alone on the battlefield behind a stalwart, blackened shield. No radiance veiled her. No glory concealed the face of the woman she resembled, a woman had once loved long ago but whose name he couldn't remember, as if she were from a dream, a dream forgotten like those when you first awaken. But it wasn't her face. It couldn't be her face. Not here, not in this place.

Not here, on this field of war, not here, where his destiny, where prophecy had sent him.

"She tricked you, my love," Faerowyn urged. "She's stricken you. She is your enemy. Just tell me her name." Faerowyn drew in front of him, trailing her fingertips down the length of the spear. "That's all I need to know and then, together, we can destroy her."

She clutched her hand above her breast, then trailed it down against her womb to where a child grew. Their child.

"Then nothing will be able to stop what fate has given us," she said.

Beneath Faerowyn, the blood-stained earth changed to a verdant field. Gray and broken stone hills beyond remade themselves before his eyes into golden domes and spires.

Her dress turned to pristine white.

"All you need to do is tell me her name."

She clutched his face within her hands. She brushed her lips across his mouth. She drew her tongue across them.

"Just tell me her name, my lover, and never-ending glory and all its treasures will be ours, will be yours. There will be no. More. War. My love."

The shield maiden beyond her lowered her shield and stood silent, waiting for him.

"We are so close to victory, my love," Faerowyn said.

"I know who she is," Chaelus stammered, "but I can't remember her name."

"But you must remember, my love. So we can stop her. Every other battle is won. She is the only thing left that stands against us."

The shield maiden opened her lips to a single word. Silently, but it crushed all other sound around him. Like a silent rolling thunder it billowed through him. Faerowyn staggered against him. Even the dead were almost awakened by its breath.

Peace fell over him, and the unspoken word she told him tumbled from his own lips. It was her name, the name he had forgotten.

"Hope."

Then the sounds of the world, and those that come just after war, the sounds of the crows and the dying, returned.

They returned along with two more as well, the sound of his spear clattering against the broken stones, and the sound of Faerowyn screaming.

\*

Faerowyn screamed. She couldn't do anything else. She screamed as the dragon child within her cried out in terror and hatred and lust. It shrieked with a virulence all its own. Its cry drained from her like blood from a wound until she was left bent and broken, coughing and hacking on the rotting rushes covering the floor.

She collapsed upon them.

She glared at Chaelus' silent naked husk crumpled beside her. The Dragon's poison pooled around him, widening as it drained from him. He was coming too near to death. She was running out of time.

A strangled moan escaped his blackened, bleeding lips.

She listened closer.

But he said nothing else. Only the one word he kept repeating endlessly. Hope.

Against her.

It poisoned his dreams, the dreams she had woven for him so that he would come to her, so that he would save her.

All she needed to know was a name, the name of the assassin who kept him away from her. And she would. She would destroy whatever still stood between them.

The dragon child boiled like rage within her womb, beating at her like a thief in the night. It would steal away this one chance from her if it ever knew. It whipped and flailed against her. She staggered to her feet. It was too soon for this. It was too soon.

She wasn't going to die like this, and no bitch, no shield maiden, no prophecy, angel, or dragon was going to take him from her. Not after everything she had sacrificed. Not after everything she had done to bring him home to her. No one was going to take him away from her again.

No one.

She screamed. This time of her own making, until the stones around her seemed to bleed. Even the dragon child fell quiet beneath her.

She wiped the stain from the edge of her lips.

"Chain him back up!" A gorge of warm blood and darker things rose in her throat. "Then bring the prophet's companions to me."

## Chapter Eighteen: Consequence

Olivia pulled her scarf across her head like a shroud. She stared into the flames, between them, deeper into the place where they danced, where both light and shadow had already become one. She watched for the stares of the eleven but their fires were veiled, or they hid from her in a place even deeper still.

Around her, in the waning night of the Kessel, the mood of the Servian camp was solemn and anxious, prayerful, and fearful. Even from the Keepers who kept the flame.

She felt wary herself.

She brought the burning wick to her lips. She blew on the soft embers of woven strands, weaving it before her in gentle circles until the supple tendrils of smoke drifted around her like a veil. She breathed in, and she waited. She listened, for the still small voice of the one she had summoned to her. The one voice she did not want to hear. The voice of the only one she knew who would have the answers to the questions that needed them.

She heard her breathing first. Her still small voice had darkened.

*"Sister."*

A dull grate, almost like a second voice, waited beneath it.

*"I have missed you so."*

The voice of someone who should have been buried long, long ago.

*"So you are finally returning home."*

Bakassas' voice danced among the flames.

*"I thought perhaps you would come to me, instead."*

Her voice, and all of the memories that came with her.

"It's good to hear the sound of your voice, sister," Olivia answered. "We've been driven away from the safety of the Garden."

*"That is because war is coming."*

"I know this."

*"Yet it is not the war but what will come after that all men must fear."*

"It is not the war, or even what will come after, that I fear."

*"Then why did you summon me?"*

"To remind me of something I can't remember."

*"Memory, like time, it fades so quickly."*

"Why did we abandon them? Why did the Evarun abandon the Pale?"

*"Because it was too hard for them to stay. Because in all of their piety, in all of their virtue, suffering was never one of their better qualities. No. They were far too selfish to suffer the rest."*

"So they left so many behind to suffer for them."

The still small voice weakened to a sigh. The second voice darkened to a growl beneath it.

*"You grieve that you must do the same as they did. But you are not the same. Do not worry, sister. They left because*

*they wouldn't save them. You're leaving because you believe you can."*

"There is something else I can't remember."

*"What is it?"*

"If they were so lost, why did we not stay to save them? Why did we not stay to save our own people before we left? Why did we not stay to save the Evarun?"

*"You were only a child, so you wouldn't remember,"* the small voice returned. *"We left them and returned here because we couldn't bear to hide anymore, alone with them, hidden in their deep valleys, where the only light to shine upon them would be their own, listening only to the praise they gave themselves, devoid of even the smallest of pities that becomes this flesh life."*

"So in some ways, we are no better than they."

The flames struggled against a sudden wind.

The small voice blew away, snuffed out beneath the voice of the unburied dead beneath it. Perhaps that was good. It was the true voice of her sister, anyway.

*"War. It's funny. Have I told you that the Dragon has come to parley with me? Veiled behind a golden mask he came to me. He asked me for my army. Funny. I wonder why he would ask this of me."*

"Bakassas. Do not do this."

*"He came to me even as he prepares to sacrifice his own queen. Why would I wish to serve such a thing?"*

"Please."

*"You know I do not claim to believe in prophecy as you do, sister. I never have. And I do not care who utters it. Be it the servant of the Dragon reborn, or the vessel of the deceitful prophet who abandoned me. He will soon pay his price, as well."*

A chill greater than the warmth of the flames settled through her. "What of Rua? Have you abandoned its grace as well then?"

The flames sputtered, nearly still.

A new, colder wind awakened them.

*"No, sister. Rua abandoned this frail world long ago."*

Olivia held her breath, hesitant to speak, hesitant to ask. "What do you know of the return of the Fallen Ones?"

Her sister sighed, almost gleefully.

*"They are already here."*

\*

Login eased the reins of the nag. The wagon and its hoardings trembled to a shuddering stop.

Maedelous woke with a start beside him.

Trails of black smoke as thick as oil rose from hidden places, deep valleys scattered across the southern horizon, the northern borderlands of Goarnn.

The low outcroppings of the southern marches had quickly descended to wasteland scarred by deep ravines. The color of the rock shifted between pallid hues across jagged walls. Bent trees and tufts of wild grass sought pitiful refuge amongst their hollows and their depths.

The seamless white tower of Oarn Dur rose like a pale fist above them all. The rumbled crash of the sea rose just beyond it.

Both had grown like premonitions over the past three days, each day getting closer along with the jagged black mountains that formed an impenetrable fortress beyond them. The smell of blood and the smell of the sea are not so very different.

The happas staggered down among the lessening crags as they opened before the travelers. Ruins of stone clung to the valley walls, their towers long since fallen. Broken battlements and rusted chains. Creaks and cascades of dead things more haunting than any of the songs from the city of the dead they had only just left. Lost kingdoms perhaps that were never meant to last, their songs never meant to be sung aloud. Yet they had been paid for, surely, in blood and loss just the same. The bones of the dead had lined their passage the entire way.

A wide valley, a crevasse, its bottom lost entirely to shadow, surrounded the tower. A single bridge of seamless white stone spanned its dark abyss to a small gate in the tower's surround.

The hovels of a small village gathered along the nearest edge, near the bridge. A pyre smoldered at the center of the village. Black smoke conjured up from it rose in thin tendrils. It gathered like a second dark fist beside the tower, with a smell that was both sweet and foul, like that of burning flesh.

The smell of the sea bled away.

The shrewd dirty faces of the villagers, like masks, watched them as they appeared. The braids of the Goarnn dressed their hair. Yet no guard's call challenged them. The only sound was the crack of wood and of steel, and the cries of men married to them, cries of war and of death, from beyond the village, from beyond the pyre, from where the tiers of an arena climbed up the haggard cliffs above, and down in the crevasse beneath.

The sound of the sea faded beneath the sounds of war.

The happas descended toward the village, and the pyre, and the death, and the crevasse and the tower that stood watch over them all.

"Welcome to the tower of Essoris, once home to Ras Anon the Mute, one of the fallen Servian lords of old," Maedelous said. "You know that he was the one who first scribed the prophecy of Talus the Giver on the wall of a slaver's pit here with naught but a lump of coal. For a hundred years, Ras Anon ruled from here, and like the others, hid away in here, and died here, in this tower he reclaimed to be hallowed ground.

"For even before him, this land meant death. Before him, the tower was the gateway to the gladiator pits of Goarnn, even before the Gorondian wizards named it so. They love the smell of death that haunts these stones.

"And now, the tower suffers as the kingly seat of a failure of a man named Oarn Dur, who has recently returned it to its former purpose; a temple where bloodshed is worshiped, and death before a crowd is the greatest glory of all. They never really cared much for Ras Anon here."

"Is that why you've come here?" Login asked.

"We've come to restore what never should have been lost, my boy. You think ill of me still, I know, and trust me even less. But you're wrong. Trust me this much at least when I say that the Servian order died long ago, long before the Hunters even came. It died before the Servian lords fell, and a promise was made that never should have been.

"But as to your question, we've come here because we need to build an army. One that is not afraid to defend what it was made to protect, one that is not afraid to do what it needs to do to defend its vows and its beliefs. One that is not afraid to kill if it needs to. That's what armies are for. The Servian Order was only made to watch over the Pale and warn against the return of the Dragon, but the Dragon has already returned. It never even left. And idle prayers alone will do nothing to stop it."

Ahead of them, the pallid stone of the bridge showed itself a paler gray as they drew closer. Black smoke rose up from the chasm beneath it like a chimney, from hovels and arenas clustered along the cliff face and across the valley floor. Cries of the victorious and the defeated drifted up like incense, the offering of the dead and the dying.

"Take us across the bridge to the tower, boy," Maedelous ended. "And do be careful, please, it's quite a long way down."

The stone of the bridge was slick with damp from the clouds gathered above them. Scarcely a man's width across, and with no railings, the bridge spanned the wide chasm to the sealed gates of the surround, and the tall bone finger of the tower rising above them. The shadows of soldiers watched them approach.

Login's hands trembled on the reins.

Icy wind spun around them in spasms, bringing with it more and more the cries of the dead and the dying.

Maedelous stared sideways at him. "Mind the reins, boy. Don't drop us before we get across. Our journey's almost at an end."

"Whose end?"

"Did I not say trust me, boy?"

Login stared down to where the wheels rolled too close to the edge, too close for him to turn nag and wagon around.

"Will the gates even open? They've already killed the ones you sent before us."

Maedelous leveled his stare on the tower ahead. His small eyes narrowed.

"Trust me, boy. We've accepted his challenge. He wouldn't dare turn us away now."

\*

The cries of the city beneath her erupted like rapture, like the building roll of a thunderhead becoming a storm, as twilight settles across it like raiment.

Faerowyn dabbed the edge of her mouth. She rose from her throne. The drained husk of the slave girl tumbled away down the dais.

Only rapture can so aptly capture the subtle line between penance and praise.

The moment that waits in between.

The taste of it, the loss of it, the very soul of it, still burned down her throat. But it didn't fill her. It didn't satisfy her—no, the dragon's—gnawing hunger. Nothing would anymore. She traced a hand across her womb. Her fingers, stained black, drew a mark across her ivory gown. Her womb, and her soul, trembled at her touch.

Not even a promise that could never be broken.

And the stares of the three captives that her guards held down on their knees before her, who had so dared to love her savior, their stares answered her nothing. They gave nothing. Nothing lost, but something held back from her; a secret, perhaps.

The savior's companions knew something. They kept something from her, about him.

A Khaalish cur, a weakling boy, and a pitch-haired woman more dour than beautiful, they knelt, still defiant before her, in chains.

Kneeling, but not broken.

A Servian knight and those who traveled with her. Those who had come with Chaelus. Those who had come with their savior. Those she had chosen to spare, for him.

Their eyes fixed upon Chaelus where he hung, unconscious, naked and prostrate, wrapped in chains over chest and limb behind her throne.

Perhaps it was one of them who had come to him in his dreams. Perhaps it was her, the pitch-haired knight. Perhaps she was a witch, his shield maiden who dared to keep her from him.

"So you are the ones he dares to love more than me," Faerowyn purred. She smiled as she descended the blood-stained steps. "You are the ones who profess to love him."

"Then let him go to us," the pitch-haired woman said.

She took the woman's chin in her hand and lifted her face. Her nails pressed just into her skin. "That is too cruel thing to ask of me, witch. And it's something I cannot give you. You see, I loved him first."

She leaned down until her cheek and her lips brushed against the pitch-haired woman, until her own dark stare held her.

"And I will not so easily lose him again."

She pressed her lips against the woman's, just a kiss. The woman's lips were soft and fearful.

The woman struggled against her.

The infant Dragon cried out within her. Its ire and hunger screamed through what was left of her soul.

The soul of the pitch-haired woman recoiled and struggled and cried out in terror against it.

She released her. "I am sure you, more than anyone else, can understand this."

The woman wept, her gaze still fixed upon her savior.

Faerowyn stared beyond the woman, beyond the other two heretics, beyond the veiled legionnaires, into the deep breadth of the hall, into the growing darkness beyond the mother of pearl columns and blood-soaked tapestries that could do nothing to disguise the horror she herself had brought here.

All to have a kingdom and win a lover back to her.

The cenotaphs that lined the hall were already full, the mountains of the dead growing high around them. The ones who still lived had already lost their will to leave, or to live, only to serve, to serve her and the dragon within her, even if it meant to feed themselves to her if she needed. Soon it would all end though. It would end in fire and in blood.

All so that he could have her kingdom and win her lover back to her.

But a dead kingdom meant nothing, and her lover, he wouldn't come to her. Because something, someone, still kept him from her.

"Why are you doing this to him?" the pitch-haired woman begged.

Her dark soldiers moved toward the woman.

She stayed them with her hand.

"You profess to love him," she said, "but you would throw him away for your prophecy, and your faith. And if he is really your savior as you profess, then you would abandon him all the more. You would sacrifice him for dead words and the vain hope of something you have never even seen before."

She looked behind herself, to where Chaelus hung in chains, where the stare of the pitch-haired woman clung.

"And what is it you really seek from him? You see, I have read your prophecy. I have read your prophecy and it promises you nothing but death."

The woman drew up.

"No. It promises us deliverance from you."

The suffering cries of the city outside swelled. A more potent offering if ever there was one.

"No. It doesn't. It simply tells you how you'll die. Read the words. All the rest is just a fantasy you've placed upon it."

She smiled at the woman, is if to a child. Her hand, her fingers, strayed across her dragon womb.

"I have read all of it," she said. "And I have seen all of it. I have seen this love that you profess. I have washed myself in it, long ago, and I have watched it dry away. I have suffered its loss, but the scent of it, like a fragrance, has never left me. Now he has come back to me just as he was prophesied to do."

The woman's eyes hardened with zeal. "You cannot know love. You can only possess. Just as the Dragon possesses you now. Chaelus is not yours to keep, like chattel, like the pitiful souls you feed upon. Prophecy, and love, won't let you."

"Not like they're letting me keep you?"

"I don't mean anything."

"And what of your friends? Do they mean something?" She stepped away from the woman. "What do they care for? What do they love?"

The sweat and blood and wounds of faith marred the barbarian's visage. His eyes were like coals.

"A Khaalish chieftain, bought to protect those who will not fend for themselves. And what does your heart long for, cur?"

The barbarian sneered. "For you to finish talking." A smirk touched his lips. The whips of the soldiers struck him. He winced but his smile remained.

The boy's stare held her. It held onto her, not Chaelus hung before him. He was no mere boy either, she could tell, and neither was his soul. It was ageless. It was like Chaelus' own, and it kept her as she drew next to him. In the light of his eyes he held an azure flame that burned against her sight.

He was one of the holy ones. He was one of the Evarun.

A son of prophecy, here, before her.

The child beast bucked and heaved within her. Its power bled through her flesh until her pitiful sight turned crimson. She felt the blood well at the corner of her eyes.

Black tendrils laced beneath her skin like a raging fire.

One hand against her womb, she staggered until she fell to her knees before the boy. Both her hands trembled. She caressed his face and neck.

"And you, child, for what does your heart dream? What does your eternal heart long for from me?"

Even beneath his voice, she could hear His voice. She could hear Chaelus' voice, the one who wouldn't save her.

"Nothing," the boy said. "There is nothing left for you to give. The Dragon has already consumed you. I see him in you. You're filled with his shadow. Very soon, you'll be dead."

Around the boy's eyes, his flesh had burned from tears that had already ended, one more sign of a prophecy yet to be fulfilled.

She drew back his tousled hair to reveal the marks of prophecy that he bore. Sepia strokes in the tongue of prophecy borne across the broken memory of scars.

*One who was but could not be*
*One who could not be but was.*

*One to teach and One to save*
*The mark of the Dragon upon him.*

She pulled her hand away from him, her whole body now trembling. "You speak with the tongue of angels because you are the one the angels have made."

The fire of the Dragon's stare burned beneath her eyes, heating the flesh where her blood tears sat, perhaps a sign that the boy was right, a sign that her own prophecy was almost fulfilled.

"I'm not afraid of you," the boy whispered. "I'm not afraid of anything, anymore."

"One to teach or one to save," she whispered back.

Or to take the one she loved away from her in a dream.

She placed her hands carefully around his face, around his head. "I wonder, then, which one are you?"

"Leave him alone!" the pitch-haired woman screamed.

She turned to her.

"Why? Do you love him?"

She twisted his head with a snap and stood. The boy dropped silent to the rush-covered floor.

No angels had come to save him.

The woman's screams deafened, drowning out even the lament of the city beneath.

Such a fine line it was between penance and praise.

Her womb unfurled in pain. She doubled over in agony.

In her ears rang the mocking voice of prophecy. Its darkness swept over her, clouding her sight, no red aura or apathy, only the darkness of a bleeding night.

The Prophecy of the Evarun.

She staggered backward.

Its voice cried out within her. Like a rolling thunder. Like a legion, like bleeding rapture. But it was the other words, words beneath those words, whispered to her from the shadows since her birth that she knew now doomed her, the prophecy from which, though she had tried, she knew she could never flee.

The Prophecy of the Dragon.

*One who was but could not be.*
*One who could not be but was.*

*One to rule and one to suffer.*
*The mark of the Dragon upon them.*

*Born to us to die for us.*
*For only the fallen may rule.*

*To tear the veil of shadowed Pale*
*So the Dragon will be revealed.*

*Vows of Prophecy*
*Vows of Betrothal*

*A martyr to the Dragon's veil*
*Will be chosen as its queen.*

*To rule the Pale beyond the veil.*
*Brought down on bended knee.*

*A broken promise she must keep*
*To bear the Dragon's seed.*

*Twelve who died for prophecy*
*Will be returned by the same.*

*Herald the end of the Giver's reign.*
*The death of those who serve.*

*Blood that's shed by prophecy*
*Shall paint the road to war.*

*Lament the ones who will forget*
*The Dragon has returned.*

"Take them away!" Faerowyn wiped her hand against her gown, blind as she stumbled past her throne, her bare feet slipping amongst the ruin she had brought upon them all. "Burn them. Make them suffer."

Behind her, the weeping of the city bled beneath the rapturous cries and gnashing teeth of her soldiers.

## Chapter Nineteen: Loss

"Chaelus?"

The void splintered but it didn't yield.

"Chaelus."

Again the voice came. Not so much a question this time as a command. Long cracks wove their way through and across the sepia veil wrapped around him. Through them came the faintest hint of the brightest blue.

The voice, a woman's, echoed across it.

"Come to me."

Chaelus reached out to the azure light, the thin crack of a promise that it was. He reached out through the void.

The nothingness of the void shattered like thin glass beneath his fingers.

And azure glow descended to verdant fields, where cool grass clutched at his fingers as he lay.

Green fields stretched out to a far distant horizon of blue mountains. The fields looked like emeralds beneath the deepest azure sky. He knew them only dimly. They were the same fields upon which he had just fallen. The same fields of war, only there was no war. Not here. No ghosts of blood or of vengeance dwelt here.

Only good things.

On a nearby hill he hadn't seen before stood a tall white tower, of the kind built by the Evarun of the purest white stone, like the tower he had once ruled from. It stood like a pillar, a monument, a promise, overlooking all. But it wasn't his tower. It never was. It never had been. It was a promise that had never been meant for him, just like so many others. And no waves of darkness fell over it to wash it away this time as had happened when the Dragon had shown him the tower before, a lifetime ago when he had fought it somewhere behind the veil, before he had defeated it, before he had defeated his self and the Dragon both.

He turned to the soft-sounding crush of grass bending beneath gentle feet.

A pitch-haired woman in the purest white dress walked toward him through the field. She smiled at him as she held the hem of her dress above the grass, as if she knew him, as if she had known him, so many lifetimes before.

And she was familiar, distant, but familiar, like someone can remember a dream when first awoken.

Yet he couldn't remember her name.

Lifting her hem just above her knees, her skin like alabaster, she knelt down to him.

Small bells sounded across the tremor of her voice.

"Do you remember me?"

Her face, her lips, were hard to see. Her beauty was like so many suns, like a halo, like a veil.

He turned away from her.

Warm, gentle fingers turned his face back.

"Don't turn away," she said. "But only speak my name to me."

"I can't," he stammered.

"Yes, you can. It is I, your shield maiden, but that is not the name you've given me. It is not my true name. I am even more than an angel, sent to you, Chaelus, vessel of the Giver reborn, to protect you and bring you home, for angel is not my name either. I am the very reason why you were chosen to be. I am the only reason you were saved. I am the reason why you were made to serve."

The backs of her fingers brushed against his face.

"What is my name, Chaelus, oh blessed child of mine?"

His own voice came out like tar. It bled slow from the corners of his mouth. He turned his sight up to her. Tears chastened his eyes. His throat burned as badly as his heart did.

"Your face is familiar to me," he said. "But I do not know you."

"That is because I remind you of someone else, someone else you think you love," the angel who wasn't replied. "But then, perhaps that is why you do, because she reminds you of me."

"Mariam."

"And tell me; tell me what you see in Mariam's face, Chaelus. Tell me what you see in her touch."

"I see hope."

"Hope." An understanding sadness crept across her lips, her eyes, from just beyond her brilliant veil.

"Then you're right, and you only know my face, Chaelus, not my name."

Her finger brushed back his hair.

"Because I am so much more than hope, and though hope is why you follow me, it saddens me that I mean so little to you. Hope is nothing but a failing for the weak."

Her finger fell away.

"I am virtue. I am strength. I am power. I am destiny. I am all of these things, but even these things, they are not my name."

She turned away, though her radiance stayed before him. She pointed to the white tower.

"Hope is nothing more than a symbol, like a tower, like a promise. Without a name, it becomes but crumbled stone. It is a void with nothing left to stand for. But a name, in a name can be housed one's very soul. It is in my name alone that the stones of a tower can never fall."

Her face turned back to him. Her azure flame burned through him. Her face had changed. Long white hair framed it, falling beyond her shoulders. Virgin white cloth veiled her eyes.

"My name, Chaelus, is the only name you will ever need. It is the one name the Dragon can never take away from you. He will try, but he will fail, so long as you remember it. It is I who chose you. It is I who desired you above all others. It is I who prepared the way for you."

She stood. As she did, the hem of her dress fell.

Its lace scraped like heavy stones against the ground. The crush of the grass beneath her feet turned red with blood. It filled the cloth of her dress like a bandaged wound. The faces of corpses grew up from the soil to mark the fields of war.

"You thpought my face was another's. But you will know my name. I will tell it to you. Do not forget it. The time of your childish yearning, the time of your choosing is over."

The ground began to tremble.

"You attach yourself to failing things. You attach yourself to mortal weakness. The hope you claim will soon die. So too will Mariam, along with everything else you've ever loved. Every promise you have ever kept. It will be nothing more than a memory. Even then the memory will fade to ash."

Blood filled the horizon to the east. The blue mountains darkened in shadow beneath it. Their tall spires splintered. Above them, the dragons took  wing. The emerald fields burned. A cacophony of legions pounded out the drums of war before them.

Her smile faded.

Blood engorged the cloth covering her eyes.

"My name is Prophecy, and you will bow before no one but me."

*

Chaelus recoiled awake. Shackles dug into his flesh.

Faerowyn clung to him. So did the chill of her shadow.

"I wish you knew how much I've given up for you," Faerowyn whispered, "just to bring you back to me. I've given you my life. I've given you the lives of my people. So tell me, my savior, what more will you ask of me? What more must I sacrifice so that I can have you?"

His chains trembled against him.

The shadow of the Dragon stained her lips. It bled like tears from her eyes. Her long white gown hung tattered and tainted over her misshapen womb.

"I have wept the Dragon's tears for you." Her lips curled in a snarl. She stumbled. "I carry his seed. Just so I can have you. Does that mean nothing?"

She held herself up against the back of her throne. It shimmered in the radiance of the burning city outside.

"Give me a sword!" Faerowyn ordered.

The barest remnant of a legionnaire, and even less of a human, cloaked in shadow, shuffled toward her. He jerked his blade from its scabbard.

Faerowyn snatched the sword from the legionnaire. She wrapped both her hands around the hilt as if it were a talisman, as if she were in prayer. Her stare grew wild as she leveled the blade toward Chaelus.

His shattered, broken stare floated across the glistening steel, staring back at him like a ghost. The razor point of the gladius trembled just above his throat, just above his skin.

Because she couldn't do it, could she. Prophecy wouldn't let her.

She whispered, her voice a tremor.

*Neither spear nor shaft shall harm him.*

"Not even a sword!" Faerowyn screamed.

She flung the gladius. It clattered and spun in circles across the blood-stained floor. "You still have the power, yet you will not help me!"

Faerowyn's hands trembled as they reached out to him. They lingered away from him, the same distance as the blade just had. She passed her hand across her face, against something unseen. "Why don't you save me?"

Faerowyn seized him, her lips pressed against his, forcing him back. The chains bore against him. But it was no kiss and it never had been. The burning cold of the Dragon's poison poured from her open mouth into his.

He fought and choked against it.

"No," he coughed, and spat. Sepia detritus drained away.

Faerowyn pulled back.

"Do. Not. Abandon. Me. Save me!"

He raised his frail sight to her.

"Save me," she whispered.

"You can't be," he said. "Until you die, you can't be."

Faerowyn collapsed to her knees. She slunk back. She passed her hand in another coarse gesture, like a ward, like a veil across her. Shadow filled her widened eyes, rimmed in red. Tears rained from their edges. She panted.

The corner of her mouth lifted in a snarl.

The voice of the Dragon bellowed from her until the stones around them shook.

"Crucify him!"

*

Al-Mariam screamed until only silence remained, and the repeated blows from the rotting legionnaires no longer mattered. She fought beneath their decaying iron grip until she could no longer feel her limbs. She drowned beneath the overwhelming weight of loss until any and all hope of breath escaped her.

The loss of her brother.

The loss of everything.

Obidae had placed himself, bringing his guards and their whips with him, to block the sight of Michalas from her. Obidae's stare didn't leave her. He wielded no expression, only strength, just like a prayer.

And silence. Even the scrape of steel as blades were drawn receded beneath it.

No sound came from the corpse of her brother, only the silence of the dead.

Al-Mariam struggled and cried out voiceless as they dragged her and Obidae through the darkness to their own execution.

The legionnaires gabbled and gnashed their teeth. Their limbs jerked about. Their eyes were void and they reeked of deadening flesh, their bloated skin entombed in cuirass and rags.

They dragged her past the still dead, dead like her brother, their bodies stacked like cordwood, down the length of the horror-filled dungeon, beneath the blood on polished stone. At least here, the blood and darkness could meet more equally; at least the cries of the dead could have meaning.

Even their silence.

In the shuffling and gabbling darkness, the iron grip of the legionnaire lessened, then fell away from her.

The sounds of the dead returned with muffled grunts and sickening thuds.

And the harsh flare of torchlight.

And a flash on bloodied legion steel.

The legionnaire behind her dropped like a gurgling stone.

The stone face of the centurion who had marched them for a fortnight in chains appeared before her beneath the shadow of his helm.

"I'm here to save you."

A slash at the cords at her wrists.

Rage stained her vision.

She clawed and beat against his cuirass. The arms of Obidae restrained her.

But her hoarse voice only wept.

"Micha!"

But his name sounded like a hammer blow.

"I am sorry for your brother," the centurion said. He gripped her hands. "I couldn't save him. But at least let me use his death to save you. At least let me repay him that."

"Why?"

"My name is Gervasis. Your brother spoke to me. He helped me escape the fate of the damned. So now I have come to save you, because only you can save another. You're the only one who can save the Giver reborn."

Her strength ebbed away. Her rage diminished like smoke. Like a trapdoor suddenly sprung open.

"He doesn't want to be saved."

"No. He doesn't. But he asked me to save you."

"What?"

"You are the only one whose name he whispered." Gervasis released her, stepping away. "It was your name the Giver whispered out loud into the darkness. It was your name he whispered alone, as his only talisman against Faerowyn, against the Dragon reborn."

Gervasis' stare wavered. "He asked me to, and I tried to, save all of you, but I was too late."

"It was you who brought us here!"

Gervasis' face returned to stone.

"The Giver will not save himself, but if what he whispered about you is true, and if I am right about what I said about your brother, then you're the only one who can."

Obidae pulled her back and stepped between them, his hands still bound, looking down on Gervasis.

"You will take her to him?"

"I will."

"What?" she asked.

Obidae leaned over her.

"Shabek, the great waiting is over. The hope you sought has come. But it is only for you. My shabek still waits for me in the east, in the heart of my people. We have prayed, and Shoa has listened and answered, to yours, and to mine. You must go with him. I must go to what I do alone."

The drum beats of the legions and the city's dancing dead sounded out in the stones around them.

Gervasis waited like a strung bow.

"We must hurry."

Her own legs held her like a statue.

Obidae held his bound wrists to Gervasis.

Gervasis struck his gladius through them.

Obidae seized Gervasis' wrist.

"Do not fail her like you did her brother."

Gervasis nodded. "I won't, not again. Go to the east. There is a postern gate where the dead are taken. You will be safe to leave the city there. There are so many, they've stopped carrying them out anymore."

Obidae turned to her. He bowed to her. He smiled. He took her hand in his and placed it beneath her breast where the arrow had pierced her, the wound from which Chaelus had saved her.

"I think I will see you again soon," Obidae assured her. He smiled. "Be it from one kind of death or another."

Then he was gone, like a sprung trap, a ghost beyond the torchlight, lost beneath the descending cries of the dancing dead.

Gervasis sheathed his gladius. He reached down into the shadows. He lifted a long bundle of pleated silver cloth, bound with heavy rope. He handed it to her.

"Take these."

She knew what it was before she took it from him. She knew what they were before she even pulled the cloth away.

Aela's long graceful hilt, and the strength of Sundengal, glimmered in the torchlight.

Gervasis drew his gladius again.

"Before we're done, I think you're going to need them both."

*

"I don't trust him," Al-Aaron said.

He had ridden silent beside the Mother until then.

The Mother's scarf protected her head against the wind. Her small hands gripped white upon the reins. Her stare grew more and more distant across the blasted plain ahead, as if she couldn't bear to look north or south to the danger that threatened them from there. But they, the dangers there, still threatened them.

"I know," the Mother replied. She drew her mare close to him.

So many dangers that neither of them could speak of, so many whispers in the dark.

"I don't trust him either," the Mother said.

The only thing left to see was the ochre shades of the Horta Mun growing on the horizon, two, perhaps three days away. They would pass beneath their shadow as they continued east toward a home only the Mother had ever been to and he had only ever heard of in legends.

The land of the angels. The land of the Evarun.

But the Horta Mun bordered another home as well—the home of the Khaalish who now feigned to protect them.

"Then why do you let him lead us? We know the way. They will not protect us."

A heavy sigh lowered her shoulders.

Beyond their small caravan, the Khaalish kept their distance just as they always had. But now they seemed to be watching them as much as they watched the horizon for the Hunters that so far hadn't returned.

"I trust him because I have to," the Mother said. "Because prophecy has told me to. It is all I know to do. I fear there is little choice left to us now."

"Belloch is not Obidae. He doesn't claim to be. He has told me this."

"I know, child, only I don't think prophecy cares, really."

"But it will honor your choice. I can say this."

"I know you can, child, more than anyone, you know this. But how many more will die because of it? Too many have died already. I cannot bear to suffer so many more deaths again."

"You did not kill those knights. It was the Hunters. It was the legion. It was the Dragon."

The Mother reached out and gripped his hand.

"There are some choices that do not unfold, child, until long after the choice we made has been forgotten."

"You're not to blame for this."

"Blame or not, I have seen what my choice has done to others. I have seen what my choice has done to you. I hear the whispers that you share in your sleep. I am sure they are little different than my own. Tell me, child, when did your faith fail you?" The Mother's hand grew cold as she released him. "There are so many things I haven't told you. There are things I have never told anyone. There are forces darker than the Dragon at play here."

"I cannot think what they would be."

"Darker, perhaps, are the things that serve it, child. The Fallen Ones, the eleven Servian lords who serve the Dragon have returned. Somehow, their twelfth has returned with them."

"But Michalas destroyed them. And their twelfth, Malius, was saved from them. Chaelus was saved..."

"There are many different kinds of death."

He fell silent along with her.

"I still see him," he whispered.

The first dull glare of sunset washed the sky. It would be dark soon.

The pain from his old wound burned cold through him.

"I still see Malius. I see him, I see the Dragon, whichever it is. He still comes to me, haunting me. He tortures me. I cannot help but wonder why, and for how long, prophecy will let him."

## Chapter Twenty: Martyr

Login tried in vain to shield himself with his thin arms from the fists of the guards and everyone else.

The gates of the surround had opened for them, but there all hospitality ended. Dragged from their wagon, they were beaten and mocked by man, woman, and child alike; the violence, the anger, of the Goarnn was their own ugly kind of joy. Weakness and mercy had no place here, only martial things, things of war.

Thick black smoke billowed from cauldrons set about the yard. It billowed among pikes festooned with skulls and tapestries, armor and weapons, haunted pillars of the dead that lined the brutal walk from gate to gate. It burned the eyes and scattered the senses.

Guards in studded leather and halberds, polished bits of bone and steel adorning the braids of their hair and beards, herded them forward through the short passage to the edge of a landing at the top of twinned stairs.

Black smoke cloaked the air of the tower as well, drifting over it, a stain across the purest of white stone, like the mournful passing of hope.

Hastily built wooden works filled the hall, making an arena with deep sides and seating rising above; at the head of it towered a jet black throne, spears standing up from its back stuck out like wings.

Stained tapestries and battered shield mounts dressed the arena. More of each bled from the walls of the gallery that circled to an oculus of light high above. The black smoke dulled it as it passed across it, but couldn't vanquish the blazon of light left upon the blood-soaked sand of the gladiator pit beneath, two spears stuck deep at its center.

A dull chant rained down from the gallery above them.

They sang of blood, and of violence, to the stomp of booted feet as more men gathered to the wooden stands of the arena.

The guards pushed Login stumbling down the leftmost of the stairs leading beneath either side of the works. Maedelous leaned on his staff as the guards forced him down the opposite one.

The smoke and the cries and even the harsh light falling down all thickened here, at the bottom. The faces and leers of the crowd were veiled above them.

A fat hairless man sauntered toward the sepia throne. The wooden works moaned beneath him. They quaked as he collapsed onto the throne. He wiped his jowl across a silken sleeve. His bald pate held a single banded iron crown. A solitary ruby hung from it like a drop of blood. His skin was mottled by scars, a longer one, greater than the rest, led from his upper lip down across the fat jowl of his neck. Black paint marred his eyes like a beast.

"To what glory would you send the blood of your enemy?" the man asked. "What favor would you ask of me as your witness?"

Maedelous stepped forward, walking around the spear thrust in the ground in front of him. He bowed his head and then raised it.

"My Lord Oarn Dur, I would ask you for your army."

Oarn Dur smiled.

"And you know, my old friend Maedelous, that I have no such army." He spread his fat arms. "It is only the offering of blood that keeps us safe."

"Do you mean to tell me then that this land where weakling babes are left to die, and where those that get the privilege to live, learn the spagot before the rattle, doesn't have an army?"

"I say it doesn't need one."

"No. It doesn't. So then, give me your people."

Oarn Dur roared in laughter. The works trembled. Shields shook. The veiled spectators cried out along with him in curses and laughter.

"Ha! You're bold! For what price? For a boy! Or an old man?" Oarn Dur leaned forward as he gripped, his knuckles white, the sides of his throne.

Login backed away.

Sweat beaded on the fat king's brow, gathering beneath the drop of blood hanging from his crown.

Oarn Dur's leer found Login. "He is succulent, I grant you, but why would I want to see him dead? Why should I not just kill you, and still keep him?"

Maedelous turned to Login.

"You can't. Because once he kills me, he's going to kill you."

The boards of the arena pressed against Login's back. The spike of a buckler protruded past his head. The tapestries billowed with the press of men behind the hoardings.

Oarn Dur settled back into his throne and the creaking of the works.

"Really?"

"Trust me."

"My life for my people? Sounds noble enough. But it's not me, really. It's also not very beneficial to me no matter how succulent the boy may be. One must be prudent as a ruler, you know. Besides, how is it you're even here? I thought you had gone up north to die along with your holy order friends."

"I had to quit."

"Really? Interestingly, when I found you were coming, I tried to leave you that message. But when I did, surprisingly enough, your friends fought back."

Login shook his trembling head at Maedelous.

Maedelous turned back to Oarn Dur.

"My friends had to quit, too."

Oarn Dur sighed.

"Makes even more sense now. They fought well, you know, though they died poorly as any man would, to die like that, truly. It's not really a dignified way to go, you know, for a knight."

"You are a butcher."

"Yet you came to me for my army. Funny, it seems that just like them, you're both going to die here too."

*

Faerowyn slipped and stumbled away, away from the radiance of her throne, away from her failure, away from her doom. She trampled across the blood and the ichor and the darkness and into the caustic silence that veiled the empty hall.

Her hand slipped from the polished column that held her. Cold stone and gore met her as she fell.

Darkness seared her vision. It bled down her cheeks like oil. It drained from her mouth, like every soul she had ever taken it from.

The scalding heat of it boiled her tongue even as it touched her lips, like the Dragon's kiss, the kiss of her betrothed, the kiss of her doom. It drained down into the tenderness of her bodice, searing her flesh even there, where once only the hope of love had ever bloomed.

Hope and love, but neither of them had saved her. And neither of them ever would. Prophecy, and the Dragon, wouldn't let them.

He was all she had ever wanted. He was why she had given it all away, all for the hope of a promise he refused to fulfill.

Wasted like the supple allure of jasmine that he had once given to her so long ago. To remember him; he, her promised one, Chaelus, the vessel of the Giver reborn, who had abandoned her to this.

Even in the face of everything she had sacrificed for him, he had sacrificed her still.

The dead eyes of a corpse stared at her from across the ruin of her hall. One of the tender souls she had taken. The flesh beneath his skin was gone, the black stain of the Dragon left seared across his lips, without hope, without love, without life.

Just like him. Just like the Giver reborn.

Slippered feet drew near her, sauntering across the gore and the stone, dancing across the dead, beneath the soft crush of velvet robes, stepping over the corpse who stared back at her. Only the dead remained now, and the wizards who still haunted her.

Vas Ore knelt beside her. He touched a gloved hand to her cheek, and his other he held over her womb. Vas Kael waited beside him.

Pain ripped through her, and cold wetness as the Dragon's shadow pooled between her legs.

She trembled.

"Get up," Vas Ore whispered above the cracking of his lips.

She wept.

Vas Kael knelt down beside Vas Ore. The cold brass of his armored fingers crushed her face as he gripped her. "Now."

"You said he would come for me!" she choked.

"No," Vas Ore said. He traced a finger down her neck, past her bosom. It rested with the other on her burgeoning womb.

Her flesh rolled beneath his touch. The dragon within her boiled and consumed her.

Her insides threatened to explode.

"I only said that he came to you," Vas Ore continued, "not for you."

She screamed, for the first time with her own voice.

"It is too late for that," Vas Kael said. "You've made a promise that now it's time to keep."

A last tear fled from her. But no more solace. Only void.

"If it helps you to know," Vas Ore whispered, "there was no way he could have saved you. His purpose was for something far greater than you."

"The dead can only save the dead," Vas Kael said. "And your death is only just beginning."

To weep without tears.

Vas Ore traced languid circles across her womb. "The day of your recompense has finally come."

Vas Kael stood. Blood gathered upon his stricken cheeks just beneath his fervent eyes. He was weeping. "The blessed day of the Dragon has come."

Faerowyn tried to crawl from them. Her fingers clawed across wet stone, through blood, both hers and from a thousand other souls as well. Her breath shook. Her skin pulled against her flesh. The press of the weight of her unnatural womb, the terror of her sacrifice, beat against her heart and her soul like a drum. Like a march of the dead, if there was even a soul in her left to be had. She doubted there was.

She wept without tears.

Vas Ore stared at her, his eyes dark behind his golden mask. His mouth opened slightly in rapture.

"You were a fool to believe you could escape this," Vas Ore chuckled, "that your will and your desire would help you against the power of prophecy, against the will of the Dragon."

"You tried to claim something that was never meant to be yours," Vas Kael said. "You could never be the master of something you were only ever meant to serve."

## Chapter Twenty-One: Transfiguration

The azure flame descended, but it didn't turn to shadow.

Michalas opened his eyes to a gray morning light.

A hill of stones and the rotting hubris of tumbled corpses, discarded here because there was no other place for the dead to go. So many dead just like him, just outside the blood-soaked walls of the Holy City of Paleos, along the corpse-strewn slopes of the valley of Hennos. The dead don't dig graves for the dead.

The stiffness of his neck lessened, fled from him, as he moved his head around, healed as his life returned to him, again.

So too would the memories flee that he glimpsed only right now, of the many lifetimes he had lived before this one. A boy always returned to save, but never a man; first come back to save his father, and then to save himself, and now, he knew, returned to save the world.

But not Chaelus, the savior the soul of his father, Talus, now possessed. Not Chaelus, who still died slowly, this very minute, his scream etched out upon the flesh of the eternal soul. Not Chaelus; only the world. He was always, he was only ever, meant to save the world.

Just like his father; Talus, the First Prince of Harloth. His father, Talus, who he still found he remembered, and missed, from his lifetime before, in those brief moments like these when he still got to remember him.

And each of the times before, there was always a lesson to be learned. Each so that he could learn the next, so that he could do this. Perhaps he had learned this one, because the angels had returned. He had learned to wait. He had learned to hope. What he had learned more than anything, perhaps though, was to trust. At least he hoped that's what he was supposed to have learned. It seemed to be.

She looked so much like his Mariam, the angel, so very much like his sister.

She stood before him upon an upturned outcropping of stone. Corpses lay scattered beneath her. The death of their eyes couldn't see her. But she was so beautiful. Just for him to see and no one else. Not even the dead. A supple azure flame held about her like a halo. Her hand waited out-stretched to him.

"Do you know now what you must do?" the angel said.

He reached out and took her hand.

Like a salve its gentle warmth coursed through him, awakening every bit of his newly re-born flesh.

"I want to save Chaelus."

"But you can't. You must go instead to the east, to the broken lands of the Khaalish. You will finish what you were always meant to do there. The fruit of grace there will soon be ripe for the harvest."

"But what of Chaelus?"

"His path is still unfolding. His lesson is still not yet learned. But not so for the ones he was sent to teach. They still have time to save him, so his path may finish unfolding."

"And what path is that?"

"To save our home."

"And my sister?"

"She is safe. She goes to save him now."

Her smile diminished.

"Only you are not. Not yet."

She nodded to a place beneath her feet, to an armored corpse just beneath the standing stone. "War is coming to you. The harvest you go to will be naught without its reaping. Protect yourself as you can in the alms of the dead."

The blessed stare of a dead legionnaire waiting beneath its chainmail coif looked back at him, an azure glow held across the steel rings around his face with the first outstretched fingers of the morning sun.

"I don't think he'll be needing it anymore," Michalas said.

"No. But you will."

Then the angel's hand diminished beneath his own until only the memory of it and her gentle assurance, and her voice, remained. "And you must hurry."

She drew his attention to the east.

He closed his eyes.

The warmth of the new sun washed over him, rising over the blood-red mountains of the Horta Mun.

"You are so strong now," her voice lingered, "and Obidae is waiting for you."

## Chapter Twenty-Two: Death

Void shattered to burning flame and a mallet blow. The nail drove through his wrist into the wood of the prostrate cross where he lay.

Chaelus cried out. But not to save his brother and win his kingdom back.

The warmth of his blood sprayed him. The pain splintered into blinding noise.

*Neither spear nor shaft shall harm him.*

But only a nail.

Chaelus screamed.

He cried out to the void of death for its solace, that would surely flee from him again as he gathered himself to suffer once more, his legs and arms splayed apart, fixed upon the crossed timbers of the prostrate cross.

*Born to us to die for us.*
*For only the Fallen may rise.*

But there would be no death. No lasting one, at least. No peace. No relief. Not for him. It was prophesized to be that way.

So he screamed at the soulless stare of the Remnant legionnaire who carried out his sentence. At the stares of the others who helped him. He stared at the ones who watched them, the dancing dead who promenaded down the happas, singing the songs of their own doom. He screamed at all of them, at the darkness, the shadow of the Dragon both around and within their eyes.

He screamed at the fact that he couldn't save any of them. Because only the dead can save the dead.

Another mallet blow.

Chaelus screamed at the Dragon that consumed them all. The Dragon he had yet to face since his last death, beyond the veil across the nightmare shore of the Shinnaras. There, where he had faced its grappling maw and the darkness of the shadow. He had stood against a legion there, as well. He had died there too, only to be remade.

But not here. There was no azure flame to save him. No Dragon to take him, only the Remnants of men, and no voice, no whisper of the Giver to remake him.

Only nails, and the sharp blur of broken flesh and blood to repay him.

A nail drove through his other wrist above the bloodied ropes that bound it there, where no nails were needed except to make him suffer more.

If only they knew they couldn't do that to him; make him suffer more. His flesh would heal even as he hung before them. It wasn't even his flesh that suffered but his soul, and even it wouldn't die.

The canted cross was lifted up. Its shadow crawled across the horde of dancing dead who shuffled by in answer to the Dragon's call.

The Remnant legionnaires shoveled dirt into the pits around the legs of the cross. The legs of the cross needed room as they pulled away from each other. It wouldn't be long before Chaelus learned if his limbs would heal once they were torn apart from him as he waited. Perhaps then death might take him.

The Remnant legionnaires shuffled away to their doom.

*To lament the ones who will forget*
*The Dragon waits within.*

They left him there; not to die, but to suffer.

He screamed a broken, sordid scream. He screamed at everything; at the fact that he was alone again, devoid of hope, devoid of everything he had left. But mostly, mostly he screamed at the sordid bitch named Prophecy who had damned him to be here at all, alone upon a cross, waiting the long, gray, hopeless wait of damnation.

*

Login stumbled back to the relative safety of the hoardings as fast as he could.

"Listen to me, and listen carefully, boy," Maedelous hissed, closing on him, thrusting his spear forward.

The roar of the warriors of Goarnn ascended. The stomping of their boots and the pounding of their fists upon the wooden stands descended until it shook their very bones. Cries of blood and cries of war.

"Listen, because the world you know is about to end."

Shields and tapestries trembled where they hung, like a second thought, or fearful rapture, like the voices screaming in blood-lust behind them, in a tremor just like the laughter of Oarn Dur, their king.

"No!"

"You have to, boy. It's why I brought you here."

"You really did bring me here to kill me!"

"No, boy, I brought you here to save you. So that there will be someone left to save everyone else."

"From what? From you?"

He moved warily, keeping the other spear, still standing upright in the sand, always between them.

"Begin for blood's sake!" Oarn Dur yelled out. "Begin or I'll come down there and gut the both of you myself."

The crowd roared.

Maedelous glanced up.

"No, child, from the beast, from the Dragon. The day of our hope has ended. The day of the Dragon has come."

"You're mad!"

Maedelous lowered his spear.

"Perhaps, but only one of us will leave here. I would prefer it to be you. My body is already broken. Dammit! That's why I brought you. You're still pure enough to have a chance at this, and not so blind in your faith to not be afraid to do what must be done, whatever that must be."

"And what is that?"

"Well, first, if you'd been listening, you've got to pick up your spear and kill me, boy. Go on! Take it!"

Maedelous knocked the other spear to the ground.

"Then, of course, don't forget, you've got to kill the king."

Maedelous prodded at him, but didn't strike him.

Login fumbled for and grabbed the spear.

"Good. Now you're getting it. You see, it seems my old friend Oarn Dur has made a deal with the Dragon. A marriage, of sorts. In a fool's grasp for power, he promised to carry the Dragon's seed. But now it's time for the little bastard to be due." Maedelous spat.

"What do you mean?"

"You've got to stop a dragon from being born, child."

Maedelous grimaced. He glanced up at the bellicose fervor of Oarn Dur.

"You've got to cut it out from its mother's womb."

"Less bark! More blood!" Oarn Dur yelled.

"But first things first," Maedelous continued.

He grabbed the shaft of Login's spear. He led the tip toward his chest.

"No!" Login screamed. "I'm not going to kill you!"

"Yes, you are, boy. You have to. It's why I brought you here. Nothing less will do."

The edge of Maedelous' spear point raked his thigh. "No matter what I have to do."

Login winced. Warm, wet pain shot through him.

Maedelous smiled. "You're just going to have to trust me on this, aren't you?"

Oarn Dur stood up to the cry of the hoarding beneath him, his face red, his eyes bulging in their sockets.

"Kill him!"

The crowd echoed in chorus, their faces held in rapture.

Maedelous screamed, throwing himself at Login.

His spear sank into Maedelous' belly.

Maedelous' face contorted, his stare fixed upon Login. Tears welled in his eyes. His hands gripped the shaft of the spear. He pulled himself further onto it until it protruded from him.

Maedelous took Login's hands in his.

His hands grew warm with the old man's blood as it ran down the shaft.

"Do everything I asked of you, boy," Maedelous choked, "if you want to live, if you are to save the Pale from its slumber. You're the only one left who can."

"What?" Oarn Dur yelled.

Rage swept through the crowd.

"I want murder, not suicide!"

A veil drew down over Maedelous' stare.

"Just make sure, whatever you do, give them a show."

## Chapter Twenty-Three: Recompense

Faerowyn awoke to the sound of a baby crying.

That's what it sounded like. That's what it seemed like. That's what it felt like, what she wanted it to be. It was soft and it was needy; needing warmth, and succor, and gentle things.

But that wasn't what it was. The phantom infant's cry bled dead beneath the screams of the dying city beneath her, and the vomitus chanting of wizards.

Her naked body hung from thick bloody ropes around her arms and legs, splayed out over the oculus high on top of the tower. The heat of the fires burning far beneath her offered nothing to warm her flesh. Dried blood matted across her pale naked skin, smeared amongst the black runes, incantations and vows written across her swollen breasts and bloated womb.

Above her, a tempest brewed.

Storm clouds swirled and billowed to a place of starless darkness high above, a darkness that held no heavens for her.

She tried to scream, but only a choking weeping came out.

She couldn't feel her arms. She couldn't feel her legs. The only thing she could feel, aside from the cold of the night, was the pressing out of the unholy beast within her womb.

"No," she whimpered.

The flesh of her womb pulsed and writhed. Beneath the blood, the black tendrils of the dragon's poison raced through her stricken flesh, over every inch of her. Its black tears wept from within her, from her mouth, from her eyes, from everywhere.

The cold and golden stares of Vas Ore and Vas Kael watched her from beyond her opened legs. Vas Ore's cracked lips bled across his chin. The whole of Vas Kael's visage held blistered with fresh wounds beneath his thin and wicked veil.

"The time has come," Vas Ore said.

"To finish what you promised," Vas Kael said.

The two wizards chanted with the other wizards as one:

*Twelve to share the Gift.*
*Twelve who did forget.*

*Herald the Dragon's return*
*As the Fallen they will rise.*

*To bring to fell the shadowed Pale*
*When the Giver does return*

*To lament the Ones who will forget*
*The Dragon has returned.*

The cold wind blew. The storm above her fled before it. It billowed about all of them, around all of those who were gathered. The mutilated faces of the wizard high priests of the Taurate leered against it in lustful anticipation as they bleated out their own soundless song.

Spires of red flame, colder than the wind or anything she had ever felt, descended from the maelstrom above to surround her. Dark whispers of men billowed among them. The wisps of faces and of crowns and of the arms and armor of ancient times coalesced within them.

The wizards chanted through the terror forming at their center, around her and the abyss over which she hung.

*Twelve who died for prophecy*
*Will be returned by the same.*

*Herald the end of the Giver's reign,*
*The death of those who serve.*

*Blood that's shed by prophecy*
*Shall paint the road to war.*

*Lament the ones who will forget*
*The Dragon has returned.*

She couldn't scream, only choke out whimpering gasps of pain.

"You cannot curse the damned," Vas Ore answered.

"It's the damned that you serve," Vas Kael added.

"The Fallen Ones have returned," Vas Ore said.

"To herald their master's return," Vas Kael said.

Tearing pain ripped through her womb. A line of red flesh raced across her buckling skin in the blood light of the flames. She screamed like a damn unleashed as it billowed past her lips.

"The Fallen Ones have returned," Vas Ore said.

But it fell beneath the scream that the beast unleashed within her.

"To lead their master's army to war," Vas Kael said.

Her womb ripped open.. A thin line turned black, then red. A swarm of creatures, worms with wings, pooled out from her, pouring over her womb like oil. She saw them, but she couldn't feel them, their legs, their wings, crawling out of her. Her flesh was numb, like a void. She could only watch them tearing it away from her.

"The Fallen Ones have returned," Vas Ore chanted.

The dragon spawn, her children, swarmed across her limbs, across her chest, snapping at her with their wicked mouths, tearing off pieces of her bleeding flesh.

Vas Ore bleated, "You took the Giver's seed and the twelfth was made whole."

The columns of fire diminished to darkness as smoking shadow cloaked the flames, the shapes of men in black armored plate, of kings, of gods, formed within them. Red fire burned beneath helms shaped like beasts, a crown set upon each of their heavy brows. One of them, his helmet in the shape of a ram, bore a rusted iron cage around his head. The twelfth bore the mask of a child. Their swords were wreathed in fire.

"Save. Me," she pleaded. She screamed. She wept. "I'll...do..."

Vas Ore smiled. His cracked lips bled. He slowly licked them. He reverently stepped away from her, from them. "We are the Hands of the Dragon."

"They are the Fallen," Vas Kael said.

"They will not help you," Vas Ore said.

"No one will anymore," Vas Kael sighed in rapture.

One of the kings, the head of a dragon shaping his helm, stepped toward her. She remembered his face, wreathed now in twisted shadow, his dark armor, his bearing, from what seemed a lifetime ago but hadn't been, when her father had commanded his legions, when he had sat upon her golden throne.

His voice was like coal. His shadow filled her vision; his eyes burned with cold fire.

*"We are the Fallen."*

"My lord," she pleaded. "Help. Me."

The Dragon King, Dalamas, thrust his armored hand into the beasts swarming out of her womb. He seized one of them and held it before him. It screamed in vim and ire.

*"We have returned at the Dragon's will,"* Dalamas said. The chill of his flame burned through her.

Dalamas thrust the beast into her face. The dragon tore at her, its black claws and teeth and wings ripping open her brow and cheeks. Blood filled her vision. It drained into her open mouth.

She couldn't do anything. Not even scream.

*"And the will of the Dragon is for you to die, so that its prophecy will be fulfilled."*

\*

Chaelus tried to turn away, but he couldn't.

Through the frailness of his sight, from the dark maelstrom gathered above him, black oil, bitter tears of the Dragon, fell down on him like burning rain.

They fell upon his flesh. They fell upon his cross. They fell upon the dry parched sand and cracked stones beneath him. They gathered around him in pools. The tears of the Dragon rained down darkness upon the Pale.

Its substance gathered upon his lips. It gathered upon his eyes. It gathered upon itself, bleeding up from the sand around the base of the prostrate cross on which his carcass hung. It rippled and convulsed. It gathered upon itself until even the high stones around him were covered, until only the legs of the cross upon which he was crucified stood bare above it.

The tentacle of the Dragon arose from it.

The Dragon coiled about itself. It coiled around the base of the cross. It coiled upward, around his legs, its flesh at once slick and grating. It boiled his skin; the shadow of its wake burning like a cold winter's frost.

Its tip hovered just before his lips. Its skin uncurled, revealing bright red flesh. From its maw, bestial teeth ground and gnashed. They gnashed through his soul, through all the memories of every life he had ever lived in its shadow. The Dragon's voice dragged deep across the bowels of the world.

*"It's so good to be with you again, my love."*

He could only stare into the depth of its open jaws.

"Are you the death that prophecy has sent me?"

The Dragon pressed its maw against his face. Cold poison dripped from it. It whispered into his ear like a kiss.

*"No. No more death, my love, I've come to save you. I've come to save you from everything that has led you here. I am here to save you from the one you named Prophecy, and all that she has done to you.*

*"The one you name Prophecy is not what she seems. She beguiles you. She leads you to think she is another. But she means to destroy you, to bring your death upon you. Don't believe in the things she says. Do not believe that what she says to you is true, my love."*

The foul vision of the Dragon wavered and diminished, melting into a pillar of oil and collapsing. Only the chill of its touch remained.

Its chill lingered as well around the figure of Magus standing beneath him, at the foot of the cross, where the darkness still pooled and rippled. The fiend who had pursued him to the gates of madness itself, a whisper in the dark from a lifetime ago. The shattered silver mask of a child still hung from his face. His own face looked back at him from beneath it, just like when he had struck down Magus before.

*"Know that I do not share the desire of prophecy,"* Magus said. *"I have no desire to see you die, here upon this cross. No, my only desire, as ever, is to have you. I am you, and you are me. Are we not? You know this from before. You've known it always. Is not the death of you the very same death of me?"*

"No," Chaelus stammered. "Death would save me from you."

*"No, not even death can do that. You of all know that too well. Death comes many ways and you have seen so many of them. How many have you suffered so far? How many more must you suffer before you trust me? Before you believe in me? I told you when we last met that prophecy would destroy you. Now here you are, as death tries to take you again, but I know it is not the death you see. Oh, how I would save you from it. Here. Now. All you need do is ask."*

"No," he muttered. Darkness cloaked his eyes.

*"I want you, my love. I want you as much as a mother longs for a child, a longing I have suffered far too long. But not anymore, for even now our children spring forth from the very womb of the one who would dare to claim you as her own, and who would dare to steal you from me.*

*"I would offer from her our children, to watch over, to command, to lead, like your father was meant to, and together take such joy in all the suffering they will bring."*

\*

Chaelus awoke again.

He opened his eyes. But it wasn't this time to death, nor even the Dragon revealed, but the tortured music of the dancing horde in the golden city of Paleos beneath him. It sounded like war.

A burgeoning storm turned above the city, a cloud of ire and smoke from fires long burning.

His wrists where the nails pierced him burned with a colder fire.

The crossed timbers of the cross had already begun to pull away, as the sand in which they were set slowly yielded. A deeper pain cried out from his limbs as they stretched, though no more so than from his lungs as his own weight crushed down upon them.

If he were lucky, he would be torn asunder. Death could hopefully come then—or might it not? For most, it would come long before, when the agony became too great to bear. Hopefully, it would for him too. He could only wait until then.

He lifted his head, his shoulders, just enough so he could breathe. But they might as well have carried a hundred stone, weighed down as they were with his lack of faith, his blindness, his selfishness, and his sin.

The Dragon had summoned him, and he had gone alone to it willingly.

He had gone alone to it, he had gone alone to her, to Faerowyn queen, to her whispered promise of the past that he never could let go. The mouth of the Dragon had whispered through her to him, and without a moment's thought or even a prayer, he had answered. And she, it, the Dragon veiled, had consumed him.

But he had fed the ones he loved to it as well. All of them.

Only a dull pain echoed now in his wrists. His blood had already dried upon the ropes that bound them.

There would be no rest. There would be no death for him. Prophecy had seen to that.

The gray morning light, sullen, settled in full over the golden city of Paleos, the glimmer of its domes struck mute by its haze.

A trumpet call echoed out, over the music of the dancing dead, a marshalling call for war.

For prophecy.

For power.

It was what he had been summoned here for.

He came because he understood too late what it meant to love for the desire to give.

He turned to the west. He strained until his eyes felt they would burst, trying to see his home. But he never would. It was lost, somewhere across the sea, beyond the mountains of Albanjan, within the heart of a white tower where the shadow of the Dragon consumed the pitiful soul of his brother, just like the Dragon had done to him, and his father before him.

A scream split the air.

A cloud of smoke the color of blood billowed up and out above the city. The distant shape of what looked like carrion birds circled through it.

But they weren't birds. They were dragons, circling as the sky above them unfolded, like the undoing of a veil, a storm of storms preparing to spread itself out like a mailed fist across the helpless Pale.

It looked everything like a war sky.

*

Maedelous slumped to the blood-soaked sand, pulling the spear away from Login's hands. His blood still pumped from his wound and from his lips, his exiting last breath little more than a choked whisper.

Login staggered away from him.

The shadow of Oarn Dur drew across him as the fat king stood.

The cries of the arena fell silent.

Oarn Dur leered over him from the edge of the hoardings.

"What kind of fool do you take me for, boy? This was no fight."

The whites of his eyes turned the color of coal.

"Nobody leaves my arena without paying the toll, the required price in blood. Not even one so precious to me as you. My old dear dead friend should have told you that."

The hoardings sagged beneath his weight.

"Nobody cheats it."

Oarn Dur drew a black iron spagot from his tunic.

"Nobody's free from it."

Login stumbled farther away from Maedelous' corpse.

The scrape of steel sounded out across the hall as blades were drawn, above him and around him, behind the banners and shields covering the hoarding walls, and over the snick of bolts being drawn.

Oarn Dur staggered.

"Not even when everything's burning."

A thin stream of black fluid fell from OarnDur's lips, then sprayed from his mouth.

"No," he sputtered. "Not yet."

The spagot slipped from his grasp.

"Aaauuuuuuugh!"

Oarn Dur clutched at his throat as the fluid continued to spray. The hoardings collapsed beneath him as he fell.

Login stumbled back again.

Oarn Dur's spagot sank into the sand at Login's feet.

Doors flew open from the works around him. Gladiators emerged with sword and spear and net and axe.

Login snatched the spagot up. Strange, for its size, it weighed more than the spear that Maedelous had just died upon.

Oarn Dur shook his head. He pulled himself upright on Maedelous' spear, his crown toppled to one side, his dark eyes nearly sightless and weeping black tears. He clutched at his throat.

"Where are you, boy?"

Oarn Dur shuffled one step, clutching at his stomach.

"Don't think this will save you."

Oarn Dur shuffled another step. His mouth opened to poison and blood.

He shuffled a third, screaming, swinging and thrusting the spear around him.

Login dropped low to the sand, holding the long blade of the spagot trembling before him like a ward. The long shadows of more spears gathered behind him. He could feel the cries of the men on the back of his neck.

Oarn Dur's black stare seized him at last. Thick blood had added to the black tears around the edges of his eyes. "There you are, my pretty boy."

Oarn Dur's jaw dropped. It opened once, twice.

His belly exploded, ripping a hole all the way from his breast to his loin. His ribs stuck out from him like wings. His body wavered like a tower preparing to collapse. A black wyrm the size of a small bull dropped from his shattered innards.

Oarn Dur's spear fell from his limp, dead hand.

The wyrm dropped to the bloody sand in coils. Infant wings unwrapped in vitriol and a spray of Oarn Dur's blood.

The rent corpse of Oarn Dur crumpled behind the beast.

The shield-bearing hoardings and men of Oarn Dur fell silent. The shadows of their spears faltered.

The wyrm, the dragon, stretched its jaws and screamed, its long teeth already bloody from Oarn Dur's innards. Its black stare shot around, trying to find focus.

Login seized Oarn Dur's spear. He plunged it down through the floundering wyrm's thickened middle, pinning it to the ground. Its vestigial wings, like a bat's, scraped across the sand.

He flipped the spagot around and brought the edge of the blade down across its neck.

The dragon's head bounced and skipped, its jaws still snapping, its piercing cry suddenly silent. Its black eyes, though, finally focused on him in its death. Their abyss was endless. From it screamed a cry of war.

Its body still writhed and spun where it was struck through and pinned beneath the broken spear.

A stream of waste poured from its open, flailing mouth.

## Chapter Twenty-Four: Promise

Michalas stared with his new eyes, remade like the rest of him, past the rippling foothills of the Horta Mun, across the sea of the dead, past the corpses that filled the valley of Hennos below where he stood, and still even beyond that to the fires that burned in the streets of what had once been the glittering jewel of an empire.

Infant dragons, born of the queen, swirled in a malevolent swarm high above the city like a fire all of their own. There were so many of them. They descended in legion to feed on those who still lived. There were so few of them left. But more still came, summoned by the Dragon's call. The dragons were growing, even after less than a day. Soon, they would take flight across the Pale.

The dark prelude to the night they would bring was already spreading in the growing storm, over mountain and city and vale, over rock and emerald spire and a valley made into an open tomb.

Brittle stones splintered beneath Obidae's approaching feet.

The barbarian chieftain stopped when he saw Michalas. "You have a glow about you, you know."

Michalas held out his hand. A sigh escaped his lips.

The azure blush of his people, the Evarun, the people he could never remember knowing, lingered across his skin and even the ill-fitting and rusted chainmail armor he wore.

The chainmail coif slumped down over his brow. He pushed it back up away from his eyes.

He suddenly wondered if his markings were still there, the markings of his people, the markings of prophecy that he and Chaelus shared.

There was no way for him to look.

He smiled. At least he could still remember he'd had them.

So far, at least, the memories hadn't faded like he had expected them to, memories of his many lifetimes before, of his many deaths, of his many rebirths. Nor had the azure glow of the Evarun, which was good, because neither had the deep darkness of the Dragon that cloaked him and every-thing, and everyone, around him. It was something so few could see.

"It won't last," he said. "And there is shadow there as well."

"Don't look back," Obidae said. "It's unwise to seek what's already lost."

"I'm not looking back. I'm saying goodbye to it."

Obidae shrugged.

Michalas adjusted his ill-fitting armor and pulled the sagging coif once more away from his eyes. He turned to the scarce stone path that led away to the east.

"Do you believe he's lost?"

Obidae shrugged. "Chaelus? I do not know. Of every-thing so many thought of him, yes. But even more so than this is everything he thought of himself. But no. I believe he will become something much greater. This is what must be, yes? He has always been the center of this, even before he knew it himself. If not, then none of this was meant to be to begin with."

"Do you speak of the Prophecy of the Evarun?"

"Of everything. I speak of you, of me, of the city and its sad souls down below." Obidae held out his hand and smiled. "There is always something better. We must always move toward it. I think it is the way of things."

"What about my sister?"

"She will as well. She already does. And very soon she will understand all that you have done for her. She is stronger than you think."

"I know." He frowned. Then he remembered. He reached into the small pouch he had kept tied to his belt. He felt within until he found it.

He placed the worn stone back in Obidae's palm.

But his fingers were loath to let it go.

"I can't tell myself I won't need it anymore."

Obidae's hands closed over his. "So let it stay with you a little while more."

"Until when?"

"Until you find someone who needs it more than you do." Obidae smiled. "My guess is it will be when the mark upon your brow, which ties you to the Giver, and to prophecy, finally fades."

Michalas smiled back at Obidae.

"Come now," Obidae said. His expression returned to stone. "The dragons will soon take their flight across the Pale. They will bring their war with them. They will bring their death with them. We must be very far away from here when they do."

*

"Is that her?" Al-Mariam asked.

The sky thundered and rolled behind them, back to where she had turned; a death knell to herald the end of days. The dark plume rose like a mountain over the city. It circled and spun above the dying city of Paleos.

What could only be dragons circled within it. Faerowyn's children. Their screams shook the very stones at their feet even from where they stood hidden amongst the broken crags several leagues away. The rocks towering above the happas hid them from the eyes of the dancing dead that poured into the city, and on which the dragons fed.

The shadow of the Dragon would take them all.

The dancing, naked dead cried out, calling to the dragons to take them as they passed. They cried out again as the dragons on leather wing and fang came down and took them up, to devour in flight, or simply throw back, screaming and laughing and singing, down onto the spires and broken temples below.

Al-Mariam put her hand to Aela's hilt. A tremor passed through Aela's steel into her flesh, like a comfort, like a warding.

"Yes," Gervasis answered. "Or, at least, it was. It is her death." He stood in full view of the death above and beneath them. But death didn't see him, or wouldn't.

He turned and walked past her to the slope of blistering stones. "It is the death of the closest thing I've ever had to a daughter; my Faerowyn, First Holy Empress of the Pale, and ill-begotten Mother of the Dragon reborn."

She followed him, scrambling up the stones. "Chaelus, the Giver, he loved her once."

"And she him, long ago, even as the Taurate and their Dragon claimed her."

"Before Chaelus' father, and prophecy, called him home."

"Before it called any of us to where we are now."

Gervasis paused, in word and in his climb up the rocky slope above her.

"Her father was Mattea ex Laudus, Regulus of the Holy City of Paleos, and First Princeps of the Theocratic Council and consul to Dalamas the Fallen. Mattea was a prince, but never a king. He was her father, but he was not the one who raised her. I did. I have done so all her life since I served under her father's command.

"Mattea, her father, succumbed quickly beneath the will of the Taurate, and the Dragon. The wizard priests had dissolved any power held by the Theocratic Council. It was only a matter of time before they were all put to death.

"So she was his offering to the Dragon, to save himself, though she didn't know it, and in the end, it didn't even save him. The truth was always veiled from her, hidden behind what promises only gold and power and will can bring. Her choice in it came later, after only shadow was left to surround her and she was fooled into believing it was the only choice left to her. By then it was too late."

Gervasis started climbing again. "There was once a time when she would have made a good queen, before her light was lost to shadow. So I cannot help but wonder if she could have stopped this, if I could have stopped any of this. I tried in every way I could to save her, to stop her. But I didn't. I couldn't. So prophecy let me save you instead, so together we might save Him."

Gervasis reached the summit. He grimaced at the growing cries coming from the city. He turned back to stare at a horizon Al-Mariam couldn't yet see.

"But we must hurry. We're almost there, and we're running out of time."

\*

Red ire burned beyond the dead seal of Chaelus' eyes. He struggled to see, just one last time, whether death was indeed going to claim him, or force him to witness the sun setting beyond the sea, beyond the mountains, and the lands that had once been his home.

But the foul face of the Dragon still burned over it all, just above the tragic face of Faerowyn, her veil cast off at last. The eyes of both burned cold, above a faceless maw that Chaelus had battled but never beaten, and Faerowyn's lips that still called to him in a wordless plea for help.

Yet neither of them mattered anymore, as the face of another drew across them both; the spurned face of Prophecy. But even her blind stare was broken. It was false. The face of Mariam still lingered over hers like a haunting ghost, like a promise that was impossible to keep.

Motes of sunlight descended around her face like soft rain. The glow of the sun climaxed, resounding with the gentlest laughter, the chime of distant bells, and the subtlest trace of azure hue.

The face of the Giver, Talus, smiled gently from beyond the mystery.

Yet he was different. He was no ghost.

His face unshaven, his eyes set deeper, a wariness clung about him like a mantle. Wounds and bruises still dark and bleeding beneath his aura littered his brow and also his chest and arms beneath the shredded tunic he wore.

"Chaelus," Talus said. "Your work here is nearly done."

"I am through with you," Chaelus choked.

"No. You're only through with everything you thought you ever knew."

"No more riddles."

"I promise." Talus' expression straightened. "When I died the first time, the stones that took my life I cast myself." Talus reached out and placed his hand upon Chaelus' wounded wrist. "Just as it was you who hammered the very nails that now pierce your flesh. It is in your fear that you turned your back on the only gift you will ever need."

Talus withdrew his hand. He reached with his right and placed it upon the side of Chaelus' face. Its warmth drew the last of his breath, his thumb upon Chaelus' mouth and his fingers upon Chaelus' temple.

Talus' voice deepened, trembling the very rock and stone around them. But it wasn't Talus' voice. It was another's. From beyond time. From beyond this place. From beyond the Veil.

*"There are many who would claim the voice of prophecy. Not all of them are true. But your voice is and always will be my voice, for I have chosen you."*

Chaelus clenched his eyes against the sound.

*"The desire of Man is but a mirror of my own, just as the lust of the Dragon is but a shadow of it. Your heart is my heart, your impatience, for me, but a reflection of the divine impatience that beats within my breast as well. But to know this requires patience, and patience is something my children are slow to learn."*

Chaelus cried out. "Then kill me and be done with me!"

"No," Talus' voice returned. "This truth was slow for me to learn. Just as it is slow for you to learn what the voice of prophecy really is, that its words are merely a husk, meaningless in and of themselves. It is the breath of prophecy; it is its breath that gives us life, not its words. You know it well. It isn't mine, nor is it any whisper in the dark. No azure flame adorns it, either. It is still. It is small. It is but a single word for the mouth to whisper."

"It is Rua," Chaelus wept.

"It is indeed, I say to you."

Talus' warm touch once more swept across his face.

"Your enemies are gone. Only friends now remain. I have come here to save you."

"Too many there are who claim to."

"But there is only one who ever has. Now be at peace."

Talus withdrew his hand.

The azure light descended, then resumed.

Chaelus opened his eyes.

The gentlest face of an angel smiled back at him. Close to him. He felt her breath upon his cheek. He knew her. He knew her face.

She was his shield maiden, but with no glow of prophecy upon her.

Only Mariam.

She wept against his lips.

"I've come to bring you home."

\*

Al-Mariam pressed her face into the anguish and blood upon Chaelus' breast and wept. Her limbs, her very breath grew weak, hopeless at the wounded and dying sight of him.

The rain deepened.

Gervasis struck the mallet back against the tip of the nail that ran through Chaelus' wrist.

A dull chime sounded out across the somber vale.

Al-Mariam winced.

The wood of the cross creaked as the nail pushed outward. Fresh blood pooled at the nail's edge just as the rain washed it way from Chaelus' flesh.

Chaelus' face hung empty beside them.

Al-Mariam cried out. She pulled the mallet away from Gervasis. She struck the nail again. Chaelus' hand trembled against the ropes that bound it as the spike hung loose within it.

Gervasis pulled it out and flung it away as if it were a viper. It rang with a second chime upon the rocks below. Gervasis pressed his cloak against the flow of blood that followed it as he cut at the rope that still held Chaelus.

Flow of blood. Flow of life. But at least he still lived.

Al-Mariam leaned over until she fell against the opposite arm of the cross, where his other wrist was still fastened.

Thunder echoed down the narrow pass of the valley.

From the corner of her burning eyes, beneath the dullness of her thoughts, the mallet clutched against her breast, Al-Mariam noticed Gervasis turn away.

Chaelus' head sagged toward her. His blanched cheeks were sunken, his mouth hung slack. The bleached crown upon his brow was dull with a pallor all its own; the mark of his promise, the mark of his sacrifice, the mark of the Giver reborn, the mark of everything he had given up for them.

She pressed her lips against his ear.

"I know you know there are many different types of death, and I know that you have suffered too many. I cannot forget that there are so many of these you have already saved me from. I cannot even begin to count their number. There are so many chances you have returned to me that I can never hope to repay. But I can do this. I can do this for you."

Al-Mariam forced her heart and her stare away from him. With what voice and vigor was left to her she struck against the nail that still held him; that still kept him away from her.

Its chime sounded out like an anvil's knell.

Thunder echoed against its call.

Gervasis stepped away from the base of the cross, back-lit by the fires of the holy city of Paleos.

She pressed her lips against Chaelus'. She breathed into his mouth. A kiss.

"At least I can save you from this death. And if I must die in so doing, then it is a death I will gladly meet."

She edged him slowly down. She laid him on the blanket they had already prepared. She wrapped it around him. She wrapped gossamer around the already-healing wounds on his wrists. She touched his flesh of prophecy there. She held him as he trembled. She held him until his trembling subsided and his breath became even.

Gervasis drew his gladius. The chime sounded like broken glass. Its polished steel blazed with the light from the burning city beneath.

"I have never hidden myself from my legion, from my men. I have never hidden what I believe from them. I left them to wait north of the city. They will know who was crucified here. They will have seen the fires in the city. They have seen the dragons above it. They know what they are to do. They will come."

She unfastened Aela from her tether. The silver of her steel brewed beneath the patient strips of gossamer that still bound her. A supple and deep azure glow danced along her edge, like a promise, like a comfort, like a warding.

It felt good.

Beneath them, where the broken hills descended to the valley below, the howls and screams of the dancing dead poured out from the Imperial city of Paleos like flowing blood. There were thousands of them, a horde like no barbarian or warlord had ever seen, all servants themselves to the will of the Dragon. They climbed over themselves, screaming, oblivious to each other, oblivious to the humanity they once were; men, women, children, legionnaires, all Remnants now, bristling with arms of war.

Gervasis turned to her. His crystal eyes filled with an azure veil from Aela's flame. He nodded.

"Until then, we stand. And I wouldn't worry about your oath. The things that come for us are no longer men."

Gervasis turned back to the burning city and the growing cries of the horde.

"Your sword, it seems, already knows this."

\*

The covering of coarse pine and scrub had thinned away to expose the bare jagged rock beneath. The stones of the Horta Mun had darkened now to the deep color of blood. The borderlands of the spine between the Theocracy and the Khaal were nearing their end.

So too were they. So too was their journey, in so many different ways.

Olivia wrapped her shawl around her again. She held her breath as Al-Aaron draped a fur across her shoulders.

"Night will fall soon. It's getting colder," Al-Aaron said.

She smiled up at him.

He knelt down on the stones beside her. They sat there together in silence.

The chaste and solemn band of her Servian knights made camp in the sheltered protection of the stony vale. The small gray tent of the Tenders and the sacred fire they carried with them had already been set at its center. Their Khaalish protectors kept watch from the ridges above.

She turned back to the south.

"What are you looking at?" Al-Aaron asked.

It was only then, for the first time, that she saw it. Above the empire, a dark cloud rose up in the far distant horizon. It was small from here, but no less fearsome. It gathered together in a single spire before spreading out like a growing shroud over a helpless world.

She could see them there, twelve in cold red flame. The storm rose from their center. She could hear their acrid voices. She could hear the sound of the suffering they would bring. Together, it sounded like a blood-curdling scream. The day of the Dragon had come. The Fallen Ones had returned.

Eleven fallen Servian lords who had already been denied had returned. They had been made twelve again. But she knew how, didn't she? And even the martyrdom of Malius wouldn't save them this time. The blood of the father is the blood of the son. And a prophecy, and a broken promise, and a past that should have been let go of long ago, had returned the sins of Malius back to them.

The Mother shook herself.

"Nothing."

She leaned toward him.

"It's nothing I shouldn't have seen before," she whispered. "Nothing that prophecy hasn't already allowed."

"And what is that?"

"That I've been afraid for far too long, my dear. And prophecy, and ghosts, are never something you should hide, or leave, behind."

"What do you mean?"

The Mother cradled his face in her hands. "It is time for you to let Malius go."

He stiffened.

She could tell the shadows of his wounds still burned.

She smiled. "And I will let go of my ghost—a promise I made to my sister that I never should have kept."

She withdrew her hands from him.

"We should have returned to Evarun a long time ago. There are wounds there that I should have healed before I left—wounds that never should have been allowed to follow us here."

The harsh scrape of boots on the callous stones rose behind them. The eldritch stench of Belloch rose with it.

"You see it too, don't you, Revered Mother?" Belloch asked. "Do you not see the clouds of war?"

She smiled at him, as much as she could, her lips and face edged with the sadness that overcame her.

"Do you know what it means?" Belloch asked.

"Tell me," she answered.

"It means you are too late."

"Everything is just as prophecy has planned."

"Perhaps." Belloch motioned to one of the Khaalish nearby. "Find the one called Al-Hoanar. Capture or kill him. I do not care."

Belloch stepped closer to her.

Al-Aaron began to stand.

She gestured him back.

"You're not going to Evarun," Belloch said.

"Then where are we going?" she said.

Belloch smiled. He looked out toward the not so distant storm.

"You are right about prophecy. The dark cloud that rises isn't weather, Revered Mother, it is dragons—a storm of them. It is war. It is death. Your prophet has failed you. The queen of the Pale has given birth to them just as her prophecy demanded. And you're too late to do anything about it. The Day of the Dragon has come."

Belloch motioned again.

Two Khaalish seized her from behind.

Al-Aaron cried out and lunged up at Belloch.

Belloch tossed him back down to the stones.

Olivia struggled against the men who held her.

Belloch squatted down before her. He stared at her through empty eyes. The cruel light of the setting sun burned across the hard lines of his face. It diminished beneath the harsh white scar that divided it.

"You're coming with us to Khaal as my prisoner," Belloch said. "When we get there, I will present you to the Khashik as tribute, for them to use as an offering, because when the Dragon has finished devouring this land, it will come for ours. We will not find ourselves unprotected when it does."

"You would betray your oath?"

Belloch shrugged.

"I will serve my people. My honor is with the Khaalish. It was never with you."

Belloch stood.

Beside her, Al-Aaron shrank as if he had just seen a ghost; his ghost.

"Now get up, woman," Belloch ordered. "You can walk, or I will drag you."

## Epilogue One: Bakassas

Bakassas plucked the small golden fruit away from its stem, nesting it, cradling it within her long slender fingers. For a moment her skin turned gray, withered like death, but then returned again to its perfect alabaster hue.

The gossamer covering her eyes pressed against her as always. Anyone would wonder how it was that she could see. But she did, perfectly, through the eyes of those around her. Through the bronze masks of her guards, who stood sentry along the shadows, and even through the eyes of those who looked upon her, wondering how it was that one so ancient as her could be so flawless and so beautiful and so young.

She waited for the wizard to do so now.

She tore at the now withered fruit with her teeth until the seed shot away. She chewed on the rotten meat slowly; watching, waiting, measuring.

But the wizard showed nothing of himself to her.

Only his mailed fist repeatedly hitting across the heads of the men he kept in chains around his sandaled feet.

Yet they weren't men anymore, were they? They were only Remnants of men.

Dabbing a cloth to her lips, she picked up a pair of the fruits from the silver tray resting beside her on the arm of her blood-red throne.

She dusted away the small remains of the one she had just eaten from the gossamer of her dress and the long white plaits of her hair. She clutched at the small smooth malachite stone she wore, like her sister's, hanging between her breasts.

"You may speak to me, wizard," she finally said.

The queer, slender little man smiled and bowed as a ruse. His teeth, chiseled and marred, spoke nothing. He bowed. Self-mutilations, from blade and fire, marched across his pallid pate.

He smiled and kicked at the head of the pitiful soul closest to him.

They were hairless and withered, naked, but whether men or women it was hard to tell anymore. Black spots dotted their twitching flesh, these dancing dead, who stared out at the world with only the widest eyes of rapture.

She knew not to dare to look through their eyes.

When the wizard spoke, his voice was as slender and dangerous as he was.

"The Dragon's own Hands have asked me to bring you these offerings."

She rolled another pair of fruits between her fingers.

"Why? And why would I want such wasted flesh when I could simply have you?"

The wizard smiled another feint.

"But then, who would return to him with your answer?"

His sapphire robes stood out against the blood rising through his skin, against the blood of the stone of her corbeled hall.

"He must know if you will march to war with him."

His skin bled through the thousand small scars cut across it, made at the man's own hands as a sign of his devotion, not unlike the stone of her hall, which bled the blood of memories, of those who had abandoned her here.

The smell of the two bloods was not the same. One smelled like iron, like rapture; the other like the pungent rot of death and loss.

"You may tell the Dragon' Hands that I am displeased that they have failed me in fulfilling their end of our bargain."

"Your prize was crucified!" the wizard sneered. "I saw him suffer myself."

The gray, withered voice of her past sounded just beneath her own.

"You lie to me! You know that my prize has been stolen from you, yet still you would try to deceive me. The Giver has been saved. I have seen it in the fire."

The wizard stifled a snarl.

"Your master has failed," Bakassas purred, in her own voice, softer again. "And you will both pay for your deceit of me."

The skin around the wizard's lips cracked and bled, suddenly unsure.

His blood smelled like war. His fear, as his understanding grew, smelled like rapture.

The wizard clutched at his eyes and screamed. Blood poured between his fingers. The Remnant dogs fought over themselves where it fell.

The crushed golden fruits slipped from her hand. Blood wept from their centers.

"Don't you know that only the blind can see?"

The wizard cried out.

Beneath her voice, the old witch finally took over.

"But you may tell your Dragon he can still have the help of my army. But it will be under my command. I will take the head of the Giver myself."

## Epilogue Two: Dragons

Login wiped the blood and bile away from his eyes.

He stepped away from the mutilated carcass of Oarn Dur, whose insides lay arrayed across the sand.

Oarn Dur's face still held a look of amazement, even awe, the darkness freed at last from his eyes. His blood-spattered iron and ruby crown lay in the sand, toppled from his brow.

Login stepped over the beheaded wyrm that had just been born from a man, its corpse still twitching, wretched, impaled to the ground. Only its head had stopped moving, its jaws locked open in death, its black soulless eyes no more empty than before.

Still holding the spagot in his right hand, he gripped the spear that ran through the wyrm and hoisted it out. The corpse of the dragon slumped to the ground, motionless. His hands shook as he lifted the spear and held it high above his head.

The men, the women, and the children of Goarnn, these gladiators, these spawn of war, rumbled in the stands and the gallery above him. They watched him from the edges of the shadows beneath the stands of the arena. They cursed him.

He knew that they had to. What choice had they but to curse the boy who had seemingly just killed their king?

Their king, who had just birthed a dragon. Their king, who had just sealed their fate. The sight of the pale boy who had just saved them from it.

Above them all, beyond the oculus on high, bestial screams rained down upon them.

Other dragons from other kings, perhaps.

It was what Maedelous had said would come. Perhaps he knew it more than anyone else.

The screams of beasts. The cries of dragons. The death of man.

The rumbling and the curses of the warriors and the children stalled to a whisper.

Before a boy. Before their king. Ready with a call for war.

"Come with me," Login said, his weak voice at odds with the challenging stares of the warriors above him.

But the time to question was over.

"If you're as good at killing as Maedelous said you were, come with me. Let's go kill some dragons."

## Epilogue Three: Blood

Baelus opened his watering eyes to a muted sun. Red—blood—veiled his vision, just like prophecy, just like the Dragon who had claimed him.

Blackened blood covered him where he sat slumped on his throne, the throne that had once belonged to his brother, the throne that had once belonged to their father. Rancid bits of flesh, somewhere between that of an eel and a beast, floated in the gore.

He held a long dagger in his hand, still trembling. The bright strike of blood covered its tip just above a small cut upon his bloated belly, where he had pulled away his robes, ready to cut the beast out himself. His knuckles burned white. He still couldn't release his grip on it.

The air was cool but for the warmth of the muted sun, falling down through the oculus above, above the space before his throne where he had forced his brother to kneel, where his brother had tried to save him. The light of the muted sun fell over that place like a halo.

But it hadn't on that day, a day he could barely remember from what seemed a lifetime ago.

His breath still came in short rasps, but they were slowly getting longer.

Dead men lay everywhere, just beyond the edge of the halo.

The scattered cries of the living descended from above and drifted in from outside.

His brother had tried to warn him, but the Dragon wouldn't let him listen. Yet somehow he still did. He had heard something; somewhere deep down, from a place where he still knew who he was, or what he had become, he had heard.

It was like a trapdoor that had been suddenly sprung open.

So he had fought back against the Dragon, quietly at first, secretly, through black days, through death days, until the very end of them, as the Dragon finally weakened its grip upon him; ready, just in case, to end his own life if he must, until he won. Somehow, he had won, and the black corpse of the beast had emptied from him in a stream of bile.

He jumped as the dagger slipped from his grasp. It clattered to the rush-covered stones.

For some reason, the Dragon had fled from him.

Trembling, he stood.

Cautious of his step, he descended the dais, across the remains of the dragon pooled about him. His throat burned.

He had been unsure at first whether it had been the dragon's death or his.

But not so for those who had followed him. Dead legionnaires lay scattered with legion blades sunk deep in their chests. Some were newly dead. Some had been left rotting where they had died more than a fortnight before. Those whom Chaelus had saved and those who had followed the dragon almost born from his own belly.

More dead lay piled around the stairs. Those who had attempted to flee, and those who hadn't let them.

He climbed over them all. He leaned into the doors. He pushed them open to the muted sun, and more cries of the dying.

The courtyard wavered. A black pyre burned in the shadow of the surround. The sharp smell of death and burning flesh assailed him.

He stumbled down the steps. His limbs turned feeble. He slumped to the ground. His crown slipped from his brow to the blood-spattered, trampled ground.

One man, a slave, strode toward him. Burns covered the side of his face. Blood darkened the gladius he held in his hand.

The man's face was familiar behind his scars.

He was one of Chaelus' men of old, the only one left, the one Baelus hadn't killed but had tortured instead, and had kept alive instead, as a trophy. He remembered him now. His name was Grovis.

Grovis stopped just before him, towering over him.

"Where do you think you're going?"

Baelus flinched away from the man's steel.

"There are more like me," Grovis said, "waiting just beyond the gate, men who are still loyal to your brother."

Baelus wiped the caustic fluid from his mouth. To defeat the Dragon only to die at the hands of a vengeance he himself had wrought and knew that he deserved. But not yet.

"Please," he said. "Don't kill me. Not yet. There's something I still have to do."

Something. Something to make things right.

Grovis knelt down before him.

"Of course you do."

Grovis pulled at the leather slave collar on his neck.

"You're going to cut this off me."

Grovis stuck the gladius in the dirt. He picked up the fallen crown in both hands. He held it out to Baelus.

"Then you're going to put this back on."

Baelus stared at Grovis' tortured face. He closed his eyes.

Grovis placed his father's crown firm upon his brow.

The thin band of steel felt heavy.

"Then we're going to find your brother."